MW01534561

Principessa ♡

(UN)Bounded

Kinsmen Billionaires Book One

Congrats !

Liss Montoya

LISS MONTOYA

Contents

Cover Design by Liss Montoya

Illustration by Jess Lucasievecz Joenck

Editing & Proofreading by Shawsome Reads Editing Services

Editing & Proofreading by LoxOnBooks Editing Services

Content Notes

Trigger Warnings

Abandonment (historical), kidnapping, explicit sex, profanity.

To RRW, my amazing sister-in-law. Thank you for being you.

Healing might not be so much about getting better, as about letting go of everything that isn't you—all of the expectations, all of the beliefs—and becoming who you are.

-Rachel Naomi Remen

Playlist

"Houdini" (Dua Lipa)

"Looking Out for You" (Joy Again)

"Can't Take My Eyes off You" (Frankie Valli)

"There She Goes" (The La's)

"Music To Watch Boys To" (Lana Del Rey)

"Me Gustas Tu" (Manu Chao)

"Lady-Hear Me Tonight" (Modjo)

"After Glow" (Taylor Swift)

"Never Let Me Go" (Florence + The Machine)

"Out of My League" (Fitz and The Tantrums)

"Cherry" (Harry Styles)

"A World Alone" (Lorde)

"Lose Control" (Teddy Swims)

"Chemical" (Post Malone)

"Soldier, Poet, King" (The Oh Hellos)

"Wildest Dreams (Taylor's Version)" (Taylor Swift)

"Espresso" (Sabrina Carpenter)

"End Of An Era" (Dua Lipa)

"These Walls" (Dua Lipa)

"HE KNOWS (feat. Lil Nas X)" (Camila Cabello)

"Sunflower-Spider-Man: Into the Spider-Verse" (Post Malone, Swae Lee)

"Best Part (feat. H.E.R.)" (Daniel Caesar, H.E.R.)

"BONITA" (Daddy Yankee)

Listen on Spotify

Author's Note

The Kinsmen Billionaires series follows the stories of two brothers-in-law (Gio's brother is married to Karina, Gabo's sister).

But they are so much more than the money they have. They are men trying to find happiness, love, and, yes, their place in the world. They have different personalities, and hence, their stories will be different but not less significant.

I hope you enjoy the journey of getting to know the Kinsmen Billionaires and the women who bring them to their knees.

Blurb

She wants a fling, but he wants forever.

I can't count the number of chips my parents left on my shoulder, but I'm finally free and thriving. Thanks to a trust fund and my brother's best friend, Gabo Godoy, I have the chance to curate my own gallery while spending the summer in Italy.

That's all this summer was supposed to be: a fun fling in the sun, searching for art and loving every minute of it.

But I wasn't expecting Gabo to be—to put it bluntly—a very hot, panty-melting, intriguing man, one who set his sights on me. He listens. He cares. He wants me for me, but he deserves someone willing to put their past behind them and fall head over heels in love with him.

That isn't me.

Or it wasn't me. The lines begin to blur, and emotions I never expected to take root in my heart catch fire, spurring us forward into the unknown.

When we finally find our footing and accept what could be, a man hellbent on revenge finds me. He steals me away from everything I loved and never thought I would have, sending us into a whirlwind until the very end.

Will Gabo find Isabella before it's too late? Or will this be the end of their summer fling in the heart of Italy?

(UN)Bounded is book one in the Kinsmen Billionaires Series. Each book is a standalone with an HEA, and the books should be read in order. Please see inside for the content warning.

Prologue

Isabella Bianchi

Santiago, Chile

Being back at Villa Libélula brings me so much joy; I love spending time at my brother Luca's place. He and his wife, Karina, own a beautiful vineyard in Alamo Peaks, a small town just outside of Santiago. I love walking around the endless rows of vines to clear my head in the mornings, going for a stroll after dinner, and watching the beautiful, starry skies against the imposing Andes mountains. It brings me peace and comfort, which is something I never experienced in my hometown of San Miguel, Argentina.

I graduated yesterday with a Bachelor of Arts from the University of Chile, and in the next few months, I'm supposed to be figuring out what to do next with my life. But all I want to do is let loose and enjoy life—be a carefree twenty-two-year-old—before the responsibilities that come with being an adult overwhelm me for the rest of my life.

Some people have life figured out at an early age. Exhibit A: my big brother, Gio. Ever since he was a kid, he has known he wanted to be a professor. He's currently teaching at a big university in the United States. My chest fills with pride every time I get to tell my friends—or any acquaintance, really—that my oldest brother has a doctorate in Forest Engineering, and his students call him Dr. Bianchi.

Exhibit B: Cata, my best friend and a kickass soccer player. She's the same age as me, but I can already tell she'll be one of the greatest players in the world. She's been called to the Colombia Women's National team, which is such a big honor and the reason why she won't be able to make it to my party today.

"There you are, Isa. We've been looking for you everywhere. Your guests are here." My brother Luca takes me out of my daydreaming as he comes into the cultivar.

Smiling brightly at my brother, I shake myself from my thoughts and plaster a huge smile on my lips. The day my parents decided they were done being parents, Luca stepped up and filled the role for me.

"Oh, perfect. I can't wait to introduce you to everyone." I hold onto my brother's arm and walk back toward the patio where we'll be hosting the gathering.

My oldest brother, Gio, is chatting with Karina, and the moment he sees me, he starts clapping. My cheeks turn beet red when everyone turns in my direction. Luca joins Gio, and suddenly, everyone starts clapping. I try to keep a smile on my face while tears run down my cheeks. I'm overwhelmed with emotion that all these people are here to celebrate my college degree: Luca, his wife and in-laws, Gio, and my friends Luisa and Ana with their families. Even some of the people who work at the vineyard are here, including Ines, our nanny in Argentina. She moved to Chile after Luca bought the vineyard—yet my parents are nowhere to be seen. It's amazing to feel this much love, but at the same time, it's incredibly sad to know that I can have all the love in the world but not from my parents. I mean, the people who brought me into this world don't give a crap about me, so my brothers had to fill in the void left by them.

How sad is that?

Four years ago, I moved here because my parents had already disappeared, but I don't think I will ever stop missing them. I had the best childhood; we weren't rich, but we never wanted for anything. Both of my parents were hard workers, and we used to go to Grandpa Bianchi's farm every weekend and ride horses. Sometimes, we even helped feed the chickens, goats, and cows.

But once Grandpa died, everything changed. He left a lot of money to my parents, and they did a 180. Suddenly, they started going to charity events. They would spend the night in Buenos Aires and leave us with Ines. The charities became more important than us, so they quit their jobs and became full-time socialites. That's when my older brothers stepped up and became my parental figures. And although I'm so thankful for my brothers, I miss my parents every single day.

Maybe if I became a big name in the art scene, they would look for me again.

"We're so proud of you, Isa. Graduating with honors and a bright future ahead," Gio says as soon as we're in close distance, and my two awesome brothers embrace me.

I can't help it—my tears start running faster and harder. There are so many things I want to tell my parents, but they never answer the phone. I wonder if they changed their numbers after we came to Chile.

"This is not a day for sadness. We are truly proud of you and cannot wait to see what you do next," Luca says in a serious but kind tone.

I can't help but chuckle. "When did you become the wise older brother? I thought that was Gio's job."

Gio chuckles, and Luca simply rolls his eyes. "Har, har. You know very well Karina knocked some sense into me and made me see what an amazing man I can be. And I'm not talking only between the sheets." Luca wiggles his eyebrows.

Gio and I immediately groan in fake disgust. I try as hard as I can to hold my laugh in, but a small smile forms on my lips. He doesn't need his ego to get bigger than it already is.

"What a way to kill the mood. bro," Gio says, shaking his head at Luca.

With a shrug, Luca replies, "Hey, I made her laugh. That's all that matters."

My friends Ana and Luisa join us in the circle I've made with my brothers, and I'm reminded we're not alone—I need to be a good host.

"Where are my manners? These are my brothers, Gio and Luca. The girls reach out to shake hands with my brothers. "And these are my friends, Ana and Luisa; they also graduated with me."

After introducing everyone and mingling for a bit, I peruse the buffet—a mix of Chilean and Argentinian foods on display. Tapping my index finger against my bottom lip, I think about what I should try first. The shrimp or the roasted beef sliders? Since today is my day to eat whatever I want, I put a couple of both onto my plate.

I'm about to grab a healthy load of salad when a deep and sensual voice says, "Excellent choice. I can't wait to try the sliders myself and see how the Argentinian *asado* compares to the Chilean one."

I'm feeling way more flustered about this food conversation than the last time I had sex, and that's not a good sign.

"Oh, hi. I didn't realize you were going to be here," I say, trying to sound nonchalant, but my voice takes on a high pitch at the end.

Gabo Godoy—Karina's brother and the sexiest man I've ever seen in my life—has more power over my hormones than I do. That's not something I want to deal with right at this moment.

"And miss your graduation? Not a chance." Gabo chuckles as he lowers to give me a kiss on my cheek. The moment his cologne hits my nostrils—a mix of leather, cedarwood, and allspice—I feel my knees weaken.

"Woah, careful there. Are you okay?" He quickly grabs my arm, forcing me to lean into his body. I can feel every single hard muscle in his chest—strong and steady, keeping me upright.

"Yeah, of course I am. I just think my heel caught on something."

Gabo looks at the ground, the smoothest concrete I've seen in my life, and instead of calling me out on my bullshit, he simply nods.

"Congratulations, by the way." He effectively changes topics as we both make our way toward the tables where everyone is sitting and enjoying themselves.

"Thank you. I still have no clue what I'm going to do with the rest of my life, but my brothers are throwing this party in my honor as if I had won a Nobel Prize."

I go for a shrimp instead of looking at Gabo. I don't know why I'm letting all these thoughts out in front of him. We've never been close. He's been living in Italy for over a decade, I think, so he only comes to Chile for the holidays.

"Your brothers are proud of you. Nothing wrong with that," he says with a shrug as if he completely gets it.

And maybe he does. Karina and I are both the youngest—having two older brothers each—and even though we don't speak much, I can tell he's incredibly proud of her. And with good reason! At twenty-six, Luca and Karina took Villa Libélula Wines to be among the top-ranked wines in South America. They've also started the process of exporting to Europe and North America.

"Maybe you're right, but I still feel I should have a better clue of what to do with my life, you know? I see both of my brothers achieving their dreams, and I don't know where to start," I say, feeling defeated. Though, maybe having this conversation with someone who's not close to me is a good idea.

"You know I'm the middle brother, right?" I nod, so he continues. "Growing up I thought I was so lucky for not having the responsibility of continuing the legacy of the Godoy name like Vicente. At the same time, I was jealous of Karina being the baby of the family and doing whatever she pleased. I felt stuck in the middle. Not enough responsibilities to tie me down, but not enough freedom either. I was still someone my parents were counting on to keep the legacy alive, just not in the same capacity as Vicente.

"As I grew older and saw my siblings rising to the challenge of fulfilling their destinies, I started to wonder: What am I going to do with my life? Am I going to just be a playboy and spend all the money that took my family so long to make on parties and frivolous things? Or am I going to turn my passion into something wonderful and continue the entrepreneurial Godoy legacy with my own architectural firm? I decided to go for the second option because the first one wasn't fulfilling, if I'm being honest."

I'm in awe of his words. Despite his struggles to find his place in his family—in this world—Gabo was able to create something utterly his. That's what I want to do, too.

"But wait, what you're trying to tell me is that you're a reformed playboy and ready for Mrs. Godoy?" I say in a mocking tone.

The deep laugh that escapes him is as much an aphrodisiac as having his scent near me. God, this man is just too much. Too bad I'm much younger than him.

Once his laugh dies down a bit, he looks me in the eyes. "Not really. I'm not looking for anyone in particular. To be honest, I don't even know what I want in a partner." He takes a sip of his pisco sour before continuing. "I guess I'm just tired of the bar scene, you know? After a while, looks are just that—looks. And what I find inside isn't as appealing, kind of like the empty playboy spending his parents' money."

His gaze never leaves me, and I love having his undivided attention. I know he's older, and I should feel out of place with him, but somehow, he sees me as an equal, and I like that.

"I'll tell you what. Why don't you spend a couple of months in Italy this summer? You can stay for as long or as little as you want. There's plenty of art to see, to create, to enjoy. From what I've heard, you have an innate talent for painting. Maybe you could create your next masterpiece while in Italy," Gabo says with an easy smile forms on his handsome face.

I nod slowly, picturing myself in Italy for the summer. Beautiful beaches, gelato, museums, small towns full of history—the possibilities are practically endless.

"You could even take a summer elective at the University of Bologna. That's where I went to school." He takes a bite of a beef slider, and I can't help but feel entranced by how his throat works to swallow.

So damn hot.

I immediately shake the not-so-pure thoughts out of my mind. The man is incredibly sexy, and the last thing I need is to have a summer fling with one of my brother's best friends, who also happens to be his brother-in-law.

"It's not a bad idea," I say after a few minutes and a few bites of my own slider. It's delicious, and it's no wonder he was enjoying his food so much. "I think I need to sleep on it and come up with a plan."

"That's the spirit, Bella." He smiles, and a dimple forms in his cheek.

How can this man grow hotter with every single minute that passes?

When I register what he just called me, I frown.

"Isabella, Bella for short," he explains like it's obvious.

I chuckle because it makes sense, but I reply, "No one ever calls me Bella. Only Isa."

"Well, I'm not just anyone, Bella darling." He gets up from the table and winks at me as he makes his way to the buffet, where he meets Luca, and they both embrace.

Yeah, I cannot have any spicy thoughts about Gabo. It'd be awkward as hell the moment the fling fizzles, not to mention that he's eight years older than me. He must have a throng of women at his beck and call in Italy.

"Isa! Oh, my God. Who's that man you were talking to? He's so hot!" Ana says as she takes the seat where Gabo was a moment ago.

A mischievous smile forms on my face as I tell her, "He's my sister-in-law's brother."

Ana raises an eyebrow and crosses her arms for good measure.

"You guys, he's one of my brother's best friends," I tell her as she looks at me like, *so what?* "He lives in Italy, and he's way older." I'm trying to come up with things that I think are either red flags or that would help her understand why I shouldn't go there with Gabo, but all I get is a blank expression on her face.

"I mean, if you don't like him, that's fine. But no one here is talking about marrying the man. A simple roll in the sheets with him would do," Luisa says as she joins the table.

Apparently, we've been louder than I thought.

"Yeah, the fact that he's older only makes him hotter," Ana adds. "A man who knows what to do in bed, not a boy who comes at the sight of you naked." She rolls her eyes and scrunches her face in disgust.

I can't contain the laugh that comes out of me. "Nothing is going to happen between us. I'm not even the relationship type, anyways. And besides, he only sees me as Luca's little sister."

"That's not how it seemed from afar." Ana lowers her voice so no one else can hear her, and Luisa solemnly nods.

"I'm sure you guys were just imagining things." I dismiss their observation and take a bite of my salad next.

When the girls don't say anything back, I release a long breath.

The party is in full swing: there's a band, and the buffet has been replaced by a cocktail bar. I scan the patio for my brother Gio—I want to spend as much time as possible with him before he has to go back to the United States—when I find a pair of beautiful, dark brown eyes trained on me. His stare is intense, and if I didn't know better, I'd say that Gabo Godoy was looking at his next prey. Instead of lowering his gaze, he starts walking toward me. He's wearing dark wash jeans and a black sweater that stretches along his chest, deliciously tracing his abs.

"I just wanted to say goodbye before leaving."

The way he looked at me, those weren't the words I expected to come out of his mouth. I can't hide my shock fast enough because he laughs and tries to cover it with a cough.

"I'm leaving early for Bologna and figured I'd spend the night chatting with my parents. It's something I don't get to do often."

I lower my gaze at his explanation; I don't want him to see how jealous I am that he gets to do that.

"Anyway, here is my contact info. Think about going to Italy for the summer. Of course, you don't have to stay with me, but I can be a point of contact if you need me." Gabo hands me his card and hugs me as his rich, deep chuckle sends a shot of lust through me—right to my core.

What is he chuckling about? No idea, but all I know is that tonight, I'll be replaying this encounter in my mind as I use my vibrator.

Feeling flushed by his mere presence, I remove myself from his embrace and give him a little wave.

Ugh, he must think I'm such a child.

The smile he gives me is downright panty-melting: it's so intense and masculine—just like him. With a nod, he makes his way to the parking lot. That's where I see Gio pacing back and forth with a huge smile on his face while on the phone. I decide to leave him be and go in search of my friends.

Tonight, I'll be the twenty-two-year-old girl I've been craving to be. I can think about my future another day.

Chapter 1

Isabella Bianchi

It's been two months since graduation, and I finally feel like I have a strong enough plan to move forward with my life. Karina encouraged me to take time to do nothing and enjoy the calm before the storm in the proverbial sense.

"You need to enjoy life, babe. If I hadn't met your brother when I did, I would have most likely traveled a bit before settling back in Alamo Peaks to help with the family's vineyard."

"Do you wish you had met Luca later in life?" I ask curiously. All I know about these two is once they gave in to each other, they have been inseparable.

"Oh, God, no. I'm thankful I've been able to travel the world with the love of my life. To enjoy every single thing with him, you know? Waking up next to him every day is the best feeling in the world, and I'm lucky I found him early in life."

My heart warms at her words; I love seeing her so happy with my brother. I know he feels the exact same way, but I don't think that kind of love is in the cards for me. I don't want to start a family and then regret having had kids and leave them abandoned to fulfill my greedy dreams.

After my chat with Gabo at my graduation party, my interest was definitely piqued about spending the summer in Italy. When he mentioned he lives in Bologna, I did some research—okay, some Googling—and was pleasantly surprised by what I found out. Bologna is not only a relatively big city in northern Italy that is rich in history and art, but it's also a hub for the mechanical and financial industries with a vibrant city life. On paper, it definitely looks like the perfect spot for me to spend a summer full of art, history, and good food. And the best part: it's a short drive away from the beach.

Now that I have a better idea of my plans, I need to confirm with Gabo that he's actually okay with hosting me for the summer, and it wasn't just something he said in the heat of the moment.

I stare at the blank screen on my phone as if it holds all the answers in the universe. There's no better time than the present. I need to get in contact with him and see if he did mean it, but I don't have his number—I drunkenly lost his card the night of the party—and I don't want to ask my brothers for it. The questioning would be endless, and I'm not ready to talk about my plans with them yet. Deciding to open my clock app, I look him up. I type "Gabo Godoy, Italy" into the search bar, and no results appear.

Ugh. I mean, I don't think people his age use this app. Maybe I'll have better luck on Instagram.

I check Karina's page instead of Luca's because my brother is a famous influencer. He has over a million followers, and I think it'd be harder to find Gabo's account that way. Once I find him in Karina's followers, I send him a quick message:

> Hi Gabo, it's Isa—Luca's sister. I was wondering if you were still okay with hosting me this summer? Let me know,
> IB.

While I wait for Gabo's reply, I decide to talk with my brothers. Whether he's hosting me or not, I need my trust fund. I need capital not only to get a space that I can transform into an art gallery in Santiago—my ultimate dream—but also to have a great time while looking for the perfect art pieces to showcase in my gallery. *My gallery.* It sounds terrifyingly amazing.

"May I come in?" I ask Luca after I knock on his office door. He doesn't reply, but I can hear him laughing, so I decide to go in regardless.

"Hey, Isa. Perfect timing. This *boludo* was just telling me how he almost burned his house down." Luca motions for me to join him in front of the screen as he wipes the tears running down his face.

Without even looking at the screen, I already know who Luca is referring to. Gio is the worst cook in history. I'll never forget the Christmas our parents left us with Ines, and she fell ill. Gio decided to make a cake to cheer me and Luca up—we were only ten and fourteen, after all. We were so excited to try that cake; it took Gio the entire afternoon, and the kitchen was a complete mess.

The moment I took the first bite, a flavor I wasn't expecting was the most dominant. I tried to swallow it while pretending to smile at an expectant Gio. But Luca—being Luca—spit the mouthful of cake onto his plate, and Gio's face fell.

"Dude, this tastes awful. Did you add sugar?"

Gio made a face and darted off to the kitchen. Luca and I followed him, and the moment he lifted the bag of salt from the counter, we all started laughing uncontrollably.

Since then, Gio gets shit every time he's in the kitchen.

"Nah, both of you can laugh all that you want but I've become a really good cook. My rookie mistakes are in the past."

"Whatever, big bro. We still love you no matter what," I say in the condescending tone we all hate so much.

Gio heaves a deep breath, as if to say, "Lord, give me patience with these two."

"I had just put some water on to boil to make lunch right before Luca called, and of course I got distracted, so the water spilled out of the pot, and Luca saw all the steam behind me and started howling in laughter. But the house was far from being about to burn down."

Gio emphasizes the word "far," making me laugh harder.

"Anyway, why did you need to speak with both of us, Isa? Is everything okay?" Gio asks with his serious, big brother tone, and I know the laughing at his expense is over.

Squaring my shoulders and smiling at my brothers, I start talking. "As both of you know, these past couple of months, I've been doing some research about what the next step in my life will be." They both nod, encouraging me to continue. "During my graduation party, I spoke briefly with Gabo and—"

"What does Gabo Godoy have to do with your future?" Luca squints his Caribbean blues at me like he has suddenly become a detective. It takes everything in me not to laugh at him.

"*Boludo*, let her finish her idea. We can do the inquisition afterward," Gio chirps, and I raise an eyebrow in question. "You know what I mean, we're just curious. Please continue," he says nicely.

"Actually, Gabo was nothing but kind and helpful when I chatted with him. He pointed out that since I just graduated with a BA, I could spend some time in Italy. There, I could not only see all the art and culture I want but also do some networking and scouting pieces I would like to have in my gallery." I clasp my hands in front of me and smile at my brothers, expectant about what they have to say.

Gio clears his throat and rearranges his glasses. "I really like the gallery idea. I think it's fantastic you can create a space not only for your work and self-expression, but also to bring in other artists."

I sigh in relief at Gio's blessing. It doesn't matter how far away he lives; we're in constant contact. I love how in tune I am with my brothers.

"I have to be honest; I'm not thrilled about you going so far away for months, but I need to remember you're not a kid anymore. I know you've been working hard to come up with this plan, but maybe you should take some more time to think things through. Karina has told me how impressed she is by your organizational skills. From what I understand, you've even come up with a financial plan. Is that correct?"

I blush at Luca's praise but nod enthusiastically. "Yeah, I mean, I took a couple of finance and administration class-es as electives, and I've been working on a budget. I don't want to burn all my money in my first year in business, you know?"

Both my brothers chuckle. It's funny to see how damn similar they are—not only physically but also in their man-nerisms.

"Isa, I doubt you'll go through your trust fund in the first year. I don't think we've told you how much money it is," Gio declares, and my eyes grow as big as saucers.

I'm guessing a million dollars, but whatever the amount, I'm super thankful Grandpa Bianchi left money for the three of us before our parents could get their hands on it.

"Yeah, Isa. I wouldn't worry about that. Your trust fund is one hundred million dollars," Luca says with a shit-eating grin, and my knees go weak.

"Are you guys sure? I didn't realize Grandpa had so much money," I say, shocked by the amount of money I have in my name.

"He didn't," Gio hurries to explain. "But your trust fund was set up almost fifteen years ago, so it's been gaining interest for a while. Plus, Luca and I decided to contribute to it," he says, and I gape at them.

"So what you are trying to say is that you guys gifted me millions of dollars?"

My brothers' faces are blank as if they are saying, "Catch up, girl."

"How are you guys so relaxed like it's not a big deal? How is this real life?" I shriek the last part, and this earns me a chuckle from Luca.

"So you guys are what, billionaires?" I ask with a nervous chuckle. When they don't laugh, I feel the blood draining from my face. "Really?" I ask, incredulous.

"Well, yeah. The vineyard has done incredibly well, and I've been investing some of the capital. And Gio has had investments for even longer than I have," Luca says, shrugging as if it's nothing out of the ordinary.

"Wow, so besides being handsome and intelligent, you guys are richer than sin, too? And how come I didn't I know you guys were billionaires?" I say, trying not to feel hurt, but it's inevitable. They still treat me like a child.

"Anyway, this has been fun, but I have to go figure out lunch and then go back to the university. Congratulations, Isa. I'm so proud of you. Luca will be transferring the funds to you, but let me know if there's anything else you need my help with. I'm only a text away," Gio states, and I nod at my big brother like the obedient little sister that I am.

Just kidding. I'm incredibly thankful that both of my brothers are still in my life and have my back.

Once Gio disconnects, I hug Luca because this is just surreal. *How is this my life?* One hundred million dollars in my name to start my dream?

"Thank you so much for being the best brother in the world. You provided me with a home and a family when our parents left."

Luca squeezes me, and after a couple of beats, he says, "You know you'll always have a place in this house, in my family, and in my heart. I'm so proud of you, kid. Can't wait to see the amazing art you'll create."

As relaxed and unfazed as my brother seems, his heart is as big as the sky. I'll never forget that he stepped up to be my parent figure when he was only twenty-two, trying to figure out life himself. After one more squeeze, we go over the bank transfer, and tears and more hugs are exchanged.

I decide I need to upgrade my wardrobe a little before my trip—I mean, I'm a millionaire now. This is incredible!

"Hey, girl, how did it go with your brothers?" Karina asks as she wipes the sweat from her forehead. She's been working in the fields all morning and just came back to the house for lunch.

"It was good, but I'm assuming you already knew?" I ask because I know she and Luca share everything.

"Well, yeah. But I'm so excited for you. What's the first thing you're going to do with your money?" she asks, giddiness oozing from her voice.

"I was thinking about getting some clothes for my trip. Then, I need to book my ticket to Italy. Although, I was thinking about spending a few days in Paris first because why not?" I shrug, feeling a little overwhelmed about the amount of money that is in my bank account now.

"That sounds fabulous. Let me shower and change, then we can grab lunch in the city and have a girls' afternoon," she chirps excitedly as she gets up from the dining table just as Luca comes in.

"Hey, bombón. Where are you going? I thought we were going to have lunch together and maybe take a siesta after?" Luca inquires as he hugs Karina and kisses her neck.

I see how my sister-in-law's knees literally go weak at my brother's attention, and I roll my eyes. I mean, I'm happy for them, but they're always touching. You'll never catch me being like that with a guy. What's the point of having someone in your life if you're just going to divorce later on? Or even worse, abandon your kids? No thanks, that's not for me.

"Okay, okay. I'm here, as well. Please leave the show for the bedroom," I say, and my brother rolls his eyes, tracing more kisses along Karina's neck.

"Yeah, *Guachito*. I'm going to the city with Isa. We'll be back tonight."

Luca pouts, and I can't help the laugh that escapes my lips.

"Dude, you're always together. You'll survive a few hours by yourself," I tell him as I pull Karina away from my brother, but he keeps his arm wrapped around her waist.

"You better come prepared to chant my name over and over tonight, bombón," I hear my brother whisper in Kari's ear, and I gag.

Sometimes, they're a little too much, and I don't think I've ever felt the need to be all over a guy every single time I see him. After more kissing and groping, Karina finally extends her hand to me and looks back to give a saucy grin to my brother, who not-so-subtly adjusts his junk. Ugh, these two are disgustingly in love.

"I'm so glad I'm moving out of this sex house. The two of you have scarred me for life."

Karina barks out a laugh, and I join her. As much shit as I give them, I adore them, and I'm truly happy for them.

"Wait until you find the man who makes you feel insatiable. You'll see," she chirps, and I don't reply. Besides a few flings in college, I've never been interested in a relationship.

"So are we looking for anything in particular?" Kari asks as she makes her way into the Santiago rush-hour traffic.

The drive from Alamo Peaks to Santiago is always dreamy, with the beautiful mountains in the background.

"Not really. I just want a couple of fun, summery outfits. You know, something cute and fresh. I'll get a feel for the city and the town and pick up more outfits while I'm there."

Karina nods slowly while singing one of the new Taylor Swift songs. "What do you think about going to Dani's boutique? I heard they just got her new collection."

I look at her, surprised. "Oh, I didn't realize she had a boutique here in Santiago."

Dani is one of Karina's best friends. They met while Karina was in college in Argentina. Dani, who's Colombian, went there for a summer after her parents passed away in a car accident. Then she met Marco, one of Luca's best friends, and as the old saying goes, the rest is history. She's a fashion designer and apparently now has boutiques not only in Argentina but also in Chile.

"That would be great. I've loved every single dress she's made for you."

Karina smiles as she continues to drive and sing along with Taylor on the radio. "So Italy, huh?"

And there it is. I've been waiting for this topic since we left the vineyard. "Yeah, the more I look up places to see and things to do there, the more I believe it's the best way to spend my summer. I even found a short summer class on modern art at the university where Gabo studied."

The moment I say his name, the air inside the car turns heavy. I saw this coming a mile away. My phone vibrates in my purse, and I welcome the distraction. It's a notification from Instagram.

GaboGodoy: Ciao, Bella. Of course, I'd love to host you. In fact, I have everything ready for you.

See you soon, G.

My heart skips a beat when I see his name, but I'm even more intrigued now. *How does he know I'll be there soon? And is he going to keep using the Bella nickname?*

"I'm surprised you got advice from Gabo, not because he's a bad guy. I mean, he's my brother, of course he's amazing," Karina says, bringing me back to our conversation and chuckling before she continues. "But because he's usually immersed in his own world, so the fact that he offered to be your contact while you're there is huge."

I look at Karina, confused.

Did she speak to him?

"How do you know he offered to be my contact?"

She smiles and waves off my confusion. "Oh, Luca mentioned it. You know him and Gabo have grown to be tight. I guess you came up in conversation when Luca said you were going to spend the summer in Italy."

Huh. Of course, they've been making sure my time in Italy goes smoothly. And my brother acting all innocent this morning, like he hadn't already given Gabo the speech about making sure I don't date anyone while I'm there. Ugh, Luca is too much sometimes.

"And don't worry. I already told your brother there's no need for us to fly with you to Italy."

My eyes grow as big as saucers, and my eyebrows shoot to the moon. "What?" I shriek, and Karina barks out a laugh.

"Oh, yeah, your brother thought it'd be a good idea for us to take a couple of weeks off and go with you to Bologna, to make sure you settled okay."

I shake my head as I face-palm. "I love Luca, you know I do. But sometimes he's overbearing."

Karina parks the car, and we get out, making our way to Dani's boutique.

"I know, and that's why I told him he needed you to do this on your own terms," she says as she links her arm with mine. "But just know that if at some point you need anything, Luca and I will be just a phone call away. Plus, my brother will be there. I think it's so cool you get to stay at his place. I've always loved it there."

Karina's words hit me like a grenade—I'm staying with Gabo Godoy? I mean, I thought he would let me stay at one of his places, but I didn't expect to share one with him. God, I hope my hormones behave.

Chapter 2

Gabo Godoy

The day has finally arrived. I'll pick up Bella at the airport in an hour. I never thought she would accept my offer. She has become a gorgeous woman—*bellissima*. It'd be tough to keep all the bros at bay.

When did I decide that it was okay for me to become a babysitter? Fucking Luca... had to guilt trip me: "Bro, remember. She's my little sister. I've taken care of yours with my life. I hope you do the same."

My immediate thought was to tell him that it's different because he's actually married to my sister. But I couldn't say no, and he's an excellent husband to Kari. The least I could do was offer accommodations to Bella.

Maybe I'm overthinking this? I mean, I only agreed to give her a place to stay and make sure she's comfortable—not to be her bodyguard.

I park my Bugatti Chiron at my private hangar. Luca wanted to bring Bella himself, but I dismissed him and sent my Gulfstream G700 to get her instead. The moment I see her coming down the stairs, it's like my body floats toward her. In two seconds, I'm right at the bottom of the steps to help her down.

What am I now, a teenager who has never seen a pretty girl? But no, she's not a girl anymore. She turned out to be a gorgeous woman. For some reason, I don't want anyone to help her down but me.

Damn brain, enough with the whiplash.

"Oh, hi, Gabo. Thank you so much for picking me up. I thought you were going to send someone to get me," she says with a bright smile on her rosy, glossy lips.

I need to take a deep breath before replying and making an idiot of myself. I'm a thirty-year-old man, for fuck's sake. I shouldn't be here swooning like a schoolgirl.

"*Bienvenida a Italia,*" I say as I give her a peck on her cheek. "Your brother would have my balls if I'd have sent someone to pick you up. Besides, it's good to see you. I didn't think you were going to take me up on my offer."

Her smile falters for a microsecond, and if I wasn't so focused on her, I'd have missed it.

"Oh, of course. I guess you'll be my guardian while I'm here in Italy, even though I'm a full-grown adult. If it is too much inconvenience, I can always look for a place to stay," she says matter-of-factly, and I instantly like her resolve.

"It's not a big deal. I'm sure you have plenty of matters to attend to," she adds as she starts walking toward a utility car where they have placed her luggage.

I simply shake my head. I like her spunk, maybe a little too much.

"*Principessa*, wait," I shout as I jog to catch up with her. She looks at me as if to say, "What did you just call me?" I chuckle. I've always liked strong-willed women, but I have a feeling Bella would give anyone a run for their money.

"Paolo will bring your luggage to either my apartment in the city, or my villa in the countryside. I figured I'd take you out to dinner tonight so you can get a feel for the city. My car is this way."

I point with my thumb in the direction where I parked my Bugatti. The moment her eyes find my car, her jaw hits the floor. I grab her gently by her elbow, and she falls in step beside me without saying a word.

When we get to my car, I open the door for her and ask, "Is everything okay?"

She shakes her head as she smiles and fixes her hair behind her ears. "Absolutely. I guess I'm just a little starstruck. That was my first time flying private. By the way, it was amazing. Thank you so much. And I don't think I've ever seen a car like this in real life."

I bark out a laugh as I help her inside and then jog to my side of the car. When I turn it on and the engine roars to life, I see a flicker of excitement in Bella's beautiful azure eyes.

"You're in for a treat, principessa." I floor the gas, and we dart out of the private hangar in a flash.

Usually, the women I take out in this car hang onto my arm like it's a lifeline, but Bella keeps her poise, almost impassive. Interesting.

I take a curve a little harder than I should to see if she'll finally show any emotion, but she surprises me. Instead of shrieking in terror, she throws her head back and laughs. I take it as a dare and fly through the streets, getting us to Verona—my favorite restaurant—in no time.

Once I park in front of the valet, she flashes me a wicked grin.

"That was fun," she says as she goes to open her door. I extend my arm to keep her door closed. She looks at me, confused.

As I get out of the car, I simply say, "I'm glad you enjoyed it. Please, Bella. I need to open the door for you."

She shrugs easily and stays seated, waiting for me. When I reach her door, the valet kid opens it and extends his hand to Bella, but to my surprise, she stays seated.

Good girl.

When the kid notices me, he jumps out of his skin. If he's smart enough, he'll get lost as soon as I give him the key fob.

"Mr. Godoy, I didn't realize it was you," the kid says with a shaky voice. If I were alone, I'd laugh, but I don't want Bella to think I'm a prick.

"And how many Bugatti Chirons are in Bologna?" I ask as I take his place in front of the door. Bella steps out of the car, shaking her hair like a model in a commercial, leaving everyone nearby stunned by her looks. My dick perks up, and I take a deep breath to keep my lustful thoughts in check. I should have gotten laid or at least jerked off before picking her up.

Why the fuck am I behaving like a teenager with Bella?

I hear a collective gasp around us. Even though I have no claim on her, I feel ten feet taller knowing that she's here with me. I place my hand on the small of her back, and a shot of electricity spreads through me. I know she felt it too because goosebumps form all over her back.

Once we get inside, a smiling sommelier shows us to my table and leaves us with the menu. Bella gazes in awe at the stunning restaurant. Verona is a century-old—a pearl in downtown Bologna—and boasts a three-star Michelin chef.

"So they know you here?" Bella asks as she starts perusing the menu.

"I actually own this restaurant," I say as I take a sip of my tonic water.

"Of course you do," she mutters, and that piques my curiosity.

"What do you mean?" I ask, wanting to know her thoughts.

Instead of replying immediately, she takes her time. She sips her water and fixes her hair. This would usually annoy me—I'm an impatient man—but I'm actually enjoying the view. Bella is wearing a baby powder blue skirt paired with a matching top. All silk, the outfit is flowy and ethereal, just like her. Her hair cascades in waves midway down her back, and her makeup is minimal but accentuates the intensity of her eyes and her pouty lips. She takes a deep breath, and I can't help but notice the rise of her breasts—two perfect small mountains waiting to be worshiped.

"Are you ready to order?" the waiter interrupts us, and just like that, the moment is gone.

"Actually, yes. I'd like to start with the octopus, then the lobster for the main course, and the orange and dark chocolate *bonet* for dessert. As for my drink, I'll go with whatever Mr. Godoy chooses," Bella says in perfect Italian. I raise a brow at her, pleasantly surprised by her language skills.

After ordering, the sommelier brings a bottle of my favorite wine. We toast, and I tell her, "Impressive. I didn't know you were fluent in Italian."

She chuckles at my compliment. "I mean, with my last name I had no choice."

I chuckle at her joke but press further. "Isn't that profiling? I've never been expected to speak Galician because of my last name."

She takes another sip of her wine. "Touché, but to be honest, I minored in Italian, French, and English at college. I figured they'd come in handy once I opened my gallery."

Oh, so that's her goal. I thought Luca was full of shit when he mentioned it. I feel like an asshole; I offered her my place for the summer and never spoke to her again. The only conversations I had about her trip were with my best friend.

"That's impressive, Bella. So your goal is to come to Europe, acquire art, and sell it in Santiago?" I ask, buying some time to find the right words for what I want to tell her next.

"Yes, that's the big picture. I actually would love to find immigrant artists who want to bring their art back home."

"Let's pause here. I feel we need to start this conversation over and, this time, do it right," I say.

"I'm sorry. I don't follow," she says, confusion evident on her beautiful face.

I give her a kind smile in hopes it'll erase her furrowing brow and let her know there's nothing wrong, per se. "I know I offered to be your host here. I'm truly pleased that you are here, and I know you'll make the best of your time. But instead of speaking directly with you to learn all these things from you, I kept in contact with your brother as if you were, indeed, a minor. And that's not right."

I take my glass in my hand, motion for her to do the same and start speaking again. "I would like to propose a toast to you, your ideas, and to having a summer to remember."

Bella's smile is blinding. "This means a lot to me, Gabo. I really appreciate you. Thank you."

We toast, and she passes her napkin over her mouth—it's a simple motion, but it brings my attention to her pouty lips.

The things those lips could do.

I clear my throat while trying to remove the thought as Bella starts speaking.

"I love my brother, and I'm very thankful for everything he and Karina have done for me. But sometimes I feel like I'm suffocating under his scrutiny."

It's the first time today that Bella has let me see her vulnerable side. Behind her bravado is a woman trying to make her voice heard and make her mark in the world.

I can definitely appreciate that.

"Being the middle brother was always a struggle to follow in Vicente's footsteps while still being true to myself, you know?"

Her eyebrows rise in question. "I thought being the middle brother was easy. I mean, you don't necessarily have to carry the family name. Didn't you mention this back in Alamo Peaks?"

A small laugh escapes me as the waiter arrives with the appetizers. "You're not wrong. I don't have to carry the Godoy last name into the next generation, but when you have a brother who fills the older brother's shoes so perfectly—responsible, disciplined, determined—you feel the need to live up to his greatness and not be in his shadow. Vicente is the perfect child, you know?" I tell her honestly.

"I can understand that, even though it took Luca meeting your sister to fully believe he could be as great as Gio." She takes a bite of her octopus and moans as she savors it.

Holy shit.

"I'm so sorry. I didn't mean to make that sound. It's just so delicious."

She covers her mouth with her hand, and I notice a pink flush creeping up her chest. She's fucking bewitching. I take a bite out of the octopus and moan just like she did a moment ago. She barks out a laugh, and I'm not sure why, but I love that I made her laugh that hard.

The night continues, and we make easy conversation as we get to know each other a little better. After our second bottle of wine, I ask for the check. Bella tilts her head, her brow furrowing slightly.

"What? Do you think I eat for free here?" I smirk at her as I sign the bill. "This is a business. I need to treat it as such."

I give her a wink; her blush is back, and this time, it's closer to a dark red hue. I need to chill it out—the last thing I need is for her to think I'm hitting on her.

Do I want to hit on her?

Before I can even answer that, Luca's words come to mind, and that's all the answer I need: take care of his sister like he's taken care of mine.

As we make our way through the restaurant, I place my hand on the small of her back. When we get outside, I ask her, "Are you too tired to walk? My place is just a couple of blocks away."

She shakes her head and gives me a small smile. It's re-freshing that she didn't make a big fuss about walking instead of driving. But we had two bottles of wine, and I'd rather not risk it with her in the car. I'd never put her in danger.

Chapter 3

ISABELLA BIANCHI

I know I haven't even been in Italy for twenty-four hours, but so far, I'm loving it. I had an amazing dinner with Gabo last night—his restaurant looks straight out of a movie. It was so luxurious, and the food was to die for—just exquisite. I really liked that he played it safe and decided to walk home instead of driving his car while tipsy. The boys at school were all about flaunting their cars and driving drunk. Allegedly, it made them cooler and more badass. Huh, not in my eyes, that's for sure.

Last night, I didn't get a chance to tour Gabo's penthouse; all I wanted was to shower and crash. My room is absolutely gorgeous: it has a four-post bed with a beautiful silk canopy, the fluffiest comforter, and tons and tons of pillows.

This morning, I woke up refreshed and ready to take Bologna by storm. The moment I set foot in the kitchen to prepare breakfast, my jaw hit the floor. It's a state-of-the-art kitchen, and all the appliances are industrial-grade. There's even a goddamn walk-in fridge! This place is honestly surreal. Everything in Gabo's place is out of this world. Owning my own penthouse—just like this one but in Santiago—has become my top dream. Right after I establish my gallery, of course.

I'm not sure why, but every time I'm in the kitchen cooking, my mind wanders to my childhood.

Growing up, I used to do ballet. Although I really enjoyed wearing tutus and the recitals, as I grew older, I switched to contemporary dance. I felt it allowed me to express myself better. It was another outlet for my creativity, just like painting.

I'm lost in my thoughts, dancing to the beat of a song I can't get out of my head while making breakfast in Gabo's immaculate kitchen. I turn from the stove to plate the pancakes I just made when I see the most sculpted body I've ever seen in my life. Gabo is wearing black basketball shorts that hang low on his waist. His muscles are on full display since the man decided not to wear a T-shirt, nearly giving me a heart attack. Not to mention the beads of sweat rolling down his abs. *Does he have a gym here, too?* Of course, he does. Even Luca has one at the villa.

I can't take my eyes off Gabo. I'm sure I'm red as a beet, but I'll worry about that later because now I see the dust of hair that forms a happy trail to what I'm assuming is a huge cock. Those shorts leave little to the imagination. Fuck, after seeing Gabo like this, I'm rethinking my past choices. All the guys I've been with are just kids compared to this Adonis in front of me.

Maybe I can find a man to have a fling with while I'm here. Hmm, I better add that to my to-do list for the summer.

"Oh, morning, Bella. I didn't realize you were already up," he says, cool as a cucumber as he wipes the sweat from his face with a towel that's now hanging on his shoulders.

I open my mouth, but no words come out. I must be making a very silly face because Gabo chuckles.

"Listen, I'm about to get ready to go to the office, but if there's anything you need, don't hesitate to contact me. If I can't come get you, I'll send Mario. He's my security lead." He slides a business card on the counter, and after a little salute, he makes his way to his room.

Once I hear the lock click on his door, I release a deep sigh. I know he's not the first attractive man I've laid eyes on, but damn, he's definitely the hottest.

After eating my breakfast, I grab his card and can't help but notice the beautiful design. His name is in bold gold letters against a black background—elegant and sophisticated, just like him.

I head to my room, shaking off any thoughts of Gabo. I take a shower before checking the weather on my phone. Beautiful sunny skies and a balmy 80°F (26°C) call for a cute summer dress from Dani's collection and comfortable sneakers to wander the streets of Bologna and get lost in its beauty.

I plan to start my day at Piazza Maggiore. It isn't too far from Gabo's place, so I use Google Maps to guide my walk.

Walking slowly, I take my time appreciating the architecture. It's incredible how Gabo's apartment building blends in with the traditional structures around it.

Last night, it was too dark to appreciate the charming details Gabo incorporated into his building. The beautiful arches and baroque statues he designed are stunning. Seeing this building only from the outside, I'd have never guessed all the modern amenities it contains. I wonder if all of the apartments are like his. My guess is no since he lives in the penthouse, but I'll definitely ask.

Last night, I could tell that architecture is his passion. The way he talked about his current project is the way I light up when I talk about my art.

I make it to Piazza Maggiore in no time and am breathless at the sight. There are so many beautiful stone buildings with their old-world charm that I'm not sure where to start my tour. I try to absorb as much as I can while I look for a place to sit down, but I just know it'll take me days to go through the intricate designs of all the windows and arches on the structures here. That's what happens when you have a degree in art and an eye for everyday artistic elements.

There's a cafe on the left side of the piazza, so I decide to set up camp there. I get my sketchbook out, and once the waiter comes around, I order a coffee and focaccia. My phone vibrates in my bag, and I immediately take it out, wondering who would be calling me.

"*Hermanita*, are you okay? I texted you last night but didn't hear back from you." Luca's voice is almost frantic. He honestly needs to calm down.

"Good morning, Luca. Yes, I'm fine. Gabo picked me up at the hangar and took me to dinner. I honestly haven't checked my phone. I'm sorry I didn't tell you I arrived safe and sound, but since you and Gabo talk all the time, I figured he'd fill you in."

I hear him release a deep breath, and I immediately feel bad. I need to remember he's just trying to be a good brother, not trying to control my life. At least, I hope so.

"No, the *boludo* didn't answer my calls or texts either. That's why I was starting to get on edge."

"I'm sorry I worried you, Luca. But I promise you, everything is fine. I haven't been here for even a full day yet, but what I've seen so far is gorgeous. The architecture is exquisite, and the food is delicious. I feel like one summer here won't be enough to really take everything in."

"I'm glad you're enjoying your time there so far. You don't need to call or text daily, but please try to answer when I call." His tone is sincere so I'm not going to give him a hard time for being a little overbearing.

As I'm about to reply, a request for Facetime comes in, and I chuckle. To my surprise, it isn't my brother on the screen—it's Karina.

"Isa, hi! Your brother was about to get on a plane and go find you," she says, laughing, and Luca takes the phone out of her hand.

"I was not. I'm not that deranged. Am I?" Luca pouts, and Karina laughs harder.

"So how's everything? Where are you staying?" Karina asks as she gets comfortable on Luca's office couch.

I flip the camera so I can show them where I am. "Everything is so beautiful here. I was about to grab a bite and sketch for a while before heading to the university to see where my summer class will be."

I talk to Karina until Luca starts chasing her out of his office so he can take a call. After saying goodbye and promising Luca I'd be better at staying in contact, I put my phone away and start trying to capture the essence of the piazza on paper. My favorite way to paint is with watercolors, but when I'm out and about, carbon pencil is my go-to. It gives dimension, and I can use shadows to do a better representation of the little details.

I lose track of time between sketching and people-watching, but I can tell it's lunchtime because the cafe is getting busier. My stomach rumbles, reminding me I need to eat. I flag down the waiter and order a pasta dish that caught my eye, along with a glass of red wine he recommended. All too soon, it's time to make my way to the university. Packing up my art supplies, I head off in the direction of the campus.

The University of Bologna is out of this world—the buildings are so beautifully preserved, you can smell the history of the walls—so much knowledge to be absorbed. Even though the ceilings are painted only in some rooms, I can't wait to attend class here. I know I'm being greedy, but I wish every single corner of this school was beautifully painted. It'd take me a lifetime to catalog all the details in the paintings here. It feels like just by being here, in this historic place, I'm already learning so much.

I want to double-check that I'm indeed registered and that everything is ready for me to start my modern art class on Monday, so I head toward the registration office. There's a huge line, but there's nothing else I have to do today. I'd rather stay here than go back to the apartment and fall asleep. Jet lag is no joke.

"Excuse me, are you here to register for the summer semester?" a guy asks me, and I am taken by surprise because I didn't see him get in line behind me.

"Oh. no. I just want to make sure I'm registered," I tell him, and he gives me a blinding smile.

Damn, he's cute. Tall, with dark hazel eyes and unruly hair. He almost reminds me of someone, except this guy is a boy, and that someone is a man.

"Oh, great, nice to meet you. I'm Giacomo." He extends his hand to me and gives me a peck on each cheek.

"I'm Isabella."

"So, what did you register for?" he asks nonchalantly. He's wearing white pants and a black tee, and his shoes are covered in paint. He has a very relaxed style, so I'm guessing he's an artist.

"History of modern art," I tell him, and his eyes grow big.

"No way. That's the class I'm trying to get into," he says with much more enthusiasm than I was expecting.

Was he going to take that class? Or is it because I told him I'm taking it?

"Really? Why do you want to take that class?" I ask.

"I'm studying art, and during the summer, I like working a couple of days a week and taking a class that can be used toward my degree. The rest of the time, I enjoy traveling," he tells me with glee in his eyes, and I smile at ease; he seems genuine.

"That sounds amazing. I just graduated from college." He raises his eyebrows in question, and I chuckle. "Yeah, back in Chile," I say as I rearrange the strap of my bag on my shoulder, suddenly feeling overwhelmed by Giacomo's attention.

"Your Italian is impressive. You could have fooled me, I thought you were from here."

I smile at the compliment. "Thanks. This truth is I enjoy learning languages."

"So, are you here just for the summer?" he asks, and I don't answer immediately. As nice as he seems, I don't know him.

"I'm sorry, I'm not trying to interrogate you. I'm simply genuinely interested in getting to know you," he says with a sheepish smile, and I smile back.

Before I can answer, it's my turn to talk to the registrar employee. I got all the documents I need for Monday, including a campus map and a couple of books the professors want us to work with.

As I'm turning to leave, Giacomo asks, "Would you wait for me? This won't take long." I nod, and fifteen minutes later, we're making our way out of the building.

"Do you have plans tonight? I'm going out with my friends, and I figured you could join us," Giacomo says expectantly.

Even though he seems nice, I'm still struggling with the jetlag, so I decide to tell him the truth.

"As fun as that sounds, I arrived yesterday, and I'm still trying to catch up with sleep. I'll see you next week," I say as I start making my way toward Gabo's place. Giacomo falls in step beside me.

"I can understand that, but maybe we can see if you're feeling better over the weekend?" He looks like he wants to say more, but he simply smiles and waits for me to make up my mind.

I shrug as I take my phone out and pass it to him. Once he enters his number, he texts himself from my phone.

"Thank you, Isabella. I'll see you around." He pockets his phone and gives me two kisses, one on each cheek, before he walks in the opposite direction. I watch his figure recede as he walks away, then continue on my way toward Gabo's place. I can't wait to take a long bath, maybe order some food, and sleep for a *long* time.

Chapter 4

GABO GODOY

I've been on edge all fucking day. When I gave Bella my card this morning, I thought she would text me so I could save her number, but nothing. I haven't heard from her all day. I know she's fine since I asked Mario to send someone to make sure she was safe, but still. It's not the same as hearing from her. I'm not even sure why I am so on edge about it; it's not like she's mine to protect or that someone has threatened her. But the moment I saw her coming out of my jet, it was like I felt she had become *mine*.

Which is ludicrous. I mean, who the fuck thinks like that? I think I've just been alone for a long time now, and seeing a beautiful woman took my brain for a spin. I think it's best to take the weekend off and let her settle alone in my penthouse.

You know that's not the only thing that pulls you to her. The girl is smart, ambitious, and driven, the little voice in my head says. I decide to shake off my thoughts and make a phone call on the drive home instead.

My brother picks up after the second ring.

"What?" Vicente scoffs. I roll my eyes; he's such a dick when he wants to be.

"Hello to you too, dear brother. I was going to ask how you are, but I guess I already got my answer."

"Sorry." Vicente releases a deep breath. "It's been fucking chaos today."

"Then my call is the answer to your prayers," I tell him, my idea taking more form in my head.

"You got my attention, Gabo. What do you have in mind?"

"What about a bro weekend? I need to let off some steam, too." I pray he doesn't pry for more than I can tell him right now, but even more, I pray he accepts. My brother is married to his business. Rarely ever takes time off.

"Okay, where and when?" he answers immediately. I'm utterly shocked he accepted, but I'm not about to poke the bear.

"Your choice. I can go over to London, or we can meet halfway in Ibiza."

"I need to get out of London. Ibiza will do."
"Fuck yes. I'll take care of everything. I'll email you the details soon."

"Okay." He releases another breath. *I wonder what has him so wound up.* "And Gabo? Thank you. I owe you."

Vicente disconnects the call before I can ask him what's going on, but I'll have time this weekend. I know he'll loosen up after a few drinks.

As soon as the elevator opens to the main floor of my penthouse, a delicious smell hits my nostrils. I'm immediately transported to my childhood in my parents' hacienda. I can't believe Bella cooked *niños envueltos*—a delicious set of veggies wrapped in thin beef slices and spices. But if I thought the smell was good, I'm left breathless when my eyes fall on Bella. This morning, when I came out of the shower, she was dancing while cooking, and it was a sight for sore eyes—Bella can move. But nothing would have prepared me for the barely-there shorts she's wearing, which give me a painful peek at her ass cheeks.

She moved all the furniture out of the living room to create a makeshift dance studio. She's wearing headphones, so she hasn't noticed that I've arrived. I can't hear the music she's dancing to, but the way she's moving, her entire body is telling a story—one that I'd like nothing more than to join.

She's swaying her arms, side to side, creating a storm. Her feet are quick, and she jumps from one side of the room to the other—impressively, I must add. Then she stops suddenly, wrapping her arms around her waist protectively. Her face contorts as if she were in pain, and somehow, it hurts me, too. It's incredible how affected I am just by her movements. I'm sure if I were listening to the music, I'd be bawling like a baby. It's art. And it's beautiful.

She opens her eyes and freezes in place the moment she sees me. A lovely blush brightens her cheeks, and I can't help but keep staring—she's so beautiful. Her hair is a wild mess, her chest rises and falls to the beat of her heart, and sweat glistens on her beautiful creamy skin. She's a vision.

"I'm sorry. I didn't realize you were home. I'll put everything back the way you had it after dinner. Are you hungry?" she asks as she rearranges her messy bun. When she lifts her arms, her tits also go up, and I have to inhale a sharp breath.

Hosting Bella definitely wasn't a good idea when I haven't had a chance to get laid in months. This new project I'm working on is more demanding than I anticipated. It's a good thing I'm leaving for the weekend. I can relax, decompress, and come back on Monday ready to kick ass—and avoid having unholy thoughts about her.

"Yeah, I could eat," I reply. I loosen my tie, and Bella swallows hard, and that immediately catches my attention. Damn, I need a cold shower.

"Great, I'll plate the food, you serve the wine?" she asks as if we've done this a thousand times, and it feels nice. Every single woman I've brought to my place who has tried to make breakfast in the morning gets the cold shoulder. I've never been a man to go from a one-night stand to a steady relationship. I don't even think I've ever wanted a steady relationship, so the mere thought of feeling okay with Bella cooking dinner for me is wild. It must be because she's family—she's my best friend's little sister, for fuck's sake.

We sit on the patio, enjoying the calm breeze. The street lights below and the sounds of the city are the perfect background for the evening. Amid the cacophony of people chatting and cars passing by, my place feels like an oasis in the middle of the chaotic city. I take a bite of the food Bella prepared, and my eyes close in ecstasy. Damn, it tastes just like the one Graciela, our nanny, used to make when we were growing up.

"This is delicious. Where did you learn to cook?" I ask, honestly intrigued.

Bella lowers her gaze and wipes her lips gently with her napkin. So demure, yet so sexy at the same time. When she raises her gaze to find mine, a small smile appears on her beautiful face.

"Inés, our nanny, became best friends with Graciela when we moved to Chile, and they exchanged recipes. The first time Ines prepared this at Luca's place, I fell in love." I chuckle at her response but nod in understanding.

"Yes, I've heard they became tight. Isn't it crazy that both of our families are so different, yet have so many things in common? For instance, this dish is my favorite ever. If I could only eat one thing for the rest of my life, it would be this." I raise my glass and motion for her to do the same.

"I had no idea it was your favorite, but I'm glad I decided to prepare a nice dinner instead of taking a bath and going to bed as I had originally planned. Jet lag is no joke, and I'd rather tire myself out now than go to bed and wake up in the middle of the night."

The image of her taking a bath forms in my head, and I immediately push it away, shaking my head. Instead, I go for what I think is a harmless and friendly toast. "Here's to a fantastic meal with unbeatable company."

Her eyes light up at my compliment, and I immediately berate myself. *What the fuck I am doing flirting with her? I need to stop this shit.* Instead of overthinking what I just did, I chug the entire glass of wine and help myself to a refill. She doesn't say anything, but she eyes me warily, as if she's worried about me. I should slow down on the drinking for a bit; I don't want her to think I'm a heavy drinker.

The rest of the meal goes by quickly as she smartly changes the topic and goes on to tell me what she did all day. I'm captivated by her bubbly personality. The way she describes the cafe where she sat for a while at Piazza Maggiore, enjoying focaccia with the most delicious cappuccino she has ever had—her words, not mine—I'm truly enjoying her story until she mentions she met someone. My brain halts like a rollercoaster stopping in its tracks.

"Hold on. Who did you say you met?" I try to sound nonchalant, but my tone has more emotion than I anticipated.

She raises an eyebrow and gives me a smirk that my dick immediately notices. Fuck.

"His name is Giacomo, and we're taking the same summer class," she says with a chuckle as she takes a sip of her wine.

I bite my lip, trying to take a couple of minutes to calm down, but she mimics me and bites her lip, and that only makes my dick grow harder. I'll have to wait for a while before I can get up from this table.

"Anyway, he seemed nice, so we exchanged numbers." She shrugs like it's not a big deal. A feeling too close to jealousy forms inside me. Jealous of what? I have no idea. Maybe it's because the fucker got her number, and I didn't.

"So you made plans for the weekend already?" I ask, and she shakes her head no. I release a deep breath, and she eyes me curiously.

"I told him I had just arrived and wanted to get a feel for the city this weekend. I'll see him on Monday in class, anyway."

Instead of calming down, this makes me even more jealous. She's already thinking about seeing him? It serves me right for getting hard for a girl who's eight years younger than me.

"Oh, about this weekend... are you okay staying here by yourself?" I ask, taking the opportunity to share my plan with her.

"Gabo, I truly appreciate you letting me stay at your place, but under no circumstances am I expecting you to be my babysitter. There are plenty of places for me to visit this weekend." She gives me a sweet smile, and I smile back.

"I know you don't need me around you twenty-four seven, it's just I don't want you to feel uncomfortable or anything while you're here."

"I promise I won't, but now I'm intrigued. Where are you going?" She leans down the table, closing the distance between us, and I can smell her heady scent from dancing mixed with a soft floral aroma—it's deliciously intoxicating.

Clearing my throat, I answer, "I'm spending the weekend with my brother in Ibiza." Her eyes grow big, and a cheeky smile appears on her face.

"That sounds like fun. And definitely not a place I would see Vicente going."

I bark out a laugh—she's not wrong.

"Yeah, I didn't think he was going to agree to go with me, but I guess he needs a break, too." Her face morphs at my words, and my eyebrows furrow.

"I didn't realize it was your idea. I'm sorry you need a break from me already." She gets up from the table and takes her plate inside.

"Bella, please wait." Fuck, I'm such an idiot. She places the plate in the dishwasher and turns to face me, crossing her arms on her chest. I try really hard to not let my eyes wander to her chest—I really do—but it's a lost battle.

"You have to believe me, I have no issue with you staying here. I didn't lie when I said during the toast that the company is unbeatable. But it's been a stressful time at work with this large project, and I just need to release some steam," I tell her, trying to sound as sincere as possible.

She releases a sigh, and her shoulders sag as her arms go to her sides. "I'm sorry. I'm in defense mode with you, and it's not fair. I guess I have some trauma I have to work through. So tell me, what's the project about?" she asks, visibly more relaxed than she was a couple of seconds ago.

What *trauma is she talking about? I need to find a way to go back to that point.*

"My firm specializes in renovating old buildings. Like this," I explain as I open my arms to show the building we're in. "We try to retain as many of the original details as possible on the exterior, while bringing all the modern amenities to the inside," I say, pride evident in my tone.

"This place is beautiful. I actually am curious to know if the rest of the apartments are as luxurious as this one." She bites her lip while giving me a shy smile, and I smile back, loving her compliment. It is a very luxurious place.

"Why don't we go back to the patio, and I'll tell you more about this building."

She nods and leads the way back outside. I sigh in relief, thankful I was able to diffuse the situation.

We sit opposite each other on the couch next to the dining table, as relaxed as can be.

"The original plan was to create a multipurpose space: housing on the top floors and commercial on the main floor.

But the moment I came in and saw the city views from this patio, I knew I had to make this my main residence."

She's giving me her undivided attention, focused on my every word, and for some reason, that makes me feel important.

"I designed the penthouse for myself, of course." She chuckles at my words, and I join her. "But I also wanted to have plenty of space for when my family visits. So I designed two apartments with a total of eight bedrooms. Plenty of space for anyone who wants to visit. The other two floors are my garage."

Bella's jaw hits the floor, and I give her a smirk. "Yeah, I like cars. I collect them, actually," I say with a shrug as I take a sip of my wine.

Once she recovers from her shock, she gives me a smirk in return. "Of course you do. I mean, you wouldn't be a millionaire if you didn't have an extravagant car collection or something decadent like that."

"A billionaire," I correct her, and she laughs out loud.

"Oh, I apologize. Mr. Fancy-Billionaire-Pants," she says, glee in her eyes, and I laugh at the moniker.

"So let me get this right. You have a five-floor building just for yourself in the heart of downtown Bologna, and your guilty billionaire pleasure is to collect cars. You also own an architecture firm that's quite successful. Anything else I need to know?" she asks expectantly, and I grab my chin with my thumb and forefinger, pretending to be hard in thought.

"Well, I own a yacht, a house in the countryside, another one on the beach, and you already know about the jet. I have more money than I know what to do with, and my pride and joy is my architecture firm. We've worked hard for our reputation, and I'm trying to expand my business into the warehouses and data center building industry." I don't like flaunting my assets in front of others, but for some reason, I feel like Bella won't judge me for sharing a few of the things I own.

"That's impressive for someone your age, Mr. Billionaire," she says, and I feel the heat rising in my cheeks at her compliment.

"I recently learned my brothers are also billionaires, and I couldn't believe it. I still can't believe it. I know they've worked really hard for what they have, especially Luca, but having billions of dollars is just crazy to me." She shakes her head like she's truly in disbelief that her family has amassed so much money.

"But anyways, I'd love to go to your country house one day. I enjoy the city, but the peace and quiet of the country is something I truly love," she says with dreamy eyes, and I'm already making plans in my head to take her out to my house in Monterosso.

"Definitely. We'll have all summer for me to show you around," I say, making a silent promise to help her have the best time of her life.

Bella gets up from the couch and yawns as she stretches her arms above her head. The movement causes her shirt to rise, giving me a peek at her toned abdomen. She gives me a little wave as she makes her way to her room. I nod, and the moment she's out of sight, I rub my hand across my face.

Why do I enjoy her company so much?

I need to keep telling myself she's just a family friend. I'm simply enjoying her company because she's nice, smart, and has all these grand plans and dreams, not to mention how beautiful she is. Nothing more. Ugh, I need to pack and get out of here.

On my way to my room, I make a mental note to let Mario know that he needs to have a security detail taking care of her this weekend.

She's my responsibility, after all.

Chapter 5

Isabella Bianchi

I wake up energized and rested but without a real plan in mind. Instead of getting up and looking for sustenance, I decide to stay in bed for a little longer; it's the most comfortable bed I've ever slept in. It's plush and soft, and the mattress is firm but not too firm. *Ah, I love it.* I'll have to get a bed just like this when I go back to Santiago.

Once I finally get up, I make my way to the kitchen. I stand still for a few seconds, unable to believe what's on the counter. It's a beautiful flower arrangement with peonies, roses, and carnations in all shades of pink, yellow, orange, and white. There are also little pink flowers that, after some Googling, I learn are called bleeding hearts. There must be at least two hundred flowers in total. It almost takes up the entire kitchen island—it's stunning. There's a note attached to it, and the paper has golden flowers engraved on it, and it smells just like the flowers.

Principessa,

I hope you enjoy your first weekend in Bologna. I've left a security detail outside the building, ready to take you wherever you need to go.

Gabo.

Interesting. He called me principessa again. I wonder where he got that nickname from? And a security detail? Why would I need a bodyguard? No one knows me in this city—I'm a simple girl who's here for the summer. Nothing more.

When I walk into the fridge to see what I can prepare, there are so many containers— it's incredible. When did he have time to plan all this? I didn't even hear him leave this morning. I get out a couple of containers with cut fruit and Greek yogurt. Then I find nuts and honey in the chef's pantry and decide to get a picture to send to Gabo, thanking him for the flowers.

I get his contact card from my purse and send him a text along with the picture:

Isabella: These are the most gorgeous flowers I've ever received. I love them. *Gracias*! I'll see you in a few days.

I eat my breakfast while browsing social media, but after a couple of spoonfuls, I decide to FaceTime Karina. I'd rather check in with her than with Luca.

When the video connects, I see she's working in the greenhouse. I'm so glad I'm missing the cold ass winter back in Chile.

"Hey, Isa. How's it going?" Karina asks with a big smile on her face as she wipes her forehead. I guess the greenhouse is warm.

"Good. Great, even. Yesterday, I went to see the campus, and it's out of this world! I even met a classmate." I stop talking so I can breathe, and Karina chuckles at my excitement.

"That's awesome. I'm glad you're loving it so far. How are things with my brother?" Karina asks nonchalantly, but I can see her smirk. She's dying to know if there's any tea.

"Everything is good. We had a nice dinner the night I arrived, and this morning, he left for Ibiza with Vicente." Karina's eyes grow big, but she doesn't say anything immediately. After a couple of minutes, she finally speaks.

"Interesting. I wonder why he had to go out of town."

I lift my shoulder as if to say, "I have no clue." But then I decide to ask what I've been dying to know.

"So he left me a note this morning saying there's a security detail outside waiting for me. What's up with that?"

Karina frowns in confusion. "Isa, do you realize my brother is a billionaire? You're staying at his place, so you need to stay safe."

"All this billionaire talk is a little crazy to me. Last week, I learned that my brothers are billionaires, and now I'm staying with a billionaire. I mean, I knew our families had money but *billionaires*?" Karina chuckles as I move my hands around, as if to say, "What the actual hell?"

"The fact that you've never seen security here in Chile doesn't mean we don't have it. The moment you moved to Santiago for college, your brother hired a company to keep you safe."

My jaw hits the floor; I feel so dumb and little. How is it possible I've had someone following me for the past four years, and I never noticed?

"But why didn't anyone tell me?" I say, my jaw clenched. "I might be the young one in the family, but I'm not stupid, you know?" Tears start pooling in my eyes, but I take a few deep breaths to keep them at bay.

"Oh, Isa. Please don't be upset. Your brothers were just trying to protect you," Karina says in a soft tone, and it only makes me angrier. I love my sister-in-law, but she's not gentle. She's strong and determined and never minces words. Right now, I feel like she's trying to calm me down, but it's having the opposite effect.

"You know what? You're right. You all always do what's best for me. Talk later." Without waiting for her to say goodbye, I disconnect the video and get ready. I'm going out, and I'm going to do whatever the fuck I want. I'm not a baby who needs to be protected from anything.

⟶⊸✦⊷⟵

The moment I walk outside, I see two men standing by a Mercedes Benz SUV. When they see me, they both come my way. I'm thankful Gabo let me know there would be people waiting for me because if I didn't know, I'd be freaking out.

The men are wearing black suits, Ferragamo loafers, and sunglasses, and they both have coms in their ears. They look like they're a little older than Gabo, but not by much—maybe in their late thirties. It's probably a good thing that they're older, considering they're bodyguards and all.

It's like I'm living in an alternate universe.

"*Signorina*, good morning. I'm Rocco, and I'm in charge of making sure you're safe at all times." He tries to smile, but I don't think he's used to it because it comes out like he's in pain. I smile in return and look behind him, waiting for him to introduce the other huge man with him.

"Oh, yes. This is Aldo, he'll be your driver," Rocco says. Aldo nods at me, and I nod back.

After squaring my shoulders and taking a deep breath, I look at Rocco in the eyes and tell him, "Very well, the first place I want to go is a classic car dealership."

None of the men moved, like I wasn't clear enough. And if I weren't so riled up about being treated like a baby, I'd just admit defeat and go shopping for clothes instead, but I'm trying to make a statement, dammit, and I want to buy a car I know no one will approve of.

"Listen, I know you have a job to do, and Mr. Godoy is the one paying you, but if you want me to give a good report back about the two of you, I need you to listen to me and actually take me where I'm asking you to." They look at each other instead of paying attention to me, and I see red. "You know what? I can take myself there. Don't worry about it."

I start walking in the opposite direction, thinking I need to download the Uber app, but after a couple of steps, a strong hand grabs me by my arm. I turn around, immediately moving out of reach. "Do not touch me. And do not think that because I look young and naive, I actually am," I say, my chest rising and falling quickly, ready to scream bloody murder if I have to.

"I apologize, Miss Bianchi. We'll take you where you want to go. Please, come with me." He extends his arm, showing me the way to the SUV, and I nod at him.

Once he opens the door for me and I'm seated, I take out my cell phone and send a quick text to Gabo.

> **Isabella**: I understand that I need your security people looking after me, but I'm not a child with restricted places to go.

I'm still fired up as Aldo drives effortlessly through the streets of Bologna. Any other time, I'd be enjoying the ride, looking at the buildings and the people, but no—right now, all I want to do is yell at someone. Even though I'd like to say a few things to Luca, I don't want to regret anything later. He's been a pretty awesome brother, overall.

Taking a deep breath, I call the person I know will understand my anger.

"*Hola, hermanita ¿Qué hacés?*" (Hello, little sister. What are you doing?) Gio answers after only one ring, and I immediately feel lighter.

"Not much here. Being driven around Bologna by Gabo's security team," I explain to my brother, and he's dead silent.

"Wait a minute, where is Gabo?" Gio asks, finally breaking the silence.

"He's in Ibiza with Vicente, but you know he's not supposed to be with me every single minute of the day that I'm here. Right?"

After releasing a sigh, Gio agrees. "Yeah, I know. I just think it's in poor taste to leave you alone on your first weekend there."

I don't disagree with Gio, but I won't tell him that. "Yeah, well... Maybe he had that weekend planned with Vicente before he decided to let me stay with him."

"You're right. They're both busy businessmen; they must have their lives planned for the next couple of years."

I don't say anything because what do I know? I'm the youngest of the bunch and everyone treats me like I'm an illiterate baby.

"Hey, Isa. What is really going on? You know I love chatting with you, but you usually go to Luca instead of me."

A knot forms in my throat, and suddenly, I can't speak. I don't want to cry in front of these men who I don't know, and I don't want to worry Gio with my immaturity; He has enough on his plate as it is.

"You know what? I'm on my way," Gio says, and that takes me out of my pity party.

"What? Don't you have to work?" I say almost in a panicked tone.

"It's the weekend, and even *I* take breaks," Gio says, and I chuckle. My brother is always in his research lab.

"There's no way I would convince you not to come, right?"

"You know it. I'll be there as soon as possible." Gio ends the call, and I relax a little bit in the backseat. Damn, this is one nice, comfy car.

It doesn't take much longer for us to arrive at a car dealership. It's exactly what I asked for—nothing fancy, just normal cars. Rocco opens the door for me and helps me out. I smile at him, feeling a little better after knowing my brother will be here soon.

I start perusing the lot, and there are so many cars. Every single brand under the sun is here, but I'm looking for something unique, something that screams ME!

Rocco and Aldo walk behind me, a little too close for my liking, and I feel trapped.

"Guys, I understand this is your job, but I'm pretty sure nothing is going to happen at this dealership."

Reluctantly, they nod and give me some more room to walk. I continue my search, hoping to find something that catches my eye. Suddenly, I spot a few Volkswagen Beetles at the end of the row. I speed up, unable to believe what I'm seeing. The cutest Beetle is at the end of the row. It's a convertible, it's pink, and it couldn't be more perfect. I start inspecting the car as I walk around it; it seems in pretty good shape.

"Buongiorno, can I help you?" A woman in a white pantsuit and black stilettos comes my way and smiles kindly at me.

"Yes, I'm interested in this car. Any chance I can test-drive it?" I'm not sure if that's the way things work in Italy, but I'm assuming a test-drive is pretty standard everywhere around the world.

"Well, to be perfectly honest, I don't know if this car works. Let me find the keys, and we can check," the lady says.

I can tell Rocco and Aldo aren't happy. They're currently giving me a *what the fuck* face, and I can't help the laugh that rumbles out of me. I know I'm being ridiculous, but if people are determined to treat me like a spoiled child, I'll sure as shit act like one. At least for today.

When the lady returns with the key, she opens the car door, and I get into the driver's seat. Rocco and Aldo approach, but I stop them before they can get any ideas.

"Hey, guys, why don't you follow us in the Mercedes?" I say.

They look at each other and then look at me. I'm sure behind those sunglasses, they're glaring at me, so I decide to crank up my charm. "I mean, I don't want you guys to be uncomfortable. Do you really think you both will fit in the backseat?" I give them a saccharine smile, and after a couple of seconds, Aldo makes his way to the SUV, and Rocco follows suit. Once they're out of earshot, I shout, "Yeah!" and the salesperson beside me chuckles.

We cruise around the dealership, and the car drives perfectly fine. I mean, it's not super smooth, but I actually like it; it has character.

Back at the dealership, I tell the clerk that I'm buying the Beetle and that I want it today. She simply nods and goes into the office, I'm sure to start on the paperwork.

While I wait, I take out my phone. I need a selfie with my new baby Bug. When the screen comes on, I notice I have a couple of texts waiting for me.

> **Gabo**: Good morning! I'm sorry, but Rocco and Aldo are a little pushy. They're just trying to do their jobs.

Gabo: Also, what's this that I'm hearing about you buying a car? I told you I have an extensive car collection. I'm sure you could have found something there to drive while you're here.

I chuckle at his second text. I'd pay to see his face when he sees my Bug. I send him a quick text back.

Isabella: Well, I wanted something unique. Something more my speed. Isn't she a beauty? *eye heart emoji*

Instead of waiting for his reply, I pocket my phone and make my way toward the sales office. I need to make this purchase official.

Chapter 6

Gabo Godoy

The moment I see the picture Bella sent me, I choke on my wine.

"What the fuck?" I ask out loud to no one in particular since Vicente has been on his phone since we arrived this morning. I'm having lunch alone and was about to head to a cabana on the beach and do some people-watching while my brother decides to stop working, but this picture has me out of bounds. Bella is a fucking vision in a dress with a corset on top, her hair cascading down her shoulders. With a huge smile on her face, she stands in front of an old pink Volkswagen Beetle. What is it that has me so attracted to her? I've dated supermodels in the past, even dated a beauty pageant queen at one point. But for some reason, Bella is the most gorgeous woman I've seen in my life.

Instead of reaching out to question her about her choice of car, I call Rocco. I need to know what's going on.

"Rocco, what the fuck is happening?" I ask, and Rocco clears his throat.

"Well, boss, Miss Bianchi decided she wanted an antique car. When I told her we wouldn't take her to a dealership, she threatened to report me to you. So I decided to just bring her in."

I can't help the chuckle that forms in my throat. This woman threatened two huge motherfuckers. She's no taller than five foot six, yet she made these two behemoths do exactly as she wished. I'm enjoying this way too much.

"Okay, that's fine. Let her be, and just be mindful of her space. Try to be unseen," I say, finally relenting to her wishes myself. "But I need you to contact my mechanic and ask him for a whole refurbishing. If it can be done overnight, even better. Tell him to spare no expense. I need that little Volkswagen to be the safest car in all of the European Union."

Maybe not all of her wishes. I still have my heart in a vise with a need to protect her, to the point that I'm becoming obsessed. *What the hell?*

"You got it, boss." I'm about to end the call when Rocco continues talking. "Oh, I almost forgot. She called one of her brothers, and he's on his way."

"What? Do you know which brother?" I ask, heat rising in my chest.

"No, boss. I didn't hear his name."

"Okay, thank you, Rocco."

I take a sip of my wine as I think this through. If she had called Luca, I'd have already heard about it. He'd be giving me shit the entire flight from Chile to Italy. That means it can only be Gio. Maybe leaving the States for a while would be good for him. Time will tell.

"What are you thinking about so hard over there? I thought by now I'd find you making out with a girl or two by the beach." Vicente pulls me out of my thoughts as he sits beside me, and a waiter brings him the menu.

We're staying at a private villa, and the service is top-notch. I always enjoy coming here. The views are spectacular, and yes, as my brother loves to point out, I've had my fun here.

"Nah, bro. Those days are over. The last thing I want these days is to catch a disease or get someone pregnant."

Vicente laughs at my answer, and I simply smile at him as he orders his lunch.

"So I just got word that Bella bought a cheap car, and Gio is on his way to Bologna."

My brother's laugh dies quickly, and his eyebrows shoot to the sky.

"Oh, shit. Gio...?" Gio rarely ever travels anymore. So yes, it's a big fucking deal that he's going to Bologna.

"I honestly don't understand what's going on with Isa," Vicente continues. "When you said you were hosting her for the summer, I just thought you were going to let her stay in one of your apartments and call it a day. You don't need to babysit her, you know?"

I pass my hand across my face as I heave a frustrated sigh. I know Vicente is right, but for some reason, the moment I saw her at the airport, I decided to claim her as mine.

"I don't know, man. That's what I thought, too. That was the plan, actually, but then Luca called and gave me the guilt trip and..." I don't know how to say this without sounding like a crazy person.

"And then what?" Vicente asks, not missing a beat.

"And then I saw her," I tell him honestly.

"What do you mean 'and then you saw her'?" Vicente is fucking relentless; he won't let me get away with not spelling it out for him.

"I know I've seen her many times in the past, but the moment I saw her walking off my jet... I don't know. I felt an urge to protect her." I know I'm not making any sense, and it frustrates the hell out of me because I've never been like this before.

"So you decided to leave Bologna to avoid her? Wow, brother. That's a great way to protect her and very on-brand for a thirty-year-old," Vicente states with too much joy in his voice. I glare at him, but it only makes him dissolve into a fit of laughter, and I can't help it; I join him.

"Fuck, man. I'm like a teenager ogling her like I've never been with a woman before," I tell him. He tries to cover his laugh with a cough, so I toss my napkin at him and continue. "Last night, when I came home, she was dancing in the living room. Did you know she used to dance ballet and then transitioned to contemporary dance? And, I kid you not, she almost brought me to tears just by seeing the passion in her every move. It was just beautiful. And then she prepared *niños envueltos* for dinner. I almost melted on the spot."

"She can dance and cook, so what? Don't you have enough money to hire chefs for a restaurant? Oh, wait a minute. That's right. You already own a restaurant, which, by the way, has three Michelin stars," Vicente deadpans, and I want to erase the smirk off his face. I really dislike it when he's so shallow.

"It's not only that, *weón*. She has a pretty amazing plan. Did you know her goal is to open a gallery? One of the reasons she's in Italy is to scout Chilean and Argentine artists to bring their art back to their home countries. She's just simply amazing, smart, beautiful, strong. She's the whole package."

I take a deep breath and think about all the little things I like about Bella. "She has this bubbly personality that I've never been into before. It reminds me of when I started my architectural firm. Now, I feel like I'm just working because I've created this huge name that I can't escape. I feel like if I try to reinvent myself, the industry will push me down." I take a big gulp of my wine, asking the waiter for a refill.

"You are Gabriel fucking Godoy. You're a hell of a good architect—your eye for intricate designs with a modern flare is what has given you your name. But don't think for a second that's the only thing you can be. You've worked hard for where you are, brother. You are your own boss. If you decide to take on a new venture and it flops, guess what? It's not the end of the world. You can rebuild and recoup the investment. It's not like you're using your entire fortune. Right? So if that's what's holding you back, don't waste more time thinking about the potential outcomes and just do it."

I'm stunned at Vicente's speech. He has always been so stuck in his ways. I wish he'd take his own advice.

"You're right. Thank you for the advice." I look at him sympathetically. "Now, how about you apply it to your own life?"

His face immediately transforms—the walls he usually keeps up to protect himself from the outside world resurface, blocking out even his brother at the mere suggestion of introspection. Damn, I should have waited a little bit longer to tell him that.

"Let's circle back to the issue at hand. What are you going to do with Isabella when you get back? I don't think you're planning to stay here for the next three months." A damn smirk appears on Vicente's face, and the asshole I'm used to is back.

It irritates me to no end that Vicente refers to Bella as an issue. My nostrils flare, and it suddenly hits me: this is what she must feel when all of us men make decisions on her behalf.

Fuck.

"What? What's going on?" Vicente asks, but I don't reply. I need to make things right.

Taking my phone out of my pocket, I dial one of my best friends.

"Yes, yes. I'm on my way," Gio says instead of hello, and I chuckle.

"Hey, man. I'm sorry you had to come all the way to Europe. I assure you, your sister is well," I tell him, and I can hear him chuckling on the other end of the line.

"No need to apologize. This conversation I'm hoping to have with Isa is long overdue. Besides, I'm in dire need of a getaway, so it's truly no big deal." I release a big breath, and Gio continues speaking.

"Just so you know, Isa got her trust fund. There's no need for you to babysit her or think that you need to help her pay her way while she's in Bologna. I'll be staying for a couple of days at The Majestic, and Isa will be with me. So you can also tell your security detail to back off."

So much for being understanding. I roll my eyes at Gio's statement, even though he can't see me.

"Look, man. You're a good friend, one of my best friends actually, but you're completely missing the point here. The reason your sister is so damn frustrated is that she's trying to start her life as an adult, fresh out of college, full of dreams and goals, and all we're doing is telling her how to live it. I get it, I'm part of the problem, but to be completely honest, you and Luca are a part of this mess, too."

My rant is met with silence. I know Gio hasn't hung up because, when I look at my phone, I see the call is still connected. He's a very calm and rational man, but the anticipation building from his silence is killing me.

"That's a very good point, and I appreciate you seeing my sister's wants and needs for what they are. The reason why I decided to go see her is because I need her to know that no matter what, I'll always have her back. But I've been treating her like the child she was twelve years ago when I left to the United States. So yeah, I need to go say I'm sorry in person. And I'll let her decide whether or not she wants your security following her all over Bologna. Maybe even embarrassing her at the university."

I wince at Gio's words. I didn't think about how it'd look to have Rocco following her around campus. I sure as shit would have been embarrassed if I had an overwhelming security detail.

"I hope to see you before I have to go back to the States, man. Thanks for the call." The phone disconnects, and Vicente looks at me expectantly, waiting for me to spill the tea.

"What?" I ask, the pure picture of innocence.

"I take it Gio isn't mad because you're being an overprotective host to his sister?"

I chuckle at my brother's comment. "Of course, he's not mad. It's Gio we're talking about."

"Good, now let's go find a girl or two to get your dick wet," Vicente says as he gets up from the table after barely eating his lunch, and I flinch at his crass comment. "What? Are you serious? You brought me to Ibiza, and you're not going to hook up with a girl?" he asks, incredulous.

"Yeah, *weón*. I'm dead serious. I don't want just any girl. I need to at least try to charm my way into Bella's heart."

"You're fucking crazy. Do you realize if things go south with her, Luca will hand you your balls?"

"And who said I was going to fumble my chance with Bella? I'm Gabriel fucking Godoy, after all."

"That's right, *The* Gabo Godoy. Let's go. Be my wingman, at least."

"That I can absolutely do."

Chapter 7

Isabella Bianchi

After visiting so many stores that I lost count, I'm back at Gabo's place. My room is a mess, with everything I bought today spread across the floor. Driving my Bug around this afternoon definitely helped my mood. Aldo and Rocco followed me in the SUV and kept a respectful distance at all times. They're not so bad when they're not crowding my space.

After making a smoothie, I take a quick shower and throw on a tracksuit to get my brother from the airport. As I walk outside the building, my phone vibrates with a text. When I look at the screen, a small smile forms on my lips.

> **Giacomo**: *Ciao*, Isabella. I was wondering if you would like to hang out with me

> tonight? I'm going to a bar with a couple
> of friends.

This guy is cute, but I'm actually looking forward to spending some time with my brother. I hope he doesn't give up on asking me out because, at some point, I'm going to say yes.

> **Isabella**: Hi Giacomo, I can't make it tonight, but I'll be sure to try my best to make it next time. Have fun!

> **Giacomo**: Thank you. Maybe you want to have coffee with me on Monday after class?

> **Isabella**: That could actually work. See you later.

Once my phone is back in my bag, I look around, and my Bug is nowhere to be seen. A cold chill rises through me, and a wave of panic invades me. Did I park in a prohibited zone?

"Miss Bianchi, we put your car in the garage. We can take you to pick up your brother, or you can take a bigger car from Mr. Godoy's garage," Rocco informs me, and I just nod at him. Although they are overstepping yet again, I'm not going to sweat the small things anymore. I can show Gio my car tomorrow.

"Is Aldo here, or are you driving?"

Rocco smiles, and I think it's the first time I've seen his pearly whites.

"Aldo is bringing the car around," Rocco says, and the next thing I know, Aldo is in front of us. I quickly get in the backseat, and Aldo starts driving.

"I'd like to apologize to both of you for my behavior today. I acted like a spoiled little brat, and that couldn't be further from the truth. You were only doing your job, and I overreacted," I tell them honestly.

They both look at each other, a silent conversation passing between them, but now that they're not wearing their sunglasses, I can see their eyes. They're full of mirth.

"It's okay, Miss Bianchi. This lifestyle can be overwhelming at first, but rest assured, we'll do a better job not being seen while still keeping you safe," Rocco states, and Aldo nods.

We make it to the airport in no time, and by the time I get out of the car, Gio is walking toward Gabo's hangar.

"*Hermanito*," I shout as I run toward my brother, who hugs me.

"*Hola, linda. ¿Cómo estás?*" (Hey, gorgeous. How are you?) Gio asks, looking at me with those kind eyes, and I simply smile at him. I know how hard it is for him to leave his place these days.

"I'm good. Had a fantastic day today, and now I hope to have a great couple of days with you," I tell him, and he ruffles my hair as he chuckles at my excitement.

"But tell me, how are you?" I ask him, hoping to hear some good news on his end.

"Same old, same old. But this weekend is not about me; it's about my amazing sister and all the plans she has for her future." I know he won't share any details with me, so I decide not to press and instead enjoy his company.

"Are you hungry? Gabo owns an amazing restaurant downtown. I'm sure he could hook us up if you want to go there," I ask, and my brother nods at me.

I shoot Gabo a quick text asking him to see if he could make a reservation for us, and he replies immediately.

> **Gabo**: Of course, just tell Aldo to drive you there. The table is already waiting for you. Maybe next week you'd like to go to another restaurant with me? I promise it's just as good, if not better, than this one.

Isabella: Sure, we'll talk next week.

I reply with something short and simple since I don't really have time to think about his change of heart. He couldn't get away fast enough, and now he wants to take me out? This is exactly why I don't do relationships.

My brother is looking at me with a kind smile on his face.

"What?" I ask with a chuckle. Sadly, I'm not used to spending time with my older brother anymore.

"Nothing. I'm just here thinking when did you become an adult? I still remember helping you with your homework in middle school." He chuckles, but I can tell his eyes are full of unshed tears.

"I know, right? Sometimes I can't believe it myself. Life goes by way too fast."

"Isn't that the truth? Sometimes I wish we could stop time and live in a beautiful moment for a while, you know?"

He doesn't need to say it; I know he's thinking about her: Ruin. The only girl he has ever loved and who vanished without a trace. I wonder if Gio will ever recover from his heartbreak.

We make it to the restaurant in a flash, and sure enough, as Gabo said, the moment we step foot inside, there's a server waiting for us.

"Before we talk about anything else, I want to tell you why I decided to come here this weekend," Gio says in his big brother tone.

I take a deep breath, preparing for whatever he says.

"I feel like you've been trying to figure out who you are now that you're done with college, and maybe you've been struggling a little bit?"

I know he's not judging me; he's just trying to figure out how to say it nicely. I smile at him, encouraging him to continue. *What on earth is he talking about, me struggling?* I thought I was very clear about my plan for the gallery, but maybe my brothers think I'm not good enough.

"The thing is, you're experiencing many big changes in a short time. I need you to know it's okay not to have everything figured out at once. Luca and I didn't give you the money to add more to your plate. We just felt you were ready to know the amount of money you can count on to start any venture you might have in mind. We know you and trust you not to blow all your money in the first month." Gio looks directly into my eyes, and I can't help but chuckle. "But in all honesty, all we want you to do this summer is have fun, learn a few things here and there, and maybe start scouting artists for your gallery. But under no circumstances are we expecting you to have your gallery up and running by the end of the year."

My eyes grow big. I know my brothers are amazing, but I always thought they were expecting big things from me. They are both so successful in their fields that it only felt fitting that I become the next big thing in my field, too.

"Let's be honest, Luca found his calling when he went to Chile after Karina and never looked back. I've always known that I was going to be a scientist. But you? Isa, you have the time and the resources to make the best choices. There's no rush. And remember, we'll always have your back. I'll always have your back."

Tears run down my face, and I don't care if people see—I seriously have the best brothers in the world.

"Thank you, Gio. Thank you for trusting me and giving me the tools to be who I want to be," I say as I hug him.

"We only provided the funds, Isa. All those amazing ideas came from you. And you know it's okay if, at the end of the day, the gallery doesn't come to life, right? Dreams can change."

"You guys provided more than money, and you know it. You both took care of me after Mom and Dad decided to spend their money and live life without us. You guys kept me safe, gave me a home, and filled my heart with love," I tell him honestly.

"And we'd do it again and again. Love you, little sis."

"Love you, too, big bro," I say as I hug him again. I send a little thank you prayer to my guardian angels for giving me the best brothers in the world.

As the night goes on, Gio and I feast and toast to a great weekend, enjoying every single moment we have together.

—◈✦◈—

Once we get back to the car, Gio asks Aldo to drive us to The Majestic.

"Oh, I thought you were staying with me at Gabo's place?" I ask, confusion evident on my face.

"I want to stay with you, but I'd rather stay at a hotel. I already told Gabo. He said he's cool with you losing your security team for the weekend." My brother's voice is hesitant, and I hate that the confident man I used to know is now buried under so much pain.

"Of course, I'd love to stay with you. Let me go to Gabo's place and get clothes. We can do a *Lost* marathon and eat gelato all night." This brings a huge smile to my brother's face.

"Like old times," he says, and I nod at him as I look at Rocco, who motions for Aldo to start driving.

When Gio opens the elevator for me at the hotel, I gasp. This damn thing is made of gold. Or painted in gold or something. But it's so ostentatious, I'm in awe. We make it all the way to the top—my brother got the presidential suite, of course. Each of us has a room, and the living space is so decadent and gorgeous. I might not want to leave this place.

"I'm going to call room service to order gelato and other necessities. Anything you want in particular?" my brother asks from his room.

I take a moment to think about this. God knows when I will see him again; I better make the most of the time with him. "Yeah. See if they have fries, a cheeseburger, and a chocolate milkshake."

He doesn't say anything, so I assume that he's calling room service. When I turn around to leave my room, Gio is gaping at me from my bedroom door.

"Isa, I thought we had a delightful dinner. I cannot believe you're still hungry."

I smack his chest and tell him, "Hey, I'm still growing. Okay? I need sustenance. And if you think I can watch *Lost* without eating my weight in food, you're dead wrong."

Gio's eyebrows rise almost comically, and I can't help but laugh.

"You're so full of shit, little sis. But yeah, I remember those days. Let's order everything they have on the menu," Gio says, a huge grin on his face. I fist-pump the air, excited to see my brother's old demeanor peeking out from the shell he has become.

I change into my comfiest pajamas, Gio does the same, and once the food arrives—mind you, in four carts—we sit down on the couches in the living room, and the marathon starts. The burger is delicious, and I have no guilt for eating more than I should; I can walk it off tomorrow. I can't wait to show Gio around the university. His little nerd heart will be so happy.

—◦❖◦—

"I really love this campus, Isa. It's like something out of a movie," Gio says as he takes his phone out to snap pictures.

"What are you doing? You need to do the background justice. Let me use my Polaroid to take a couple of pictures of you."

My brother chuckles at my request but doesn't deny me. I take out my camera and start instructing him on a few poses. He's so patient, and even though I get a couple of eye rolls, he does everything I ask, and we snap one last picture together.

"Isa, these are really good," Gio says as I pass him the pictures. "Maybe you should also include a photography section in your gallery."

I beam at my brother's praise. The man has a Ph.D., is a well-known researcher, and used to be one of the best teachers in the world.

"Thank you. Yeah, that could definitely work, as well. It'd also help more artists all-around," I reply as we make our way back to the car Gio rented: A red Alpha Romeo 4C Spider—this car is so much fun. When Gio removed the top of the car, I decided to wear a handkerchief on my hair—I feel like Sofia Loren in those classic movies. The breeze hits my face, and the sun warms my skin. What is this life? I've always had a good life, but I feel this time in Italy will be one to remember.

"Okay, Isa. Where to next?" Gio asks as he drives leisurely around Bologna.

"You know what? Let's do something crazy. Let's go to the beach," I tell him, barely able to contain my excitement.

"Let's go," Gio says as he looks for directions on his phone. I'm so glad to see my brother taking life as it comes—no plans, just doing whatever the moment brings.

We made it to Rimini in no time, and since Gio was driving, I was in charge of the music. To my brother's dismay, I had my summer mix on. A bunch of my favorite songs to dance to were on full blast the entire drive. Believe it or not, he's more of a country music fan.

The moment I see the ocean, a huge grin appears on my face. There's no way I'll ever be close to the water and unhappy. For some reason, the ocean has always brought me peace.

I remember summers in Mar del Plata. Mom would pack the car with food and tons of beach gear—towels, coolers, umbrellas, sunscreen, toys, you name it. Then Dad would drive, and Mom would be the DJ, with Gio, Luca, and me in the backseat singing our lungs out. We would always stay at the same beach house. The boys and I would get bikes and ride to the ice cream shop a few blocks away. We would park the bikes and walk to the beach, eating our ice cream in silence, people-watching, and watching the seagulls fly over the ocean. It was peaceful and one of my happiest memories.

Gio finds a place to park, and the moment I get out of the car, I think my brain is playing tricks on me. Gabo is walking toward us, and he's looking like a snack, wearing low-hanging linen pants and a half-buttoned shirt.

"I thought you were in Ibiza," I say in shock when he's a foot away from me.

"Yeah, well. Vicente had to go back to London, so I decided to spend the rest of my weekend at my beach house," he says

as he leans down and kisses me on both cheeks. When I get
a whiff of his cologne, my knees go weak. Damn, this man is
just delicious.

"Hey, man. So glad I was able to catch you before I have to
head back," Gio says as he and Gabo share a bro hug.

"Same, man. I didn't know you guys were coming here, but
I'm glad everything worked out," Gabo replies as we fall in
step with each other and start walking toward the beach.

"So you guys didn't plan this?" I ask, confused. This is way
too coincidental. They both shake their heads, and I frown.

"Me being here and you guys coming my way was just
kismet, Bella. No need to overthink it," Gabo says nonchalantly, even though something inside me says there's no way.
I have no proof otherwise. My suspicions deepen when I
catch a sly look between Gio and Gabo, but they won't say
a thing, so I just let it slide.

"So, what were you guys thinking of doing?" Gabo asks,
and Gio looks at me.

"It was my idea to come. I just thought we would walk
around the wharf and maybe find a shop to get swimsuits
and spend the day on the beach." I shrug, suddenly feeling
my plan is lame, but the smile that appears on Gabo's face is
anything but.

"I know you guys are spending quality sibling time, but
maybe we can walk to one of my favorite restaurants in town.
Then we can get some gelato as we go shopping, and we

can spend the afternoon at my beach house. The views are unbeatable from there."

Gio looks at me, waiting for me to decide. Even though I wasn't counting on spending more time than necessary with Gabo, I can't help but agree with his plan. The man has charm. Not going to lie.

"Sounds like fun," I tell them, and Gio nods in agreement.

"Great! This way." Gabo extends his arm to show us which way to go.

"Is it your first time in Italy, Gio?" Gabo asks, and my brother's face falls.

After a couple of very uncomfortable, quiet minutes, Gio speaks. "Yes, it was Ruin's dream to visit Italy someday. We were planning to come over and do a road trip all over the country but..." My brother shrugs, and I absolutely hate this for him.

"And you still came to see me? I'm so sorry, Gio," I say, giving him a side hug as we continue to walk.

Being the amazing brother he is, he ruffles my hair as he says, "There's nothing I wouldn't do for you, little sis. Plus, it's been four years. It's time I get my life back." Gabo and I stop in our tracks like a hammer or something has hit us.

"Dude, that's great. I mean, it's awful you were never able to find out what happened, but I'm glad to hear you're ready to leave the past behind you. You're a bright scientist, and you deserve to be happy," Gabo says to Gio, and I really, really appreciate him right now. This is what my brother needs: lots of support and understanding from his friends.

"I agree. I'm happy you're finally starting to leave the past behind." I give Gio one more squeeze and let him go to focus on the beautiful view in front of me. There's a Ferris wheel by the pier, people milling around, eating gelato, or with a huge sandwich in hand. Some people are on bikes or skates; others are singing and dancing. The vibe of this city is amazing. The pictures I saw online don't do it justice.

"Gabo Godoy, is that you?" A saccharine voice brings me out of my thoughts. The next thing I know, a woman is hanging on Gabo's arm. When I look at Gio, his face full of amusement says it all.

"Oh, hey, Brenda. Long time no see," Gabo says to the woman while trying to remove the vice grip she has on his arm, but she's not getting the message.

"Well, baby, that's on you. I've been trying to reach out, but you never pick up the phone."

Gabo's nervous chuckle should be all it takes for her to let go, but no. She hasn't even acknowledged our presence.

"Yeah, well, I'm a busy man. What can I say?"

Brenda doesn't have time to answer because Gio starts talking. "Nice to meet you. I'm Gio Bianchi, and this is my sister, Isa."

The woman finally takes her eyes away from Gabo. The moment she looks my brother up and down, her claws release Gabo's arm, and she jumps up and down in excitement as she reaches for Gio's hand.

Gabo stands next to me while we watch the woman trying to charm my brother, but Gio has always been very particular about who he dates, and this woman simply doesn't fit the bill. She's wearing a dress that hugs her curves and leaves nothing to the imagination, her hair is bleached and has lots of damage, and her face can't take any more Botox.

Gio disengages in a way that leaves Brenda shocked. After a handshake, my brother starts walking in our direction. Brenda is left standing alone until she spots another group of handsome men walking by and heads their way.

"Wow, that was an interesting encounter," I say, trying to figure out who that woman is to Gabo, even though I have a hunch.

"I apologize about that. Things you do when you're young sometimes haunt you years later," Gabo says, placing his hand on the small of my back. That zing I felt the first night was back in full force.

Gio notices but doesn't say anything, and I really don't mind it, so I move a little closer to Gabo. The moment I do, his fingers squeeze my waist, and when I look up at him, I see a blinding smile already waiting for me. I don't think Gabo is a relationship kind of guy, but I guess if he's looking for a summer fling, it wouldn't be too bad. I mean, he's ridiculously hot, he's smart, and I'm sure he can show me a good

time. I could definitely do worse than a hook-up with Gabo
Godoy. Only time will tell.

Last night with Gio at the hotel was fun; we had more gelato, and he reluctantly agreed to watch something else other
than *Lost*. As much as I love my brother, I couldn't take more
of that show. We ended up watching funny videos on our
phones. It's amazing how much one can laugh at silly stuff.

After taking Gio to the airport, Aldo and Rocco follow me
to uni to ensure I arrive safely. After giving myself a quick pep
talk, I hop out of my Bug, square my shoulders, and put on
my brightest smile.

When I get to the classroom, everyone has the same
vibe—happy but a little nervous. I guess the first day of
school is the same for everyone; it doesn't matter if you're
in your hometown or if you're an international student,
first-day nerves are universal.

Giacomo waves at me as he enters the classroom. Once the
initial introductions are made, the instructor takes over, and
I relax a bit, feeling more in my element as he starts talking
about modern art and the biggest Italian artists to date.

I'm lost in note-taking, and before I know it, the bell rings.
Armed with my first assignment, I gather my things and
head for the museum.

After going to the museum to start our first piece for school, Giacomo stops me on my way out and asks if I want to grab a coffee with him. I'm not going to lie; I was a little hesitant about accepting after Gabo returned unexpectedly from Ibiza. He was fun and carefree, and the electricity between us was palpable. But Giacomo seems like a nice guy. Since there's absolutely nothing going on between me and Gabo, besides maybe a silly summer crush, why not? I want to make the most out of this summer.

"So Isabella, what do you want to drink?" Giacomo asks as he helps me settle into a seat at a little cafe near the museum.

"I'd like a cappuccino and one of those pastries over there," I say as I point to the fluffy pastries on top of the counter in the cafe. They remind me of the *medialunas* in Argentina, and I'm sure they'll taste just as good.

Giacomo nods with a smile and walks gingerly to the counter to place our order. As I look at him interacting with the barista, a smile forms on my face. He's such a nice guy, always brightening people's days. I wonder what he's telling her to have her blushing so hard.

"Okay, our order will be here soon," he says as he sits next to me. There's a soft breeze, which brings a whiff of his cologne my way, but instead of being pleasant, it's overpowering. I scrunch my nose, and his eyebrows arch in confusion.

"Is everything okay?" he asks, and I chuckle. I really need to work on my poker face, or should I say poker nose?

"Yes, I just thought I smelled something, but it must have been my imagination," I tell him as I fix a piece of my hair behind my ear.

"Is this your first time in Italy?" he asks, sparking conversation, and I'm thankful for the change of subject.

"It actually is. I've traveled to other countries in America, but it's my first time in Europe."

"Oh, that's cool. I've been to almost all the European countries. It's really easy to travel around here." I nod. I've heard about traveling by train and whatnot around Europe.

"Have you ever wanted to travel to other continents?" I ask him.

"Not really. I have everything I want here: plenty of beautiful sights and delicious food," he tells me as his eyes brighten. And mine immediately dim. Traveling is one of the best things in the world—learning about different cultures and seeing different art. Those are experiences I hope to collect in my lifetime. But I don't tell him any of that since he has clearly made up his mind.

Our coffees and pastries arrive. I do a happy dance in my seat, and Giacomo rolls his eyes at me.

"What's wrong?" I ask.

"Nothing. It's just... we're in public, so..." His uncomfortable glance around the room makes it clear he's embarrassed by my enthusiastic response to our food. I just stare at him, and he gives me a blank look.

It takes everything in me not to throw this hot coffee on him, but it's only the first day of uni, and I want to have a great time. Instead, I switch topics, and it doesn't take long for me to realize that we don't have much in common.

"So what did you decide to work on as your project for this week's class?" I ask.

Giacomo goes on and on about how he wants to recreate a painting by Giorgio Morandi, one of the greatest Italian artists of the twentieth century. I should be thrilled to learn more about an artist who's new to me. I should be asking questions about his work and what Giacomo finds so interesting about it, but all I can think about is the note Gabo left me this morning on the kitchen counter.

Buon Giorno, Principessa.
I'm looking forward to having dinner with you tonight.
No need to cook; I have it all figured out.
-Gabo

I mean, this man couldn't leave fast enough last week, and now here he is being an outstanding host and letting me know he has dinner covered.

Am I overthinking this? Or is Gabo really putting in an effort to spend time with me?

"Earth to Isabella," Giacomo says as he snaps his fingers in my face. The action startles me, and I jump in my seat, which makes Giacomo laugh.

"Sorry, I was lost in thought. What were you saying?"

"I was telling you how much fun I've had having coffee with you, and I was about to ask if you would like a repeat some time soon." I smile at him. I don't want to make him feel bad; he's a good guy, but I don't feel anything. I enjoy chatting with him, but the spark I feel lighting up my insides every time I'm near Gabo is nowhere to be found.

"Thank you so much for this, but I really need to get going. I'll see you tomorrow at class, yeah? Bye," I say as I stand up and start walking to where Aldo and Rocco are waiting for me, three tables from where I was sitting with Giacomo.

"So is that a yes about the repeat?" Giacomo shouts, and I roll my eyes.

"I'll see you later," I reply without looking at him. Aldo and Rocco fall into step with me. I hope Giacomo takes the hint.

Gabo has taken up residence in my mind, and there doesn't seem to be room for anyone else.

Chapter 8

GABO GODOY

"So how was Ibiza? Any hot models?" Dominic, one of my closest friends and business partner, asks, coffee in hand, as he enters my office first thing Monday morning. The events of the weekend immediately flood my mind.

I ended up leaving my brother in Ibiza and headed back to Italy the moment Rocco mentioned Bella decided to stay with Gio. I've had a couple of scares since being publicly proclaimed as a billionaire, and I know Gio doesn't have a security detail like I do. The man continues working at a public university in the United States, for crying out loud.

It's not only that I don't trust she'll be safe with her brother; I just don't want to continue being an idiot. I want to see, once and for all, if I'm imagining things or if I truly have a thing for my best friends' little sister. If I do, I need to be all-in from the get-go; I can't screw this up. It wouldn't just do a number on Bella; it would ruin my friendship with Gio and Luca for life.

Finding them wasn't hard—I might have had a tail on them. Sue me. The moment I saw Bella with her carefree smile and relaxed posture as she walked down the pier with Gio, a pang of jealousy hit my chest. I needed to be the one enjoying her company, not him. Maybe that makes me an asshole—Gio is her brother, after all—but I want this summer to be about me and her. Getting to know each other, learning what makes her tick, what makes her sad, so I can erase it from the face of the earth. I need to see if this feeling that has invaded my brain is genuine or if it's a simple infatuation.

The moment Brenda approached me, I tried as hard as I could not to flinch; I really didn't want to make her feel bad, but she was a one-night stand, nothing more. I thought Bella would get jealous and possessive, but to my surprise, she didn't react. It might be a sign of maturity, or it's a sign that she doesn't give a fuck about me. I hope it's the first. But when I placed my hand on the small of her back and she leaned into me, I couldn't help the dumbass smile that spread across my face.

Gio ended up leaving this morning, so Bella spent last night at the hotel with him. Even though we had a great time in Rimini, I wish I could've spent more time with Bella. I need to take her back to the beach soon; it's the most fun I've had there in years. Seeing her happy made me happy.

I snap back to the conversation when I see Dom staring at me. " I think Vicente met a couple of women, yeah."

"What? Vicente? Your grumpy asshole of a brother hooked up with a model, but you didn't? I should have gone on that trip." Dom shakes his head.

"Yeah, yeah. You're a good friend. But not even your persuasive methods could sway me from my plan," I inform him as I fall into step with him. Our weekly team meeting is about to start in the main conference room at my firm building.

"Good friend? I'll have you know I'm your best friend. Heck, your only friend on this side of the world. And if what I'm thinking is accurate, I might be your one and only friend left after your dick damages your friendship with the Bianchis."

I hate it when he has a point.

"Good thing my dick won't damage anything. It'd only solidify our relationship."

Dom stops in his tracks, and I wince as I replay my words in my head.

"Sorry, that sounded creepy as fuck. But you know what I mean. I simply want to see if there's anything beyond desire with Bella. I won't fuck up my friendship with Luca and Gio just to get my dick wet. I'll wine her and dine her before we get to that part."

"You're an idiot. I just hope this doesn't backfire." He pats my back as we get our seats, getting ready for the weekly meeting.

"Good morning, everyone. What's good today?" I ask no one in particular. One of the summer interns raises her hand hesitantly, and I motion for her to speak.

"Good morning, Mr. Godoy. Today is the day we will send the global merchandise company our proposed model for their new warehouses here in Italy," she says, pride in her voice.

Fuck, how did I forget about this?

"Let's pull up the design real quick."

She nods as she works with the video system. After a few clicks, the design is up on the main screen, and I don't feel a thing. Anyone could have come up with this design—it doesn't scream Gabo Gadoy. After my conversation with Vicente, I'm ready to go all in and stop following trends. It's time to shine.

"Okay, how can we make this design blend in better with the environment? Because the way it's looking right now, it sticks out like a sore thumb." My comment is met with silence—I'm usually better when delivering a critique, but there's no time for niceties. We only have a couple of hours to improve the design.

The room erupts in chit-chat. Groups are assembled, everyone buzzes around, and I simply take out my notepad. I know there's software available out there to do this, but to me, nothing will ever beat the feel of pencil on paper and the sound of the carbon contacting the fiber. Plus, it gives me more freedom to do the tracing. After a few minutes, I give my sketch to our lead designer and the room grows quiet. Everyone is looking at me like I'm an alien.

The truth is, I haven't made any of our designs in a while. I've become more of an observer than a hands-on boss. And maybe that's what is bothering me—I need to feel completely in charge, not only approve designs and sign paychecks. Sitting down in endless meetings while my creative team shows me their latest designs and ideas, I always think about how I'd have done it better. It's time to get out of this routine, which I have no idea how I ended up in.

"Mr. Godoy, are you certain this is the design you want to go with?" the design team leader asks, and everyone is looking everywhere but at me. They think I'll get upset at his questioning.

"Yes, why do you ask?" I inquire calmly, but I can tell the designer is starting to sweat. "Look, this company is a big team, and if we don't trust each other, we will never be able to grow. Please, speak freely."

After clearing his throat, he finally tells me what's on his mind. "With all due respect, Mr. Godoy. This doesn't look like a warehouse." I smile as I unbutton the vest of my three-piece suit and make my way toward the big screen on the left side of the room.

"And that's exactly what I'm going for. The outside of these warehouses will blend effortlessly with the beautiful and peaceful geography of the Emilia-Romagna terrain. The inside will be as efficient and plain as any other warehouse in the world, designed to meet the customers' needs. However, the outside will scream, "This is Italy, and we are proud of it." Soft angles instead of a cookie-cutter box is what I'm going for. Fresh materials that are not only local but also environmentally friendly are what I want to offer our clients. I want everyone to know that here at Godoy *Construzione*, we not only build the most gorgeous buildings and homes, but also the most state-of-the-art and environmentally friendly warehouses. Understood?" Everyone nods, and when I look at my friend Dom, I see that he has a proud smile on his face.

"Good. Let's get to work, then. We have a deadline to meet."

As much fun as I had today at work, helping the team get the design ready to share with the global merchandise company, Bella was on my mind all day. How was her first day of school? Did she make more friends than that Giacomo kid she mentioned the other day? What did she wear? I can't wait to get home and figure all this and more out.

"Smells good in here, but I thought I said I had dinner covered?" I say as I enter my penthouse.

Bella's smile is blinding. She's wearing another pair of short shorts, a distressed white shirt, and her hair is up in a messy bun.

"Hey, Gabo. Yeah, I know, but I felt like cooking for you," she says with a shrug like it's the most natural thing in the world. "How was work?" she asks as I stand in front of the stove and pick up a spoon to try whatever she's cooking. If it tastes like it smells, I'll eat it all. But Bella smacks my hand gently with a washcloth, and the spoon falls to the floor. We both chuckle.

"It was good, you know. Same old, same old." I tell her as I pick up the spoon. "How was your first day at uni?" I ask her as she bends to wipe the dirty spot the spoon left on the floor. I try to look somewhere else, but her ass is perfect; I can't help but ogle.

"Oh, it was amazing. I can't wait to tell you all about it. I also went for coffee afterward with Giacomo," she says gingerly, and my eyebrows shoot to the sky as my heart rate picks up. "It was nothing. He wanted to have coffee with me, and I said yes, but there's nothing there. He's just a friend."

My heart rate slows down a beat. The mere thought of that guy potentially having a chance with her makes my stomach twist.

"Well, it's good to have friends. Glad this guy Giacomo can be one." I shrug as I busy myself washing the spoon.

I internally slap myself. Can *I be more lame? Is that all I could come up with?* Bella definitely makes me feel and act like a teenager. She smirks at me like she knows I'm full of bullshit, and my dick can't help but notice.

Sorry, dude. No playdate for you for the foreseeable future. We have to woo her first.

"Go wash your hands and put on some comfortable clothes. I have an idea for dinner tonight." Now, she's got me wondering what that idea is about.

"As the principessa wishes," I say with a flourish and head to my room. I can hear her chuckles until I close the door behind me. It's incredible how, in a matter of days, we went from not knowing how to act with one another to a totally domestic couple. Whatever was said in her conversation with Gio must have put her at ease, and I'm eternally grateful for that.

I decide to go for a quick shower instead of just washing my hands, and after toweling myself off, I grab a pair of sweatpants and a white tee. When I returned to the kitchen, Bella had already plated our food and was standing next to the kitchen island waiting for me.

"So I thought it'd be a good idea to have dinner outside while we watch a movie?" The hope in her azure eyes makes my heart flutter as if there's anything in this world that I'd deny her.

"Sure, it sounds fun. What movie do you have in mind?" I ask her as I grab the bottle of wine and two glasses.

"Hmm, I'm in the mood for a classic. Any favorites?" I'm surprised she's letting me pick, but I won't shy away from a challenge.

"Have you watched *La Dolce Vita*? The director, Federico Fellini, was born in Rimini," I tell her as I set up the movie system.

"I don't think I have, but that sounds like a great movie. Let's do it." I smile at her as I queue the movie and head back inside for the food. When I get back outside, she has poured two glasses of wine and has a fuzzy blanket on her lap. I wish I could join her under that blanket, but I don't trust my dick to be the gentleman I'm trying to be.

"Let's toast," I say as I raise my glass, and she does the same.

"To a great first day at uni," I say, and Bella beams.

"How did you know I had a great day? Did Rocco say anything?" she asks after taking a sip of her wine.

"I haven't spoken with him all day, but you're in a great mood and prepared another delicious meal for us, so I assumed you had a great day." I shrug as I taste the wine she chose for us tonight—a delicious red.

"That's true. I am in a good mood tonight. But how can I not be? Turns out, we'll have different instructors each week, and this week, it's the curator of the Bologna Museum of Modern Art!" She screeches, and I chuckle at her excitement.

"I take it you are pleased with having him as your instructor?" I smirk at her, and she grins back.

"Very. We'll be going to the museum the next two days to create a painting based on something that catches our attention. Isn't that amazing? Our own take on a classic!"

"That sounds pretty awesome, and who knows, it might be the first piece you sell at your first expo," I say nonchalantly, but I know I'll buy every single one of her pieces.

"Enough about me, how was your day?" Bella asks expectantly. It's refreshing to have someone genuinely asking about your stuff, not because she wants a slice of what you have in the bank.

"It was actually better than I expected. I had a meeting to approve the design of a set of warehouses we are bidding on for a huge merchandise company here in Italy. I got to change the model within two hours of missing the deadline for submitting our proposal," I tell her, excited to share my day.

"That sounds amazing and nerve-wracking at the same time. When will you learn if you won the bid?"

"I'm hoping by the end of the week, but it could be next week."

"Well, at least you have more work to do, and I can keep you entertained with my daily uni updates while you wait," she says, a blinding smile on her face.

I can't help but thank the stars for giving me a chance to spend time with and get to know this woman. She's a light I've never had in my life before, and I hope I can keep her with me for a long time.

The night goes by quickly as we eat the delicious pasta Bella cooked and finish the bottle of wine while we comment on one of Fellini's masterpieces. I also caved and joined Bella under the blanket—her idea, not mine. Tomorrow, I have to take her out for dinner; it's safer without blankets in the proximity.

Chapter 9

Isabella Bianchi

This week flew by, and as I told Gabo during our mid-week dinner, I'm absolutely in love with the piece I came up with while at the Museum of Modern Art. I decided to paint a live scene instead of doing a take on one of the exhibits.

A woman came in both days and stood for several hours in front of the same painting. The first day, I was intrigued enough to sketch her, tilting her head to the left and observing the painting without moving her hair. For a moment, I felt as if I was her—mesmerized by the art, trying to figure out what the painting was trying to tell me—and the result was beautiful. I wasn't counting on finding her at the same spot on the second day, but it helped me to create a more detailed version of my painting.

It turns out I have a great group of classmates; everyone is so kind and so fun. It's going to be really hard to return to Santiago in a couple of months, but I would be lying if I didn't admit that the best part of the week has been spending time with Gabo. He leaves every morning before I'm awake. I can tell the moment he walks back through that door that he's exhausted. But when his eyes lock with mine, it's like he gets a second wind. After freshening up, he comes back out, ready to have dinner and talk about our day.

I've never done this with anyone—except my siblings, and there's nothing sensual about that—but the way he gives me his undivided attention every single time I'm with him makes me feel like the luckiest girl in the world. The first night, he kept his phone with him, and he had to put it on silent more often than not.

Who needed him with such insistence?

I'm assuming it was his assistant or his business partner, but whoever it was, Gabo said they could wait until the next day. He hasn't pulled out his phone at night ever since.

Today, we're heading to his house in the countryside, and I'm so excited. I asked him if we could drive my Bug instead of one of his fancy cars. After a lot of back and forth, he agreed. It also helped that he had secretly taken my Bug for refurbishing. I wasn't really mad—I thought it was cute that he wanted me to have a comfortable car, but I was also surprised by it. I mean, I'm still not sure why he cares so much about me. At the end of the day, I'm just his friends' little sister.

By the time Gabo comes back from work, I'm all packed and ready to go. His eyes grow impossibly big when he sees the suitcase I'm taking with me, and I simply shrug.

"Hey, you never know what kind of clothes you're going to need," I say, and he lifts his hands in surrender.

"Oh, I wasn't judging. I would never dream of it," he says as he approaches me for a hug.

So far, that's all we've been doing: hugging and occasionally holding hands. If it were up to me, I'd have climbed him like a tree days ago. I guess he's testing the waters first and seeing how we feel together.

"Good, because I didn't feel like justifying myself," I reply as I take a big breath, inhaling his delicious scent—a mix of whisky, tobacco, and sandalwood. So masculine.

"Did you have a good day?" I ask him as we remain hugging and swaying to an imaginary tune.

"I did. We heard back from the global merchandise company, and they loved the design. They want us to design warehouses all around Europe, modifying the design to fit the terrains in each country. It's the biggest client we've ever had," he says, pride evident in his tone.

"Congratulations, Gabo. That is amazing. I hope you have some good wine at the country house because tonight we have to celebrate," I tell him as I squeeze him tighter to me, hopefully he can tell how proud I am of him. He melts in our embrace and I can't help but love this little moment.

Ugh, I can't wait for this man to make a move. I think I'm going to have to pack my vibrator for the weekend. Otherwise, I might do something that I will regret later, like sneaking into his room in the middle of the night and pretending I saw a ghost just to have my way with this handsome, smart, and thoughtful man.

"You might say I have a good wine collection, but I guess you'll just have to wait and see for yourself," he states as he kisses me on top of my head. He lets me go to grab my luggage. I practically melted on the spot—the kiss wasn't sensual, but it sure made me feel like the most cherished person in the world.

"Ready?" he asks as he hits the elevator button.

"Ready."

"Mario, Rocco, and Aldo will follow us in the SUV. You and I will go in your... car." He shivers as he looks at my beautiful pink Bug, and I throw my head back in laughter. This trip is going to be a blast.

"Wait, where's your luggage?" I ask, confused.

"I have everything I need there already." He winks at me as he extends his hand. I give him mine, and he chuckles but places a kiss on my palm, and I feel my knees going weak. He's such a gentleman.

"No, principessa. I was silently asking for your car keys."

I open my eyes as it dawns on me that he wants to drive. Heat rises all the way to my cheeks; he must think I'm a child.

"Oh, I see. No need. I'll be the one driving tonight." I look at him directly in his eyes, letting him know there's no room for negotiation here. I don't expect him to give in—he's used to getting his way. But to my surprise, he goes to the driver's side, opens the door, and motions for me to get in.

"Thank you, kind sir," I tell him as I get into the car.

"You're welcome, signorina," he says, kissing the back of my hand again, and I need to fan myself as he makes his way to the passenger door.

It turns out Gabo is a great copilot. He plugged in my phone instead of his so I could play one of my playlists. Every time I was hesitant about a turn, he simply told me where to go. No mocking, nothing but kindness and respect.

The moment I slow down to turn into his property, my mouth falls open. This is not just a countryside house—this is an estate, a villa, a mansion. Oh, my goodness. It's absolutely breathtaking. The road that takes us to the house is guarded by tall field maples, and when the road ends, we are met by a massive stone house that creates a perfect harmony with its surroundings.

"So what do you think?" Gabo asks, and I just look at him. "Come on, let me give you a tour," he says as he gets out of the car and walks around to open my door.

The house is absolutely dreamy. There are several living spaces, including a kitchen that rivals the one in his penthouse. When we step outside, there's a huge pool in the backyard. I can't wait to go on a hike in the morning, the hills surrounding the property look absolutely amazing.

"Signore Gabo, hi." A lady in the kitchen greets him as we come back inside, opening her arms and waiting for a hug. She seems to be about Ines and Graciela's age—our nannies back home—and just as sweet and nice as they are.

"Margareta, ciao," Gabo replies as he hugs her.

"I haven't seen you around here in a while. I was starting to get worried that you had sold the place and hadn't told me," she says as she squeezes his cheeks.

"You know I would never do that to you."

"Good answer," she says, patting his cheeks, and then her eyes are on me.

"And who is this gorgeous signorina we have here?" She opens her arms for me to hug her, and I do so without hesitation.

"That's Bella, my guest and dear friend," Gabo replies as he scratches his head.

"Oh, I see. Welcome, Bella. You're as beautiful as your name," she compliments me, and I smile at her.

"Thank you so much, Miss Margareta." She pats my cheeks and motions for us to take a seat at the dining table.

"*Mangia, mangia,*" she says, placing two plates full to the brim in front of us.

"Grazie," Gabo and I say in unison, and we both chuckle.

After eating, Gabo shows me to my room. I cannot believe he hadn't brought me here before. All the decorations in this house are antique. The bed has four posts with a sheer cover hanging from them, giving it an ethereal feel, kind of like the one in his penthouse. However, the details on the ceiling are painted in gold. It's stunning.

"Gabo, this is such a gorgeous room. I can't believe this wasn't the first place you brought me to when I arrived in Italy."

"I didn't realize you would be so taken by this villa, but if I'm honest, it's probably my favorite property of all the ones I own."

"Yeah, it'd be my favorite, too. I don't even need to see any other of your properties." Gabo chuckles and heads toward the door.

"If there's anything you need, my room is next door." I nod, and he closes the door. I thought we were going to hang out like we've done at the penthouse, but maybe he has work to do? Ugh, who knows. This man is an enigma.

After showering, I decide to send a quick text to Luca, just to let him know everything is going well.

> **Isabella:** Hey, dear brother. I'm still having a ball here in Italy. The class at uni has been amazing so far. This week, we had an instructor from the Museum of Modern Art here in Bologna. Next week, another instructor is coming from the

Museum of Art and History in Switzerland. How cool is that? I'm working on finding young or up-and-coming artists. I'm at school with many of them, actually. You don't need to worry about me achieving my goal before I have to head back to Santiago. Love you lots, Isa.

I'm not expecting him to reply immediately since it's the middle of the night in Chile. I flop down on the bed, stretch my arms, and wonder what I can do with all this time on my hands since the night is still young. The thought of Gabo disappearing into his room so early makes me think of something I could definitely do. I get up from bed in one swift movement, and I go looking for the magic wand in my luggage.

Chapter 10

Gabo Godoy

This week, I barely had time to do anything with Bella other than have dinner and hang out afterward. I need Dom to take a few responsibilities off of my plate so I can spend a couple of hours during the day exploring my favorite places with her while we're here.

I'm thinking about what to do tomorrow in town with Bella when I hear a noise coming from her room. Her headboard is against the same wall as mine, so technically, if she twists and turns in her bed, I'll hear. I should have thought this through better because the more I listen, the more I realize that the sound is coming from a vibrator.

Fuck. My. Life.

I try to take deep breaths and not think about what's going on in Bella's room, but it's simply impossible. It doesn't really help when she starts making little noises, moaning as she pleasures herself with a damn vibrator. My dick is at full mast just by hearing her moan, and I can't help but think that it should be me making her scream.

My hand finds my dick, and I start moving it up and down, using a bead of precum to spread over my length. Bella increases her pace—I know because I can hear her rapid breathing—and I know she's getting close because now her moans are unintelligible. I think I'm going to jump off the proverbial cliff with her when I hear her moan, "Oh, G. That's it. That's how I like it, G."

My hand immediately releases my dick, and I freeze. *Does she call me G in her head? Or is she thinking about someone else?* Fuck, what if she's picturing that kid Giacomo from uni? I thought she said he was just a friend. She hasn't mentioned him lately, but that doesn't mean anything. They've been hanging out every day at school. Fuck if I'm going to let a kid take Bella away from me.

By the time Bella screams in ecstasy, my erection is gone. Fuck, I guess I have my work cut out for me tomorrow. It's time to see if Bella is as into me as I am into her. I've been restraining myself from making a move on her out of respect for Luca and Gio, but I just can't deny the chemistry between us.

—◦❖◦—

I couldn't sleep all fucking night, twisting and turning, thinking about Bella's orgasms being for someone who isn't me. Fuck that.

Around five in the morning, I finally give up on the idea of sleeping and fire off a text to Dom, letting him know I wouldn't be available under any circumstances the entire weekend.

I go for a run to clear my head, but my thoughts just go back to her as I pick up the pace. I know Gio saw me wrapping my arm around Bella's waist. Instead of giving me a murderous look or making a comment, he just gave me a look as if to say, "I see you." Maybe he's okay with me dating her. I know Gio, being the oldest of the Bianchi's, is more mature than Luca.

But Luca is another story; he's been determined to keep Bella under his supervision like a dictator. It's weird because I remember when he reached out to me before he went to Chile after Karina. I told him I'd be watching but never interfered in his plan. And I sure hope they both know I'd never just have a fling with Bella. If I pursue things with her, it would be a genuine effort, not just to scratch an itch or, as my brother so bluntly put it, to get my dick wet. Bella is an amazing woman, talented, driven, passionate, not to mention gorgeous and funny. She's the whole package.

Maybe I should talk to Luca... but then that feels like I'm validating his stance, and Bella doesn't deserve that. She deserves to be treated like the adult she is. Yes, she might be younger than me, but she's an adult. And more importantly, she's worth any headaches that Luca might give me because of this. I finish my run exhausted but with renewed determination.

"Morning, Gabo," Bella says from the breakfast nook in the kitchen. She's a fucking vision in one of those running sets women wear—little shorts and a sports bra. Her sky-blue outfit looks stunning, perfectly matching her eyes and making them pop. She has her hair in a braid, and my first thought is to tug it hard so she can look me in the eyes and tell me I'm the only man she sees when she's using her vibrator.

"Gabo?" she asks, and I clear my throat.

"Yes, hi. Sorry. Good morning," I say and her eyes grow big, curiosity evident in her gaze.

"I'm okay. I just couldn't sleep very well. I kept hearing weird noises."

The moment her brain registers my words, her cheeks turn beet red. I turn around and get busy making a plate of food so she doesn't see the grin I'm sporting.

"Hmm, weird. I actually slept really well. I was able to relax after a hot shower," she says. I look her in the eyes, and she's the picture of innocence. This woman drives me crazy.

"Well, I'm glad at least one of us could sleep. Anything in particular you want to do today?" I ask her, effectively changing the topic.

"Well, I was hoping to go for a hike around your property and then maybe go to town for lunch. I'm not sure yet."

"That sounds like a nice plan. Are you in need of a tour guide?" I ask her, and she starts playing with her braid. I need to look away because the ideas in my brain are making my dick hard, and I can't be sporting an erection in running shorts; it'd leave nothing to the imagination. I don't want her to think I only want sex with her. I need to woo her, not scare her away like a perv.

"Of course. I thought you were busy, so I was planning on asking Rocco to run with me." The smug smile I had on my face a couple of moments ago is replaced with an icy glare, and her laugh only makes me glare harder.

"Oh, you think you're funny?" I ask.

"Hilarious," she replies, and I just know in my veins that this woman was made for me. It doesn't matter how much older I am or who her family is—this woman is mine.

My body gets a mind of its own, and I close the space between us. She walks backward until she's against the counter, and I cage her in, placing my arms on each side of her body. Bella's eyes grow big, expecting my next move. I see her swallow, and all I want to do is kiss her, make her mine in this kitchen right now, throw caution to the wind, and deal with the consequences later. But all I do is lean down ever so slowly, my lips caressing her cheek. She closes her eyes and parts those pouty lips, ready for a kiss. I take a deep breath and step back, standing up straight. Her shoulders sag.

Is she disappointed I didn't kiss her? Good. That's good. I'm going to make it worth your wait, Bella. You'll see.

"Okay, eat up so we can go for a hike, little miss funny." I toss my napkins on the counter, making her chuckle at the nickname, but she continues to eat her fruit.

—◈◆◈—

"Wow, and all this land is yours?" Bella asks as we get to the top of a hill that oversees all my property.

"Yes, I've been adding land over the years. When I first bought the villa, it was just a small parcel. But the thought of adding more land seemed right," I answer her honestly.

"And do you have a special goal for all this land? Or is it just for pleasure?"

"I have no plans to develop this land; it would take away from the charm of the town. I just don't want others to ruin it for the townsfolk, you know?"

"That's very chivalrous of you. I hope people appreciate it."

"They do. They weren't sure of my intentions at first, but with time, they have come to know me. They accept that while I might be a billionaire, I'm not a greedy person. I actually enjoy the laid-back atmosphere the town provides me, and I sponsor a lot of the things the town needs. I also provide scholarships for kids who don't have the resources to go to uni but do have the grades. They have taken me into their fold, and I like to repay the favor however I can."

"That's pretty amazing, Gabo. You are amazing," she tells me, and her eyes shine brightly. I've never felt more proud of my actions than right this moment.

"You are the amazing one here." I boop her nose, and she twitches it. I would give away all my money if it meant I could kiss the living daylights out of her right now.

The sun is shining bright but isn't too hot since it's still early morning. There's a light breeze that's dancing with the trees and the bushes, creating a beautiful tune just for the two of us. I need to know for certain that she really wants this, that I'm not making things up.

Somehow, our bodies are flushed together; my arms are around her waist, and hers are against my chest.

"Gabo?"

"Yeah?"

"Are you going to kiss me?"

"I want to."

"But?"

"I want to do this right, you know? I want to get to know you before I undress you. I want to make you fall in love with me so when we are finally together, there's no doubt in your mind who you belong with," I tell her honestly. I need her to understand that it's not that I don't want her; it's that I want her for a long time.

Her smile falters, and now it's my turn to frown and be confused. "Did I say something wrong?"

"Not wrong. There's nothing more I want than to be with you and have a great summer with you, but the moment you start talking about a long time together, I will start to retreat," she tells me with a smile, but it doesn't reach her eyes.

"But why? You must know I would never hurt you, at least not on purpose. Right?"

"You're a good man, Gabo, but I don't believe in love. Attraction, lust, desire, passion. Absolutely. But love? No, I don't believe in that," she tells me in a serious tone.

I know there's way more behind her words, but I need to tread carefully here—she's opening up to me, and I need to make her feel safe enough to tell me why she doesn't believe in love.

"I'll tell you what—let's head back to the villa, freshen up, and head to the town for lunch. Maybe, afterward, if you're in the mood, we can talk some more about this 'love is not my thing' deal." This time, her smile is blinding like the sun, and right now, that's enough for me.

When we get to town, we find the traditional farmers market in the town's plaza. Bella does a little happy dance, and I raise my eyebrows at her.

"I'm just excited. This place is magical. I mean, look at all the little stands. The fruit looks so fresh and delicious. You think they'll let me buy only one peach?" I smile at her enthusiasm as I pull her to my side. Once she's in close proximity, I place my hand on the small of her back, dangerously close to her ass. She doesn't move my hand. Instead, she puts her hand inside my jeans pocket and squeezes my ass. Damn, two peas in a pod.

Chapter 11

ISABELLA BIANCHI

I can definitely see why Gabo loves this place—this town has charm. With cobbled streets, medieval architecture, and even a castle, it's enchanting. The locals seem to be kind and friendly since every time I approach a booth, I get free samples of whatever they're offering. But when they realize I'm with Gabo, their smiles turn up a notch. He's like their town celebrity; everyone hugs him and invites him to take whatever he wants from their stands. The more time I spend with him, the more I believe what he told me earlier today. He might be a billionaire, but he's not greedy. He grabs fruit and veggies from the stands but never leaves without paying, refusing to take no for an answer.

"So what are we going to do with all this produce?" I ask him as I eye the tote bag he's carrying.

"Well, I thought I'd cook dinner for us tonight since you've cooked plenty this week," he tells me like it's the most natural thing to have a billionaire cooking dinner for you.

"I didn't realize you cooked."

"I know my way around the kitchen. I just don't do it often because there's nothing more boring than cooking for one. Plus, I'm always busy at work or going out for dinner meetings. But your company has me completely motivated to create an amazing meal tonight." He winks at me, and I fan myself, which causes him to chuckle.

"Come on, let me show you the best gelato in all the Emilia-Romagna region." Gabo takes my hand, and we enter a tiny gelateria. They have countless options, and I'm drooling just by reading their sign with all the day's flavor.

"They've been making gelato since they graduated from high school. They're high school sweethearts," Gabo says as he greets the old couple behind the counter. After lots of hugs and kisses, the lady makes her way to me while opening her arms. I feel such joy at this moment, being in a peaceful and beautiful place with amazing people who haven't questioned why I am here with Gabo. Now, receiving the same welcoming hugs he's been getting? I don't want to think too hard about this, but I wouldn't mind living here.

"Oh, Signore Gabo. She's gorgeous," the lady says as she looks back at him while cradling my face with both hands. "What's your name?"

"Isabella Bianchi. Nice to meet you," I tell her, and she gives me a megawatt smile.

"Bianchi, eh? Are you Italian?" I smile at her comment.

"My grandfather migrated from Gazetta to Argentina. That's where I'm from." She nods, seemingly satisfied with my answer. After patting my cheeks a couple of times, she motions for me to follow her.

"Eat," she says bluntly. But she's offering gelato, so there's no way I'm going to pass it up. When the rich pistachio flavor hits my taste buds, an involuntary moan escapes me, and everyone chuckles.

"I'm sorry, it's just so good," I say sheepishly.

"It's okay, we know. I'm Giuseppe, by the way. And that's my wife, Maria," the old man tells me, and I finally have a name to put to their faces.

"Any other flavor you want to try, principessa?" Gabo asks while looking intently at me, and I'm about to melt on the spot. Those brown eyes of his are soulful and have a glint of a promise. A promise of a good time. Clearing my throat, I ask for the coffee-flavored gelato, and Gabo nods. This one tastes like espresso—intense but delicious.

"Okay, yeah. This is the best thing I've tried in my life. Can we get a liter to go?" I ask no one in particular, but Giuseppe busies himself getting my order ready.

"I'm glad you like it. I make a mean tiramisu with this gelato," Gabo informs me as he kisses the top of my head.

"Yum, you'll never catch me saying no to dessert," I tell him, and he replies with a chuckle. After paying for the gelato and with the promise of coming back soon, we leave the ice cream shop.

"Anything else we need for dinner tonight?" I ask, looking around the booths to see if there's anything we missed.

"I don't think so. Are you ready to go?" Gabo asks, and I'm about to say yes, but on the far side of the plaza, there's a small booth with carved wooden pieces.

"Can we go see those?" Gabo starts walking toward the booth, my hand in his. I do my happy dance, which earns me a chuckle and a hand squeeze. I'm really enjoying the fact that he lets me be me and even encourages it. Not like the boys I've been with in the past, who were too embarrassed whenever I did my little happy dance. Screw them.

As we get closer to the booth, I can see the intricate details of the wood carvings. They are exquisite.

"Gabo, look!" I call him to get closer to the bed board I have in front of me. It's made of maple wood, so the coloring is honey brown with lighter speckles here and there. What I love most is the pattern. It's a beautiful set of arabesques, delicate and simple, but as a whole, this piece is a work of art.

"Ugh, I wish I had a place to put this piece here in Italy," I say in a low voice because the more things I find and see, the less I want to go back to Chile.

"Funny you say that," Gabo says, startling me. "I was going to ask you if you wanted to use one of the salons on the main floor of the villa for dancing and displaying your paintings. This piece would fit perfectly there."

"You would do that for me?" I ask, astonished.

"Yeah, it's a huge villa, and nothing would make me happier than to give you some space for your art."

I don't think. I simply jump and lock my legs around his waist. I hear an "oomph" come out of his lungs, but Gabo doesn't miss a beat. His hands go around my waist, holding me in place.

"Thanks, G. I've never had my own studio before," I say against his lips, and I'm praying every single prayer I know that he'll kiss me this time. Just a kiss—that's all I want. For now, at least.

A gorgeous and cheeky smirk appears on his handsome face, and I twist my eyebrows in question.

"I'm G," he affirms, not asks. When realization dawns on me, I open my eyes wide. He heard me last night. That was what his comment was about this morning. I bite my lower lip, and Gabo grunts.

"Don't tempt me like that, Bella. We need to have a conversation before I can kiss those gorgeous lips."

I press my core against him, and his hands squeeze my waist.

"I promise you, I'll make it worth the wait," he says as he releases me and places me on the ground. I shake my head to get rid of the lust fog my brain is in, and when I look at the man behind the booth, he's grinning like a loon. Welp, I guess we gave him all the action he's going to see this month.

"I'm interested in this piece," I say as I point to the bed board.

"It's two hundred fifty Euros." I open my eyes wide; I was thinking at least a thousand.

"Are you sure?" I ask him. I don't want him to think he needs to give me a discount.

"Okay for you, two hundred Euros."

"No, no, no. I was just thinking that you should charge more; this is a gorgeous piece."

"No, signorina. That's the fair price," he tells me, and I see Gabo getting his wallet from the corner of my eye.

"No, this is mine. Please let me pay for my stuff."

"You're right, I'm sorry. I just want to give you the world," Gabo says, and it takes everything in me not to jump his bones.

"You cannot say those things if you want me to behave, G," I whisper, and he just chuckles.

After paying, the artist promised to bring the wooden piece to the villa at the end of the afternoon on his way home. Gabo drove his Ferrari to the farmers market, so there's no way we'll be able to fit it in there. I should have known he let me drive my Bug because he had another set of cars at the villa.

Tonight is shaping up to be one of the best nights of my life. I just have to open up my heart to Gabo and tell him why I don't believe in relationships. Easy, right? I sure hope so.

Chapter 12

Gabo Godoy

If I thought the farmers market was a great date with Bella, cooking with her is even better. Her soft summer vibes playlist hums through the kitchen speakers. I must admit, it's not terrible and somehow captures the summer vibe I'm leaning toward these days—fun days under the sun, enjoying her company. I wish I could take Monday off and spend more time with her here, but she's beyond excited about the professor coming from Switzerland.

I also need to oversee the completion of a couple of buildings and start researching the other countries where we will be designing warehouses. I need to make sure that every single detail I change in the original design will look flawless against the different terrains.

Getting back to reality, I look at Bella, whose back is turned to me. I need a medal or something because all I want to do right this minute is sit her up on the kitchen counter and spread her legs wide open for me. But, for the sake of starting things with her on the right foot and for being a good friend to Luca, I must wait until we talk. I hope she'll share her fears with me tonight, but we shall see. One thing at a time, and right now, we have to make the pasta.

"Have you made pasta from scratch before?" I ask against her neck, and her skin immediately gets goosebumps.

"Excuse me? I'm Argentinian, *che*. Of course I have; we make gnocchi every 29th of the month." I smile at her. I love how proud of her roots she is.

"Oh, that's right. My bad." She huffs a breath and turns to face me fully.

"Yeah, Grandpa Bianchi taught us how to make pasta. But tonight, I want to see you in action." The smirk on her face has my dick twitching. I'm about to say, "Fuck dinner, let me have my way with you," when my phone starts vibrating. I wonder who it might be—I gave Dom specific instructions not to bother me with work stuff. A cold chill runs down my spine when I get the phone out of my pocket and see who's calling.

"It's your brother. If I don't get this, he'll be on the next plane to Bologna."

Bella chuckles and pauses her music on her phone.

"Hey, bro. What's up?" I say as I hit accept and put the phone on speaker.

"My man, we're good here. Enjoying winter. How's everything over there?" Luca says, and my sister retorts in the background, "No, we're not enjoying winter. I'm miserable. Being pregnant during winter is no fun."

"I'm sorry, you're what?" I ask Karina, even though Luca is the one who called.

"Surprise! We didn't want to say anything until we passed the first trimester. Then life just got busy, so only Mom and Dad know." I look at Bella to see if she knows, but she's as flabbergasted as I am.

"Fuck, I'm going to be an uncle and I didn't know? You guys suck."

"Yeah, what Gabo said. I'm the only auntie this baby will have, and I didn't know? I need to go tomorrow and buy out the entire Versace baby store for this kid."

Karina is howling in laughter in the background as Luca continues to talk. "So that answers my question. You two are together."

Bella rolls her eyes almost comically, and I have to cough to cover my laugh.

"Yes, brother dearest. I'm with Gabo, my host. What a crazy thought, huh?" Bella retorts, which only makes Karina laugh harder.

"I'm sorry, Isa. I just worry about you. That's all."

"And you know I love you for it, Luca. But you need to chill. I'm an adult who can make her own decisions."

"I know, I know. It's just Gio said maybe he saw something between the two of you. I just wanted to make sure you're not fooling around with each other. You guys know that would be fucked up, right?."

I don't even have time to react as Bella grabs the phone from my hand and shuts off the speaker.

"Enough is enough, Luca Bianchi. I love you. I'm forever grateful for everything you've done for me, but if you ever think, even for a second, that you have a say in who I date or who I fuck, you're sorely mistaken. It's none of your business, or Gio's, or anyone else's if I decide to have a one-night stand, a fling, or whatever with Gabo or any other mortal on this earth. If you think you have a say in my life because you gave me money, I'm sorry to break it to you, but you don't. I'll be depositing your money and Gio's money back into your accounts tomorrow morning. And until you can accept that I'm an adult who can make my own choices, don't contact me again."

Bella hangs up, not waiting for Luca to say anything back. I don't think—I just kiss her. Holy fuck, where has this woman been my entire life? The way she stood up for herself is the hottest thing I've ever seen.

The kiss isn't gentle or measured. It's bruising and passionate and all-consuming. I hold her by her waist and lift her to the kitchen counter, just like I've been dreaming of doing all day long. The way she responds to me, letting me explore her body with my hands while she explores mine, it's like she was made for me.

She must like what she feels because she pulls me flush against her. The moment she starts lifting my shirt, I know we need to stop. I don't want to, my dick for sure doesn't want to, but we still need to talk.

"Fuck, Bella. You drive me out of my mind. The way you handled your brother was so sexy," I say against her lips, and she bites my lip. *Damn*. "But we need to make dinner, and then we have to talk. Remember?" I bite the pout that forms on her lips before trying to busy myself by setting out the ingredients to start the pasta.

"I hope I didn't get you in trouble with him. I know you guys are close, but the man is about to become a dad, and he still gives me shit about *my* life. I just couldn't take it anymore," she says as she starts prepping the produce we bought earlier today to make the sauce.

"As I said, what you did was incredibly sexy. Don't worry about getting me into trouble with him. We're just two adults trying to figure out this pull between us. It doesn't concern anyone else."

She stands behind me and hugs me against her. It's cute to see this petite woman trying to embrace me.

"By the way, any chance you know of a job I can get this summer? Since I'm returning the money, my funds will decrease considerably."

"You don't need to work, I can provide for your every need," I tell her honestly—there's nothing I want more than to spoil her.

"I know you can, but I still want to pay for my things, you know? It's a pride thing now. Besides, without that money, I won't be able to open my gallery as fast as I thought I would. Every little bit of money I can start making now would help."

And this right here is one of the things that attracts me to her the most: she's resilient, determined, and brave.

"I'll tell you what—let's enjoy the rest of the weekend, and on Monday, I'll see if we can create an extra intern position at the design firm. I'm sure we can work around your uni schedule."

"Thank you, G." She spanks my ass as she goes back to her chopping board, and I chuckle at her antics.

After dinner, we decided to eat the coffee gelato directly from the tub instead of making the tiramisu and sit down by the pool in a huge lounge chair that comfortably fits both of us.

"What a beautiful night. The only thing that would make it better would be to have a telescope to see the stars," Bella muses, and I make a mental note to buy a telescope for the next time we're at the villa.

"It is a beautiful night. It's actually perfect for talking." I smile at her as she groans.

"Ugh, I forgot we still have to have this conversation. Okay, what do you want to know?" she asks, squaring her shoulders.

"Well, first of all, why does the idea of a relationship make you want to run away?"

"I see we're starting slow, huh?" Bella chuckles, and it's not lost on me that she takes a fortifying sip of her wine.

"I'm not sure how much you know about my family, but the reason I moved to Chile for college was because our parents decided to check out of our lives. When Grandpa Bianchi passed, they inherited a lot of money, and they changed. Gio was supposed to start college in the US that summer, but our parents decided to go on vacation for almost three months and only told us right before they left. So he stayed local so he could take care of us."

I'm speechless. What kind of parents do that? This makes me understand Gio's quietness on a deeper level. He had to become a responsible adult before he was ready.

"Then, when Luca met Karina, he decided to move to Chile, which would have left me alone in our hometown. I asked if I could move to Santiago. Both my brothers offered for me to move in with them. It was a very tough conversation we had with our parents, but at the end of the day, they chose the money and the life it brought them over us. Ever since I moved to Chile four years ago, they haven't made an attempt to talk to me or check on how I am doing. I even invited them to my graduation but didn't hear back from them." Bella's beautiful azure eyes fill with emotion, and I bring her to my lap. Those assholes are not her parents; they're simply the people who made her.

"They don't deserve your tears, principessa. They lost everything worthy in life the moment they decided to walk away from their kids. I'm even more proud of you now, after knowing that growing up wasn't easy, that you have a void in your heart, and yet you're still thriving in life."

Bella hugs me as her tears flow freely, and I let her—she needs to mourn this loss. I'm not sure if her brothers have let her vent, but I'm incredibly touched that she trusts me enough to bare her heart to me.

"You're right, they don't deserve my sadness. But the fear of becoming them is what's stopping me from being in a relationship."

I look her in the eyes and wipe the tears away from her face. Her skin is blotchy after crying for a while, but she has never looked more beautiful—raw and exposed to me.

"And what makes you think you'll become them? You're nothing like them. You care about your loved ones."

"I know my fear is irrational, but it's how I feel." She shrugs, and I can tell she's winding down; tiredness is evident on her face.

"Let's make a deal. We can start dating casually; no need to talk about the future. We'll focus on the present and see how you feel," I suggest, fully intending to do everything in my power to make her feel everything I feel for her every single day.

"You got yourself a deal," she says as she presses her lips against mine, sealing the promise.

Chapter 13

Isabella Bianchi

"Good morning, everyone. I'm Martín López, and I'll be your instructor this week." I immediately lift my eyes from my sketchbook—that name doesn't sound Italian at all.

"I'm Chilean, but have lived in switzerland for a while now, and last year I started teaching a module of this class."

Everyone nods, and I grin like an idiot. What are the odds that I would have a Chilean professor in bologna? I can't wait to chat with him and ask for advice on getting artists to send _____ Chile with me.

_____ stuff quickly and make my way to the _____ Val L_____ _____ were _____ our work

"Thank you, I'm Isabella Bianchi. I went to school at the University of Santiago." His eyes go wide, and I chuckle.

"Oh wow, I didn't expect to meet a fellow Chilean here. Are you from Santiago?"

"No, I'm actually Argentinian, but moved to Chile for college."

He stops packing his canvas bag and looks at me from head to toe. His demeanor immediately changes. I frown, confused. He shakes his head quickly, and his easy smile returns.

"Sorry, I just thought you looked familiar for a second."

Hmm, interesting. I doubt he knows my family, but you never know.

"Any chance you've ever been in Alamo Peaks?" I ask him, wanting to know if he knows Luca.

"No, never heard of it. I'm from Valdivia, which is 520 miles south of Santiago," he says as he starts walking toward the door. His answer is kinda strange, since Alamo Peaks is part of the well-known wine region, but I don't think he's lying.

"Oh, I see. Yeah, I've never traveled south. It must be beautiful though." He nods at me as I fall into step next to him.

"Professor López, I have this idea about opening a gallery back in Santiago, and my hope is to be able to provide a space for immigrants to send their art back to their homeland. I was wondering if you know any up-and-coming artists here in Europe?"

We walk in silence for a couple of minutes. He seems deep in thought, and I take the opportunity to look at the people walking around campus, noticing how the golden hour light casts a beautiful glow upon them.

"That's very noble on your part, Miss Bianchi. But have you thought if it would be profitable? Is there a market for such a niche in Santiago?"

"To be honest, I don't think there wouldn't be. I mean, people are dying to have fresh and authentic pieces in their spaces. But maybe I should include new artists from around the world, not only Chileans. Do you think I should make a poll?"

"I think your idea has great bones; it's new and fresh, but you should do some marketing research. If you have the funds, maybe even hire a marketing company. Food for thought, Miss Bianchi. I'll see you tomorrow," he says with a smile and starts walking faster.

I stop and turn around to find my Bug. He does have a point; if I want to have a profitable business, I cannot only be guided by my heart.

When I'm back in my car, I see Aldo and Rocco parked in the spot next to me. I give them a little wave, and Rocco waves back. Taking my phone out of my bag, I see I have a couple of messages waiting for me.

Gabo: Do you have time to stop by my office before heading home today? I want you to meet with HR to see if any of the open positions interest you. We can go to dinner afterward.

I smile at his text. We didn't have a chance to talk this morning, but as usual, a huge bouquet and delicious fresh fruit were waiting for me in the kitchen.

I check the other message and hold my breath before reading it.

Luca: I'm sorry, Isa. I know I screwed up big time by being a nosey ass. Let me know a good time to call and apologize. Also, I returned your money transfer. That money is yours, no strings attached.

I can only imagine what Karina told him. "*De seguro lo cagó a pedos.*" *(I'm sure she gave him an earful.)* I'll have to text him soon.

Lowering my window, I motion for Rocco to do the same.

"I need to go see Gabo in his office," I inform them, and Rocco nods as he raises his window again.

I punch the address into my phone, and as I'm making my way out of the parking spot, Giacomo blocks my way with his motorcycle. I hit the brake so hard that my car rattles, causing me to yelp in shock.

"What the hell?" I raise my hands to Giacomo. Rocco gets out of the SUV and has Giacomo off his bike and in his hold before I can even get out of my car. I need to help Giacomo before Rocco hits him or something.

"Rocco, it's okay. This is Giacomo. We are in the same class," I say as I approach them, but Rocco doesn't even move.

"I know who he is, miss. But he jumped in front of your car. Was he expecting you to run him over?" Rocco says through his teeth, and I can see the terror in Giacomo's eyes.

"Rocco, let him go. Please," I say politely but firmly. Rocco doesn't reply; he simply lets him go, and Giacomo bends his middle while gasping for air.

"I was just coming to see if you wanted to have dinner with me. I didn't mean to startle you," he says after a couple of beats.

I try hard not to laugh at how small he looks right now, still terrified from Rocco having him in a chokehold. I'm sure his intentions are good, but no man will ever match the BDE Gabo has.

"I know you didn't mean anything by it. Maybe next time, text me and don't jump in front of a moving car?" I say, and he chuckles, his cheeks blushing.

"Okay, yeah. That's fair. I'm sorry."

"And I'm so sorry to have to say no, but I really need to get going."

His gaze drops.

"Listen, Giacomo. You're a good friend but that's all we'll ever be. I hope you're okay with that."

He gives me a sad smile with a little wave, and even though I feel bad for saying no again, I can't wait to go see Gabo. It doesn't matter if I keep telling myself that all I want is a fling with him; my feelings for him are growing. He's so thoughtful, sweet, and kind to me. I'm not sure how much longer I'll be able to keep these blooming feelings at bay.

"One day, you'll say yes, Isabella Bianchi," Giacomo says out loud with a smile on his face as he walks backward. I hear Rocco grunt beside me, and I simply shake my head as I get back into my car. He's persistent—I'll give him that. But at this point, I wish he'd focus that persistence elsewhere.

I start driving toward Gabo's office while listening to my soft summer vibes playlist. A song is stuck in my head, and I need to create choreography for it—another thing to add to my to-do list.

"Hello, I'm here to see Mr. Godoy," I tell the woman outside of Gabo's office after I make it to the top floor of the building. She pulls her glasses down on her nose and eyes me like I have dirt on my face. I look behind me to see if Rocco and Aldo are around, but they're nowhere to be seen.

"Is there something wrong?" I ask because her staring is making me uncomfortable.

"Is Mr. Godoy expecting you?" she asks, and I pin her down with a glare.

"As a matter of fact, he is," I tell her in a short tone. I'm not about to be looked down on by this woman. I know I'm not wearing business clothes, but I'm not wearing anything indecent or provocative either; I have one of my sundresses on and tennis shoes.

"Is there a problem here?" Gabo's deep voice materializes behind his assistant, and she stands up like she has a rocket in her butt.

"No, sir. I was simply asking this girl if you were expecting her because she's not in my calendar," she says as she flattens her skirt with her hands.

"My bad, I forgot to mention that my girlfriend was coming to see me." Gabo emphasizes the word girlfriend as he comes to stand next to me and kisses me on the cheek. Such a gentleman.

"Oh, I'm sorry, miss. I didn't realize you were with Mr. Godoy," the lady says as she takes her seat. She can't look me in the eyes, and her face is red. I guess she's feeling bad now.

"Isabella Bianchi, nice to meet you." I extend my hand to her, and she shakes it, still not meeting my eyes.

"Did you have a good day?" Gabo asks, effectively ending the awkward encounter with his assistant.

"Very. It turns out my instructor is Chilean. I asked him about any contacts he might have with Chilean artists."

"That's amazing, principessa. Maybe we should invite him for dinner before he goes back to Switzerland." I grin at his idea; he's so thoughtful.

"Let's go meet Giulia. She's the head of HR."

We go to the elevator, and once the doors close, I hug Gabo, inhaling his signature scent of tobacco, whisky, and sandalwood. He kisses me slowly, and I melt in his arms. He looks so good in his three-piece suit, and all I want to do is take it off and eat him whole.

"How's your day been?" I ask as the elevator makes its way down.

"Busy," he replies as he releases a deep breath. "There are a lot of studies we need to conduct before we can start the new designs for the warehouses. The terrains in Germany and Sweden are quite different from here."

The elevator dings, and we make our way to Giulia's office.

"That sounds intense. I hope I don't have to work on soil studies because I have no clue about it," I tell him, and he chuckles.

"I'm sure we can find something that's more your speed." I smile brightly at him. I love how he gets me.

When we step into Giulia's office, I immediately think of *The Devil Wears Prada.* Her office is immaculate—all white and pristine. Giulia is a gorgeous woman—tall, lean, and with stunning hair. Not to mention, she's dressed to the nines. I wonder if Gabo has had a fling with her. Judging by the way she's looking at him, I'm sure it has crossed her mind at least once.

"Giulia, hi. This is Bella, my girlfriend."

And here I thought we were taking things slow, but he's been introducing me as his girlfriend left and right.

"Hi, Bella. Great to meet you. So Mr. Godoy mentioned you have a degree in the arts?" Giulia asks, and I nod.

"Perfect, we were thinking you could work on creating a color palette for each of the new warehouses we're currently working on."

I can't hide my excitement; this is right up my alley.

"That sounds amazing. When can I start?" Giulia and Gabo chuckle, but I don't care. I think it's a cool task.

"You can come back tomorrow after your class. Are you okay working three hours a day?"

"Absolutely, that's doable. Do I have to do my work here or can I work remotely?" Giulia looks at Gabo, looking for guidance, I guess.

When he smiles, she replies, "Of course. If you have a computer, you can submit your work to the design team; otherwise, we'll provide you with a PC." I smile at her and let her know I have my own computer.

"Great, here's your badge. Welcome to Godoy *Construzione*." Giulia and I shake hands, and Gabo places his hand on my waist, leading me back to the elevator.

"I knew you were going to like this project. Color is your thing."

"Impressive how well you know me in such a short period of time," I say, internally swooning. I can feel the walls I've built around my heart starting to crack.

"I pay attention to what matters." I lay my head on his shoulder and press a kiss on top of his jacket.

"Do you have work to finish?" I ask him, hoping he says no.

"I was waiting for you. I made a point of finishing everything that was pressing before you arrived. Are you hungry?"

"Starving," I say as I exhale a breath. Suddenly, I'm exhausted.

"Okay, let's go find some food. Anything you have in mind?" he asks, and I look at him sheepishly.

"Actually, yes. Not sure why, but I'm craving seafood. Do you know a place?"

"I have the perfect place," he says with his signature smirk, and for a moment, I forget we still need to talk about this girlfriend thing.

"G, I came in my car. Should I follow you to the restaurant?" This stops him in his tracks.

"Rocco can drive it back to the penthouse. You're not leaving my sight, principessa." I huff, feigning annoyance and pouting for good measure, but secretly, I love that he can't be away from me.

"Seriously? I don't think Rocco will fit in my car."

Gabo chuckles. "He will if he wants to keep his job." With a wink, this conversation is over. Gabo's ability to find a solution for everything in a matter of seconds amazes me.

Once comfortably in his car—he drove the Rolls Royce today—Gabo splays his right hand on my thigh, and a shot of electricity runs through me. It's like there's a kinetic current between us. He almost makes me forget we still need to talk about this girlfriend deal... almost.

"So, G, what's this thing about you calling me your girlfriend?"

"I thought it was clear already. We're taking it slow, but you're mine," he answers like it's the most natural thing in the world. I can't help but throw my head back and laugh.

"Is that so? I didn't realize that made me yours." I challenge him with a smirk after my laugh calms down. I love giving him shit. He's such a caveman and so possessive. If he didn't make me melt like he does, I would be concerned about how much he's into me in such a short time.

"It is so. Listen, principessa. I can be patient and give you all the time you need to understand you're not a fling to me, but never think for even a second that I'm playing games with you. When I tell you you are mine, it's because you are," he informs me in such a low and deep voice that my insides tremble with the promise of more.

"Understood," is all I manage to say.

Yup, my walls are crumbling down.

"Good." He squeezes my thigh a couple of times before removing his hand. "We're here."

When I look outside, we're in a residential area. There's no restaurant in sight, but Gabo gets out of the car and jogs toward my door to open it.

"This way," he says as he helps me out of the car and places his hand on my ass. This man can't be subtle to save his life. He's so possessive, and if I didn't find it sexy, as hell, I'd be concerned.

"Are you sure there's a restaurant around here?" I ask as I look around, and all I see are a bunch of residential buildings.

"It's the best kept secret in all of Bologna. They only open for a couple of hours every day."

"So how do we know we're getting a table?" I ask innocently. The look Gabo gives me makes me laugh.

"Okay, I'm sorry. Sometimes I forget I'm with Mr. Billionaire." That earns me a chuckle.

We arrive at a wooden door on the first floor of one of the buildings, and Gabo knocks twice. A waiter answers, and the moment he sees Gabo, his face lights up, and he opens the door wide for us.

"Mr. Godoy, what a pleasure to have you here. We were about to close, but for you we're always open," the waiter says as Gabo gets the seat for me.

"Thank you so much. I really appreciate it. We don't need a menu; just give us whatever you have available." Gabo looks to me for approval, and I nod. I've never been surprised like this in a restaurant. I like the idea of eating the chef's recs.

"Right away, Mr. Godoy."

"So, G, any other projects going on besides the warehouse one?" I ask him while we wait for the appetizers.

He shakes his head and takes a few seconds to gather his thoughts. "Honestly, I'm itching to find a project that challenges me, you know? Lately, I feel like all I do is the same project over and over again," he says, and I wonder if he has people in his business to confide this kind of thing to.

"What kind of project are you looking for? You're known for restoring classic structures and, lately, for environmentally friendly warehouses. What do you think would be a challenge for you?"

"That's a great question, principessa." He takes a sip of wine the waiter just brought us, and after approving it, we each get a glass.

"The truth is, I don't know. I haven't felt inspired in a long time. All I do is work and work; I think I might be burned out."

"Okay, hear me out. Why don't you take a week off and just do stuff with me? We can just enjoy life here in Bologna—we don't need to do anything crazy. Recharge your batteries, and then maybe the inspiration muse will knock on your door?"

"I like the way you think, Bella mia. Let me see what I have in the next couple of weeks. What about your class?"

"I'll have a one-week break after this week, then three weeks of class. So it'd be perfect if you could take next week off. Since I can work remotely on your company's project, I can do it from anywhere in the world," I inform him.

He looks at me with those soulful eyes; all I can think of is kissing him. So I do. I lean closer to him, and he meets me halfway. I start the kiss gently, enjoying the feel of his lips on mine, but Gabo takes over, and it's like a raging inferno. It's like he can't get enough of me; he pulls me toward him, and I straddle him on his seat. The moment I feel the hardness inside his pants, I start rubbing my core against him. He's making me feel too much, and a simple kiss won't do.

The waiter clears his throat, and Gabo chuckles against my lips. I slowly remove myself from Gabo's lap, feeling the heat rising in my cheeks. When I look at him, he's as cool as a cucumber—not fair.

"I apologize for the interruption, Mr. Godoy, but here's a sampler of the appetizers we have today. Roasted octopus with potato cream, applewood smoked burrata, cream of roasted cherry tomatoes, and grilled focaccia."

"All this looks delicious, thank you so much," I tell the waiter as he makes his way back to the kitchen.

"What do you want to try first?" Gabo asks, and although I don't understand why he's asking me, like the good girl I am when I'm with him, I answer, "The octopus."

"Good choice. Come here." He takes a spoonful of the potato cream, which has a couple of octopus pieces, and feeds it to me. The moment it hits my taste buds, a symphony of flavors explodes in my mouth.

"Hmm, delicious. Here, let me," I tell him as I grab the spoon from his hand and feed him.

"It definitely tastes better when you feed it to me," he says, and I chuckle.

The food keeps coming, and each dish is better than the last; I don't think I've ever had so much food at once. But with Gabo feeding me, it feels like nothing. Now all I want is to nap. I'm in a food coma.

"Do you think you have room for dessert?" Gabo asks, and I shake my head as I rub my belly.

"If I eat one more bite, I might explode," I tell him, and he kisses the back of my hand as he helps me up from my seat.

"Okay, what do you think about a night stroll?"

"I think Netflix and chill might be a better option." Gabo frowns, and I laugh.

"What? You don't know what that means? It's just code for a hookup," I retort incredulously, and he starts tickling me mercilessly.

"I don't want to talk about the past because it is irrelevant now, but I have never dated. I've never felt the need to do things like this with anyone," he says as he sways our intertwined hands.

"So you've never had anything other than one-night stands? Is that what you're trying to say?" I ask in a playful tone, not wanting him to think I'm judging him. I've been the same way.

"You could say that. I've had a few friends with benefits, but I've never had a steady girlfriend until you."

Here we go with the girlfriend calling again, but this time, it doesn't sound so terrible.

We reach his car, and he drives us back to the penthouse. I press him one more time for good measure.

"G, I don't want this to be a constant thing between us, but I really don't feel like having a title just yet. Can we just enjoy each other's company and see how things go?" I say, releasing a frustrating breath.

"I don't do things half-assed, and I sure as shit won't fumble you, Bella mia," Gabo informs me as he starts tracing circles with his finger on my thigh.

"You just said you never had a serious relationship. Why do you have to start now? I'm not one to be bound, Gabo. Let's just say we're unbound. Yeah?" I bat my eyelashes and pout for good measure.

"I don't think I'll ever be able to say no to you, Isabella Bianchi. You and I are (*Un*)Bounded," he says with a deep, almost defeated, sigh.

"Thank you, G. Thank you for listening and accepting me the way I am."

"Always."

Chapter 14

Gabo Godoy

T... ...ek w...t b...
...pro...ects...
with n... ...la Prof...
of con... ...Bel...
Acco... ...el...
arti...
in...

...nd...
...sn't dr...
...ollege. Ye...
another b...
her. *My n...*

However, I wasn't too happy to learn that Giacomo had almost caused an accident with Bella's car. I had to hear it from Rocco, who also reported that the kid had been almost harassing her for a second date. *Why can't the guy take the hint?* Maybe I'm expecting too much of a *ragazzo* who's still in school.

I know Bella is with me, but the fact that she doesn't want labels still makes me feel uncertain. I don't want anyone to think they have a chance with her. Because they don't. I trust no one, especially when she's involved, so I had Mario run a background check on him.

'Earth to Gabo," Dominic says as he enters my office, Mario hot on his tail.

"Is everything alright?" I ask, noting the urgency with which they both entered.

"Yeah, we were just power walking after lunch. And by the way, I won," Dominic says to Mario with a wink, to which Mario just rolls his eyes in fake annoyance. These two have been beating around the bush for far too long—I wish they'd just fuck and see if they can get it out of their systems.

"Boss, I ran the background check on Miss Bianchi's classmate as you asked and the guy is squeaky clean," Mario states, face unreadable.

"And is that a bad thing? I'm glad he doesn't present a threat to my Bella."

"Good, that's good. He just seems too perfect and no one ever is." I know what Mario is trying to tell me: we need to dig deeper.

"Can you get in contact with your friends at Interpol?" Dominic barks out a laugh that soon morphs into a coughing fit. Mario passes him a bottle of water, and Dominic eyes him, appreciative of the gesture.

"Gabo, don't be ridiculous. The kid is simply a good citizen, he must be one of the people who goes to the bathroom with the lights off. He's just pure like that." Mario and I laugh at Dominic's ridiculous assessment, but I need to know for certain the kid doesn't present a threat to Bella. One can never be too careful.

"Alright assholes, you all are funny and shit, but my woman is waiting for me to start the weekend," I say as I motion for them to say whatever it is they came in to say.

"Sounds good, boss. Aldo and Rocco going with you? Or do you need me to go?"

"Yeah, they're coming with us. You take the weekend to continue investigating." Mario nods in understanding and starts making his way out of the office.

"Did you already tap that? Or that's why you're acting like a psycho, investigating everyone who comes in contact with Isa?" I cannot believe Dominic just said that. I have him pinned against the wall in two seconds flat.

"Don't you ever refer to Bella like that ever again. She's the most important person in my life, and I'll stop at nothing to make sure she's safe at all times," I say with a clenched jaw. I've never been this furious with Dominic.

"Okay, okay, relax. It was a joke. What happened to bros over hoes?"

"Bella is not joking material. Understood?" I ask before releasing him, and he nods, massaging his neck.

"I see you've finally met the one," Dom says with a smirk, and I release a breath.

"Yes. She's everything I see." I hear his laugh as he leaves my office. I can't wait to finish what I have to do so I can go to the villa with her.

After a couple more hours of work, I'm about to close my laptop when Dom comes into my office.

"Sorry, man, but you're going to have to delay going home to your girl."

"Unless someone is dying, I'm out of here," I tell him in a tone that doesn't allow any arguing.

"Trust me, Gabo. We need to do this together."

"What is it?"

"Sheikh Khalid is here." That catches my interest.

"The sheikh is here? What for?" I ask, incredulous.

"Oh, I don't know. Maybe because he wants to do business with you? Wake up, bro." Dom snaps his fingers in front of me, and the first thing I think of doing is to call Bella.

"Hi, G. Are you on your way?" she answers after the second ring.

"Hi, Bella mia. Actually something came up."

"Huh?"

"Yeah, a sheikh is here, and I need to take him to dinner—a business dinner. Are you okay with starting our week off tomorrow morning?" I hate it. It hasn't even been a full day since I committed to making time to hang out with her, and I'm already asking for time to work.

"Oh, sure. It actually works out perfectly," Bella answers in a chirpy tone.

"Is that so?"

"Yeah, my classmates are going out tonight, and I had said no because we were leaving but now I can go. Good luck with the sheikh! See you later, G." Bella hangs up, and I stay with the phone against my cheek. I thought she would be disappointed, but I guess she can bounce between plans like no one's business. I can't help but feel the jealousy forming inside my chest. The thought of Goody Two-Shoes Giacomo being there makes me uneasy. No one is ever that clean.

"What? She hung up mad?" Dom asks.

"No. She said she could just make other plans, then." Dom barks out a laugh, and if I wasn't so intrigued by what the sheikh wants to talk to me about, I would swat his head.

"Sheikh Khalid, welcome. What a pleasure to have you here," I say as I welcome him into Verona, my restaurant. His entourage is at least twenty people. For someone who doesn't like drawing attention, he sure knows how to make an entrance.

"Mr. Godoy, I appreciate your flexibility to see me with such short notice."

"I must admit, I was surprised when I learned you were in town. What can I do for you?" The sheikh smiles at me as he sits and looks around for someone to fill a glass of water for him.

"It's quite simple, Mr. Godoy. I want you to build me a palace. Something humanity has never seen before." I raise my eyebrows at his statement.

"I see." I take a sip of my water, and I wish I had something stronger in hand, but out of respect for the sheikh, I only have water, like him.

"May I ask, why me? I'm flattered, but I would be lying if I said you didn't catch me by surprise."

"I like humble men, Mr. Godoy. That speaks highly of you. But I also like attention to detail and in that regard, in my opinion, you are second to none."

"I'm grateful for your vote of confidence, Sheikh Khalid. Is there a timeline? Any specifications? I currently have a few projects going, and I'm about to embark on one of the biggest projects of my career. I want to make sure I can give your project the attention it needs."

"I can appreciate that. I have a few projects going on myself. That's why I came personally to speak with you, because there are some matters that cannot be delegated if you want them to go perfectly."

"I couldn't agree with you more. Let's talk business." He smiles at my words and asks one of his bodyguards for a tablet.

The evening goes by with us eating and talking about his vision for his newest palace. I guess this is my sign to finally get out of my comfort zone.

———◦❖◦———

"Rocco, where are you guys?" I ask over the speaker as I start my Lamborghini Aventador SV. I can't wait to see Bella.

"Mr. Godoy, we're outside of Fuoco. Miss Bianchi and her classmates are inside."

"Okay, I'm on my way," I say as I disconnect the call and punch in directions on the navigation system. The time flew by speaking with the sheikh, and I'm beyond excited to embark on that project. I can't wait to tell Bella all about it.

It's an easy drive to Fuoco, and I'm parking in front of the place in less than ten minutes. I didn't get a chance to change, so I leave my suit jacket in the car and roll up my shirt sleeves. Everyone in line is ogling my car, and as long as no one touches it, it's fine. I guess it's not often you see one of these since they went out of production a couple of years ago.

The bouncer nods for me to cut in line, and I pass him a five-hundred Euro bill.

"Thank you, Mr. Godoy," I hear him say before I disappear into the throng of people inside this place. I make my way to the bar and ask for a whiskey on the rocks. I take a fortifying sip as I scan the area, looking for those azure eyes that I can get lost in. Finding her doesn't take me long—she's the most beautiful woman on the dance floor. She's wearing a barely-there black strapless dress and sky-high silver heels. Her hair is down in flowy waves, covering her back. She's dancing to the beat in a circle with other girls, all of them dressed to the nines, but I only have eyes for the Argentine fairy who has enchanted me since the moment I saw her descending from my jet.

I'm enjoying watching her dance, waiting for the perfect moment to join her when a kid, who I can only assume is Giacomo, gets behind her and dares to put a hand on her waist. This wimpy motherfucker decided to hit on the wrong woman.

I finish my whiskey in one big gulp and reach the dance floor in four strides. People make way the moment they see me barreling through the crowded space—they're smart to do so. When I get to Bella, I see she has stopped dancing and is saying something to Giacomo, but he's still holding her. I get between them and look down at the kid, effectively breaking their connection. I'm not the tallest person, but I'm taller than this idiot.

"G. What are you doing here?" Bella asks with a gorgeous smile on her face, eyes sparkling. She's happy to see me.

"I came for you," I tell her as I place my hand on her middle and see her visibly relax. I relax a smidge, too.

"Isa, do you know this dude?" the kid asks, still in our space.

"Of course, this is Gabo. My..." She looks at me with a smirk.

"I'm hers and she's mine. Now get lost." Bella chuckles, and Giacomo simply stands there. I'm guessing he's in shock.

"You're with this dude? He could be your older brother," he shouts, and I tense at his words because I'm not that much older than them, and my patience is thinning fast.

"He's not," Bella informs him. At the same time, I say, "I'm not, but I can be your worst nightmare if you don't leave alone what's mine." I practically growl.

"Wow, okay. Have fun with the geriatric." That's it. I'm done with the disrespect. He's about to finally leave when I grab him by the back of his shirt.

Mario is next to me a second later. He came with me after the meeting. "Do you need help, Mr. Godoy?"

"Please help this kid find his way home. I think he's passed his curfew." Mario nods and holds Giacomo by the back of his shirt.

"I'm not a kid. I'm twenty," the kid shouts, and I chuckle.

"You just proved my point, please don't embarrass yourself and leave."

"Mr. Godoy, is there a problem here?" A man wearing all black joins the conversation. I'm guessing he's the club manager.

"I'm not a kid. My name is Giacomo, and I came with my friends to have a good time," he retorts as he tries to get out of Mario's hold but can't.

"Do you know who he is?" the man in black asks Giacomo.

"No. Should I?" he answers in a defiant tone.

"Well, Mr. Godoy is one of the most influential men in the city. I'd suggest you do as he says."

"Why should I do that? Is he mafia or something?"

"No, I'm not involved with the mafia. But it just so happens, I own a lot of businesses and a design/construction firm, so if you ever want to get a job in your field, I can make it impossible for you. I usually don't like to show off my status, but when someone messes with what's mine, I will stop at nothing to make them understand," I tell him in a tone that doesn't allow room for arguing.

"And you're okay with this, Isa? I thought you were different," he spits, and I'm about to get him out of here once and for all, but Bella surprises me when she gets in front of me with her hands on her hips.

"Look, Giacomo, you've been a good friend. I enjoyed having coffee with you and you're a good classmate, but I told you I didn't want to dance with you, and you didn't listen. Not to mention the fact that I've said, as nicely as possible, that I'm not interested in a relationship with you. Maybe you need to go home and reflect on what just happened. Because when a woman says no, it actually means no." My Bella shrugs as she turns her back to him and grabs my hand, leading me to another area of the dance floor. I bark out a laugh as I follow her. I'm pretty sure I'd follow this woman to heaven and hell if she asked.

"Hey everyone, this is Gabo." She introduces me to her friends, who stopped dancing when Giacomo decided to make a scene. They all wave, and I wave back; no one says anything about the incident, so I let it pass, too. The one who looked like a clown was Giacomo, trying to fit where there was no room for him.

"Oh, I love this song. Come on, G," Bella says, and I follow her through the dance floor. She stands in front of me, and I can finally wrap my arm around her middle, bringing her flush against me. She moves her hips to the rhythm, and I follow her lead. I keep telling myself I can't have her. Not yet. But the pull I feel toward her is stronger than anything I've ever experienced before. Bella raises her left arm and pulls my head down by grabbing the back of my neck. It's such a simple yet sensual touch that I can help but buck my dick against her ass. Bella starts rubbing her ass against my dick, and I need to take a couple of deep breaths to not come in my pants. Fuck.

"Are you wet, Bella mia?" I ask her as my right-hand travels down her chest and onto her thigh, dangerously close to her core.

"That's something you have to find out," this little minx replies, and I can't take it anymore.

"Okay, let's go," I say as I start making my way toward the exit and she giggles.

"Somewhere I can check how wet you are without any witnesses. That pussy is mine and only mine," I turn back to whisper against her ear, and she does her little happy dance, making me chuckle.

When we leave Fuoco, I see a crowd mingling around my car. When one of them spots me, he motions for everyone to make way for us. Luckily, it doesn't seem like they were touching it. I help Bella inside, blocking her from view. I don't want anyone to see her pussy, and that excuse of a dress she's wearing doesn't leave much to the imagination.

"Where to, Mr. Godoy?" Mario comes to stand next to me as I close Bella's door.

"We're just going to my penthouse. Once we enter the garage, you guys can go home. Thank you, Mario." He nods with a smirk like he knows what's about to go down. And I don't even correct him because tonight I'll taste Bella Bianchi for the very first time.

I get in my car, and the engine roars to life once I turn it on. I notice Bella pressing her thighs together, and my dick jerks up in response. She wants this as much as I do.

"Hey, G. Would you be okay if I do this?" She doesn't even wait for me to reply. She opens her legs wide, placing her left foot on top of my junk—I hiss at the touch. The heel is digging dangerously close to my cock, but I widen my stance, giving her more room to play. She starts twisting her foot, left and right, adding the right amount of pressure. I grab her heel-clad foot and start massaging my cock with it. It's so damn sexy that if I weren't driving, I would have come already. I have one hand on her foot, the other one on the steering wheel, trying to focus as much as I can on the road, but I notice from the corner of my eye that she's starting to touch herself. Fuck, no.

"You can't touch what's mine, principessa," I grit through clenched teeth, really trying to reign in my emotions. She simply chuckles and wets her middle finger with her arousal and licks it clean, making a show out of it. I drive as fast as I can; I can't let her come without me tasting her first.

I enter the garage and watch the SUVs disappearing on the other side of the gate. Mario, Rocco, and Aldo won't be back until tomorrow.

An idea pops up in my brain. I park the car and make my way to help Bella out, and the moment I see her standing in front of me, lust evident on her face, I know what to do.

"Come here and spread your legs for me," I command, and Bella follows me. "Lie down," I tell her next, and she looks around.

"Where?" she asks, confused.

"On the hood." She immediately sees where I'm going with this, and she spreads her legs as she sits down on the hood of the Lamborghini. She leans down to untie her heels, and I stop her in her tracks. "Leave them on. Now, go all the way up on the hood," I instruct her as I remove my vest and tie and toss them to the side. "Put your feet against the hood, Bella mia."

"But I'll scratch the paint with my heels," she chides.

"It'll be a reminder of the first time I made you come, principessa."

Bella smirks and does as I asked. I get on my knees, and the view takes my breath away. She's wearing a tiny, lacey black thong that's wet with arousal. Her black dress is ruched all the way to her waist, her ass is against the red hood of my car, and her heels are digging into the hood. They'll leave dents, for sure. I couldn't care less.

"What is taking so long?" Bella whines, and I chuckle.

"Patience, principessa. I'm admiring the view." She widens her legs in response, and that's it. I start placing kisses from her ankle to her calf, leaving goosebumps as I make my way to her inner thigh. Once I'm within reach, Bella tugs my hair, and I welcome the sting. I have never felt so turned on in my life. I trace circles with my tongue, and I feel her squirming, so I place my hands on top of her feet, hoping she'll stop moving. I truly enjoy seeing her come undone for me. The moment I place my tongue on top of her core, she bucks up, and I chuckle.

"It's not funny, G. I want to come," she whines again, so I repeat the tortuous act over and over. When I feel her breathing increase, I pull her thong with my teeth, ripping it in the process, and spit it on the floor. The moment my tongue touches her clit, I feel ten feet tall. The moan Bella shouts is something I've never heard before. I open her lower lips with my hands and use my tongue to enter her, eating her mercilessly.

"Yes, G. Like that," Bella chants, and I start making circles with my tongue on her clit as I enter her with two fingers. "G, I'm going to come. It feels so good."

I pick up my pace with my tongue and fingers as she starts moving erratically. I know the moment she comes because her walls start pulsating against my fingers, and her heels dig deeper into the hood of my car, making a screeching sound. I'd be pissed if I wasn't enjoying this so much. I let her ride out her orgasm, and when I see her breathing start to even out, I stand up and open my arms to her. She takes my hands, and I kiss her once she's standing, letting her taste herself in my mouth. I reluctantly let her lips go and lean down to grab my tie, vest, and her panties, which I pocket.

"Let's go, G. It's your turn now."

We hold hands as we make our way to the elevator, but what she doesn't know is that I won't come tonight—at least not with her. I want to save our first time together until we're at the villa, so I stay quiet as I lead her to her room.

"Wait. So you gave me the best orgasm of my life, and now you're telling me I have to sleep in my room by myself?" Bella pouts, and it almost breaks my willpower. Almost.

"There are a lot of emotions running wild tonight, and I think it's best if we sleep on them and start fresh tomorrow at the villa," I say as I give her a peck on her nose.

She gets on her tippy toes to kiss me. "Fine. Good night, G."

"Good night, principessa."

I heave a deep breath as I make it to my room and undress quickly for a cold shower.

Once in my bed, I hear Bella moaning quietly. *Fuck my life. Is she using that damn vibrator again?* Not wasting time wondering, I shoot her a text.

> **Gabo**: Are you using that fake *eggplant emoji* again?

It takes a couple of seconds for the text to be delivered, but I know the moment it does because her moaning stops.

> **Bella**: Maybe… want to come and join me? *evil emoji*

"This woman will be my demise," I whisper to myself in my empty room.

Gabo: I think I'll pass. It'll just make you want more of the real *eggplant emoji* *kissy face emoji*

Bella: Ugh, I hate you.

She replies instantly, and I hear the moaning resume. I can't help the laugh that escapes me, imagining her hot and bothered for my cock. I can't wait to make her see stars tomorrow.

Gabo: No, you don't. Rest up, Bella mia. Tomorrow, I'll make you come so many times, you'll beg for mercy.

Bella: Promises, promises.

And this firecracker attaches a picture of a pink vibrator entering her pussy. I groan loudly, and now it's her turn to cackle. Well played, Bella. Well played.

Chapter 15

Gabo Godoy

I had also had a we
with pain. I
Bella a steing
ing, an oise
drea ut
hea

wh
eah, s
ve been
spend th
walking a no

"Yes, bro. I saw her last night. Let me go check on her." I hang up on him before he can keep asking questions. I put on a pair of gray sweatpants and rush to Bella's room. After knocking a couple of times and not hearing any noise inside, I try the doorknob and it turns, so I open the door. Bella is spread like a starfish in the middle of the bed, buck naked. If Luca weren't downstairs, I'd get into that bed and wake her with an orgasm, but I can't.

"Bella mia, wake up," I tell her as I gently shake her arm. She makes an unintelligible noise and turns on her side, giving me a glorious view of her ass.

"Bella, Luca is outside. Wake up." That does it. Bella sits up, disoriented.

"What is he doing here?" she finally asks after looking at the horizon quietly for a couple of seconds.

"I don't know, but he's blowing up my phone. I need to open the door for him."

"Okay, okay. Go. I'll put on clothes in the meantime."

"Okay. Are we telling him?" I ask as I make my way out of her room.

"Are you crazy? Why would we do that? We're still figuring out where this is going, remember? You said you'd give me all the time I needed," Bella practically shouts, panic in her voice and her eyes wide like a deer under high beams.

"Alright," I tell her as my shoulders sag. I won't lie; I wanted to have this conversation with Luca to get it out of the way. I know I promised her time, and I stopped calling her girlfriend—at least out loud—but I don't like having secrets with my best friend. I'm not doing anything wrong, and I don't see why we need to hide, but I promised her time, so I will give it to her.

"*Boludo*, finally. I thought I was going to have to call the police or something to investigate what's going on in here," Luca says as he gives me a bro hug.

"Sorry, *weón*. I was trying to wake B... Isa up. It took her a second," I tell him, showing him the way to the elevator through the garage.

"Damn, what happened to the Lambo? Angry ex?" Luca chuckles as we pass by the car where I made his little sister come so hard that she scratched and dented the hood.

"Yeah, Gabo. What happened?" Bella asks with a damn smirk on her gorgeous face, and my death glare only makes her laugh.

"*Hermanita, hola*." (Little sis, hi.) Luca interrupts our staring contest as he makes his way to the elevator where Bella is standing.

"Hi, brother dearest. Color me surprised to see you here." My girl throws a jab at her brother, and I have to cover my laugh with a cough.

"Well, I texted you and haven't heard from you for days. I was trying to apologize. I'm sorry, Isa."

Even though this is hard for Luca to admit—because he's never wrong, of course—I can tell he's sincere.

"And yet, here you are. Overstepping the boundaries I placed," she tells him, crossing her arms in front of her.

"Ugh, that's exactly what Karina told me. Don't tell her I said that." Bella and I bark out a laugh, and after a couple of beats, Luca joins us.

"I forgive you, Luca. I know you want what's best for me. But I need you to trust me. You have to stop monitoring my every move."

"I promise," Luca says, and if I didn't know any better, I'd say he's trying to keep tears at bay. If he cares like this about his little sister, I know he will be the best dad to my niece or nephew.

"Phew, okay. I have twenty-four hours of freedom before Karina comes to Italy looking for me. Where are we going?" Luca rubs his hands in excitement, and I internally roll my eyes. We should have gone to the villa last night.

"Hmm, let's see. What do you feel like doing?" Bella asks Luca.

"If you say going to a cabaret or a gentlemen's club, I'll hang you by your balls," I interject.

Bella laughs, and Luca shudders at the picture I painted.

"No, bro. Karina is the one and only for me. I was thinking about going to the beach. It's fucking cold in Chile right now." Sometimes I forget the weather is the opposite in the southern hemisphere; when we're in summer, they're in winter.

"We can go to my beach house in Rimini. It's just a short drive from here."

Bella does her little happy dance, and it takes everything in me not to grab her and kiss her senseless.

"What are we waiting for? Let's go," Luca says as he makes his way back to the entrance.

"Wait, I need to eat and change," Bella tells him. "I just woke up, remember?" She pins him with a stare, and he rolls his eyes and messes with her hair. I miss this sibling banter. I need to make a point of seeing Vicente and Karina more often. Maybe now that I'm with Bella, I'll visit Chile more.

A couple of hours later, we're back in the garage. We need to bring a car that fits three people, so my convertibles are out of the question.

"Really, man. What happened to the Lambo?" Luca asks again, and I can hear Bella chuckle behind us.

"Not sure. It was like that after I came out of a bar." I shrug for good measure, but Luca knows me well.

"Are you serious? And the fucker who did this is still alive? Where were your bodyguards?"

"Mario was with me inside the bar, and Aldo and Rocco were with Isa. It's not a big deal, nothing that can't be fixed."

"Okay, who are you, and what did you do with my best friend? The Gabo Godoy I know would die before letting anything happen to any of his precious cars."

"My precious." Luca imitates Gollum's voice, and Bella and I laugh. He's so ridiculous.

"Why are you so worried about it? It's just a car. I'll get it fixed in no time," I say as I open the back door of my Mercedes G-Wagon for Bella. She kisses me on the cheek. I freeze for a moment, not understanding why she did that when she still wants to keep things a secret from her brother.

"It's just, you're always crazy about your cars," I hear him say as I help Bella into the backseat, and he gets into the passenger seat. She blows me a kiss, and I blow her one back. I like living on the edge.

Once we get to my beach house, I park, and Mario and the boys park right behind me.

"Once baby Bianchi is born, we have to come here for a babymoon. This place is sick," Luca says as he does a 360 of the property.

"You know you and Kari are always welcome here. Plus, it'd be nice to meet my niece or nephew."

Bella comes to stand next to me and, in a very inconspicuous way, swats my ass, which makes me jerk in response.

"Are you okay, bro?" Luca asks, concerned, while Bella makes her way inside the house.

"Yeah, man. I think a mosquito bit me or something."

After calling the local pizzeria to order lunch, we get into our swimsuits and head to the beach. Bella decides to give me a heart attack by wearing a tiny white bikini with a strawberry print. She looks good enough to eat.

"Hey, Gabo. Could you help me with the sunscreen? There are areas I can't reach," Bella asks with a blinding smile. I look where Luca is, and he's busy on the phone—I'm assuming with my sister—and walking toward the water.

"With pleasure." I lather my hands with sunscreen and wait for her to lie down on her front. I untie her top and start covering her back with sunscreen, getting as close as I can to her sideboob without looking like a freak. Then I make my way to her legs and pay special attention to her ass. I can't help but chuckle when I see her squirming, trying to rub her thighs together.

"No, principessa. That won't work. Plus, your brother is on his way back," I tell her, even though Luca is still focused on his phone call.

"Help me tie my top, please?" she asks hurriedly, and I laugh. She's so damn cute.

"Do you want tan lines?" I ask her honestly.

"I want to walk around a bit, so yeah, I don't mind the tan lines."

I do as she asks and see her put on a black hat and black heart-shaped glasses. She looks so gorgeous, like the old Hollywood divas who used to vacation here in Rimini back in the day. I can't wait for Luca to leave so I can walk around freely with Bella, kiss her at every corner, and shout to the world that she's mine. I would tell Luca right now, but Bella wants to keep things between us. I know I agreed to it, but I'm not sure how long I can keep something like this from my best friend. The Lambo episode was a close call.

"Wanna play volleyball?" Luca asks, pocketing his phone.

"Sure, let's see if we can find enough people to form two teams." I look around the beach, and although it's not crowded, enough people are mingling around. You'd think Luca speaks Italian by how he charmed everyone and got two teams together in no time. No, he doesn't need to speak the language; he's pure charisma. Or swag, as he would say.

I scan the beach, looking for Bella, and when I spot her by the water, I jog to where she is. Like a moth to a flame, a couple of college-looking kids hang on her every word.

"Is everything okay here?" I ask her, and she turns to face me.

"Yes, G. We're good. We were just chatting."

I eye the kids up and down. My hand itches to take a possessive hold on Bella, but I can't play the possessive boyfriend card with Luca nearby. "Okay, we're going to play a volleyball match. If you need me, I'll be right there." I point toward the makeshift sandfield, and she nods.

"I'll make sure to enjoy the view. I hope you put on a good show for me." She gets impossibly close to me and places a barely-there kiss on my chest. I turn my hat backward as I make my way back to where Luca and his new friends are waiting.

"Everything okay with Isa?" Luca asks as we take positions.

"Yeah, I just wanted to let those kids know she's not alone."

"Thanks, man. You're taking your job of taking care of Isa seriously. I really appreciate it." Luca pats my back as the game starts. I can't be chill around her to save my life. This hiding gig is harder than I anticipated. She makes me feel like a boy in puberty.

The game goes back and forth, everyone having a good time. I'm not really paying attention to the score. As Bella requested, I'm trying to put on a good show for her—running to hit every ball, falling on the sand a little bit more than needed. Luca rolls his eyes at my theatrics, but the moment I dusted off the sand from my abs, I caught Bella ogling me and biting her lower lip. Yeah, she likes what she sees, so it's worth it.

Our team wins the match, and everyone returns to their beach spots. Luca, Bella, and I go back to my house for lunch. Pizza and Aperol spritzes for everyone.

"I'm going to take a shower to get rid of all the sand I got in places that shouldn't be in contact with sand," Luca informs us, and I chuckle.

Once I hear the door close in one of the bedrooms upstairs, I'm next to Bella, kissing her. Her lips are warm and inviting, and I've been dying to kiss her all day.

"Hey, G. Do you think Luca suspects anything?" she asks as she trails kisses on my jaw.

"I don't think so, but to be honest, I can't wait for him to leave. I don't like keeping you a secret. I want to kiss you and hold your hand in front of everyone," I tell her.

"I know. I want that, too. But you know Luca—we need time to warm him up to the idea." I capture her lips with mine again, and the kiss turns passionate quickly. I want her so badly.

Bella stands up, pressing flush against me, and my hard dick is pressing against her belly. She starts squirming, driving me wild. *Maybe I can make her come once before Luca comes back down.* I'm about to put her on the kitchen counter when I hear steps coming down the stairs. Reluctantly, I let Bella's lips go, and she sits back on the breakfast bar.

"This has been fun, but I need to go back home to my wife. Can you guys give me a ride to the airport?" I look at Bella, and she's wiping her mouth after eating more pizza. Damn, everything this woman does is sensual.

"I thought you said you had twenty-four hours here. What's the rush?" Bella asks him, curiosity in her tone.

"I'm not built for the single life anymore. I miss Karina more than words can say, and I'd rather go back now so I can sleep with her tonight." I chuckle at his reasoning but don't argue. If someone asked me if I wanted a bros weekend or a weekend with Bella, I wouldn't think twice. Bella would win every time.

"Sure. Bella and I can change back at the penthouse after we drop you off. Let's go," I say as I make my way to the front door where Aldo, Mario, and Rocco are shooting the shit and eating pizza and cola.

"Ready to go, boss?" Mario asks, getting up from the couch.

"Yes, we need to drop Luca off at the airport."

"We can do that for you, sir. Aldo and Rocco can take him, and I'll stay with you and Miss Bianchi."

"No need, Mario. I appreciate it, and I really appreciate the way you call my sister Miss Bianchi. No silly nicknames. Bella? What the fuck is that, *boludo*?" Luca asks.

Fuck, I didn't even realize my slip-up.

"Bella is also part of my name, Luca. It's not a big deal. Let's go." Bella makes her way to my G-Wagon, and Luca and I pile in right after her. I can't look him in the eyes; there's no way he doesn't know something is going on between me and his little sister. I feel tense the entire drive to the airport, and I can feel he's tense, too. This fucking sucks, but I won't say anything until Bella does. I promised her time, and that's what I'll give her.

Forty-five agonizing minutes later, we're at the airport, and Luca is the first to get out of the car.

"I didn't realize you had bought a jet, man. Nice," I tell him, trying to make conversation.

"I rented it, but maybe this is something I need to invest in. Now that we'll have a little one in tow, it will definitely come in handy." I nod; a jet is a great investment.

"Thank you so much for coming to see me, brother dearest. I'll be back in Chile in no time," Bella says as she hugs Luca, and he hugs her back.

"Remember, no matter what, I'm always proud of you. Even though I might not agree with your choices, I'll try my hardest to respect them," he says as he looks me in the eyes.

Fuck.

Then he comes to give me a bro hug. "Yeah, the two of you are not fooling anyone. I can see how you look at each other, wanting to rip each other's clothes off. And even though, in theory, it's not my business, you both are part of my family. So if this goes sideways, one of you is going to be heartbroken and the other one is going to be fucked. And I don't want to be in the middle of the shitshow, but we all know which side I'm going to choose. So be careful." With that, he runs up the staircase and disappears into the jet.

Fuck.

I turn to look at Bella, her shoulders sagging. I immediately wrap my arms around her, and she hugs me back.

"I wish it'd gone differently," I hear her say, muffled against my chest.

"I know, principessa. Me too. You know he's my best friend and my brother-in-law, but you are mine, remember? We'll show him and everyone else that we are bound to each other."

I hear her chuckle as she lifts her face to look at me.

"We're (*Un*)Bounded, G, remember?" she tells me with a crooked smile.

I roll my eyes at her as the jet's engine starts. We both wave. I'm not sure if Luca is looking through the window.

For Bella's sake, I hope he is. I know my girl is tough, but her brother's opinion is important to her.

Chapter 16

Isabella Bianchi

I really thought we were going to get away with not having to have the conversation with Luca on his trip, but he dropped his opinion like a bomb at the very last minute. It wasn't really a conversation; it was more like a judgment. I know the situations are different, but when Gonzalo, Karina's dad, basically told Luca never to come back to his house, we all rallied behind him to get his girl.

It's still crazy to me to think how my brother judges me no matter what. I'm too young, I don't know what I'm doing, I can choose a good partner. Never mind that. How on earth is he not happy for me? For a nice guy that's smart, there pr

"The truth?" I ask after a deep breath.

"Always."

"Two things: I'm thinking about how I don't want to keep fighting myself to not let you call me your girlfriend and how hard my brother judges me," I say as my voice breaks at the last part.

"Before we talk about your brother, I just need to make sure I'm hearing you correctly. You are telling me you are ready to admit you're my girlfriend?" Gabo says in a giddy tone, and I can't help but smile at how happy he is.

"Yeah, G. You're my boyfriend," I tell him as I grab his hand and squeeze it hard. He has become my rock, and I don't want to deny it anymore. I'm head over heels for this man.

He kisses the back of my hand over and over as he whispers, "Thank you, thank you, Bella mia." And if there were any doubts left, they're gone. This man is incredible.

After a few more kisses and whispers, Gabo's face turns serious, and I know it's time to talk about my brother.

"I know this is hard for you because Luca has been your parental figure for a while, but deep down, I know he only wants what's best for you."

"Yeah, G. He has a great way of showing it," I say with a scoff, and Gabo barks out a laugh.

"You know your brother has no chill." Gabo points out, and now it's my turn to laugh.

"You're not lying," I tell him as I take my phone out. I need to get this off my chest.

Isabella: Why did you have to out me to Luca? He just left after coming for less than twenty-four hours.

Gio: What are you talking about?

Isabella: Oh, come on, big brother. You told Luca you saw something between me and Gabo, and he came all the way from Chile to let us know how he feels about it.

My phone vibrates with an incoming call, and even though I roll my eyes at it, I answer it.

"Hi, Gio."

"Luca did what?" I chuckle at Gio shouting on the phone. Honestly, at this point, we all should know how extra Luca can be.

"Yeah, he arrived this morning and told us to take him to the beach. He played volleyball with Gabo, had lunch, and then told us to give him a ride to the airport. Then he proceeded to tell us how wrong he thinks this thing between us is and got into the jet without saying goodbye," I tell Gio everything, feeling really crappy all over again because the more I think about it, the more ridiculous I think this situation is.

"Can you please put me on speaker?" Gio asks, and honestly, I don't know what to expect from my brothers anymore.

"Please, Isa. What I need to say is to the two of you."

I look at Gabo, who's completely focused on driving. I know whatever my brother says, it's best if Gabo hears it. I know now he's in this—whatever this is—one hundred percent.

"Okay, you're on speaker now."

"Hey, man. Isa was just saying how fucked up your best friend is," Gio says, and Gabo and I chuckle.

"Yeah, bro. He came, did his little show, and then told us what's what before heading back."

"Listen, the only reason I mentioned anything to him was because I did see something between the two of you. I thought it was a good thing, you know? I actually think the two of you make sense together."

My jaw is on the floor. "You do?" I ask after the initial shock has passed.

Gabo squeezes my hand as if to say, "I told you so."

"Yeah, Isa. I do. Gabo is an exemplary man. You know me, I don't say anything lightly. He wouldn't have made a move on you if he didn't think he was being honest. Our families are already close. It wouldn't be a smart move."

"Boom. Thanks, Gio. I knew Bella wasn't the only smart Bianchi." Gio chuckles at Gabo's compliment.

"I know this is silly and you don't need it, but if it makes you feel better, Isa, you have my blessing. And if for some reason I need to knock some sense into Gabo, you just say the word. I can do that, too." My heart warms up at my brother's words. He truly is the best.

"Thanks, Gio. Please, just don't say anything to Luca. I don't want more drama. He'll accept it whenever he's ready."

"You got it, Isa. Love you."

"Love you, too, big brother." I disconnect the call and look at Gabo, who already has a mischievous smirk on his face.

"What are you thinking?" I ask, a little too anxious to know the answer.

"That we should go to the villa and start our week off right now."

"I love that idea, but I don't have any clothes there."

"That's fine. You don't need them anyway," Gabo says in a serious tone, and I open my eyes wide.

"What? Haven't you been begging me for sex?"

"I have not begged, *Signore* Godoy. How dare you," I say, mock indignation oozing from my tone.

"Oh, my bad. I thought it was you, Bella mia, chanting, 'Yeah, G. Like that. More, G,'" he mimics my accent, and I swat his arm as he tries to move away from me.

"Fine. You know what? I don't need you; I have my trusty dildo," I state as I fold my arms against my chest.

"You'll use that damn thing again over my dead body," Gabo says, and I cackle at him. He's so dramatic.

"Lucky for you, I always have it in my purse," I say as I pat my bag. Gabo raises a brow in question, and I explain, "You never know when you need an orgasm, you know?"

"The only thing I know is that you'll never want to use that dildo ever again once you ride my cock." I swallow hard at his statement. I'm so ready for him.

"So what is it going to be, principessa? Are you going to ride me? Or are you going to use that fake dick you have in your purse?" Gabo's hand gets dangerously close to my core, and I instinctively open my legs for him.

"Fuck. Just as I suspected; you're so wet for me." Gabo circles my clit with his index finger, and I can't help the moan that escapes me.

"We'll be there in five minutes. And then you'll be mine," he says as he keeps playing with my clit.

⟶⊷❖⊶⟵

"You guys can go to town for a while or do whatever. Miss Bianchi and I won't be available until tomorrow," Gabo informs his security detail as he carries me like I'm a sack of potatoes into the villa. I giggle the entire time until we enter his room, and he lays me down on his bed—almost ceremoniously.

"I've been waiting for this moment for so fucking long," he says as he gets on top of me, trailing kisses down my collarbone.

"What are you talking about? I've only been here for a few weeks," I say as I shamelessly grab his ass and push him down so I can get relief by feeling his hard length rubbing against my core.

"I have always thought you were beautiful, but when I went to your graduation back in February, not only did your beauty knock me on my ass but also your drive, your take on life. I knew then I wanted to get to know you better, so when you told me your plan, I thought it was kismet to offer you a summer in Italy." Gabo continues with his assault on my neck. I'm sure I'm going to have a bruise there tomorrow. And I couldn't care less. This magnificent man just told me he was hoping I would come spend the summer with him. Me. The woman Luca still treats like a little girl.

"If we're going to be honest, I've always thought you're the hottest of the Godoy brothers, but never thought I'd have a chance with you since you're so old."

"Old? I'll show you I'm experienced, not old," he growls the words against my neck. "And even though some people might think my experience is a point against me to court you, I'd say it's actually good. I made all the mistakes I needed to make before I had a chance with you. Because now I'm one hundred percent certain that you are the only woman I want in my life. I don't need to look anywhere else. You are everything I want."

"Then make me yours, G."

He doesn't reply. He simply starts undressing me with such reverence that I get goosebumps all over my body. I've never in my life had anyone treat me this passionately and thoughtfully. When I'm naked, he sits down on his feet and admires me from head to toe.

"Fuck, Bella. You are every wet dream come true." He removes his shirt and swim shorts, and his cock springs free. Hard and proud.

Gabo gets on top of me once more and starts trailing kisses down my chest. He grabs one of my breasts in his right hand and starts flicking my left nipple with his tongue. I press his head down gently, letting him know how much I'm enjoying his exploration of my body. He continues flicking, licking, then biting my nipple until he decides to pay the same attention to my other breast. I can feel my heart rate increasing. It's embarrassing to admit he has me so hot and ready for him by just touching my breasts, but his tongue is incredible.

"Gabo, I need you." I'm finally able to form words.

"Tell me what you want, principessa. I was made to please you." Ugh, this man says the hottest things.

"I need you inside me." I grab his thick, dripping cock in my hand so he can get the hint.

"I need to make sure you're ready for me." He kisses me sweetly and tenderly. Taking his time, he presses his lips to mine as he starts moving on top of me, giving me the friction I'm seeking. He makes his way down my chest and kisses my breasts again, then down my middle until he reaches my navel and opens my lower lips with his hands. He licks me from back to front and, fuck, if I don't buck in response. It's an overwhelming sensation to feel him all over me.

"You taste so good, I think I'm addicted already," Gabo tells me as he traces circles with his tongue on my clit and enters me with two fingers. The sensation is too much and not enough at the same time—I feel like I'm going to self-combust if he doesn't stretch me with that big cock of his.

Seeking relief, I start moving to the pace he's entering me with his fingers when he stops and moves on top of me. He thrusts into me in one swift movement. I feel the air leave my lungs at the invasion, but once he's completely in, he gives me time to adjust to his size.

"Are you okay? Did I hurt you?" he asks as he looks at me, those deep brown eyes full of concern.

"I'm okay," I tell him as I kiss him, waiting for my lungs to expand again. Once I'm breathing normally, he starts moving ever so slowly. I've never felt this way, like we could be together like this forever.

Gabo kisses me as he picks up speed, his eyes never leaving mine. We don't need words—our bodies communicate with a dance that only the two of us know. The moment I crisscross my legs around his back, Gabo pushes in even more—something I didn't think was possible—and I yelp in pleasure. He suddenly stops, likely worried that I'm in pain, so I kiss him hard to let him know I'm okay. He starts moving again, and this time, all the gentleness flies out the window. We both are moving fast, chasing the proverbial fall. After three more thrusts, Gabo and I come together.

Once our breathing has slowed down, he gets up from the bed and goes to the bathroom. I get into the fetal position, wishing I could snuggle with him right now. When he comes back out, he's holding a washcloth, and I look at him, wondering what he's up to.

"We didn't use a condom. I need to clean you up." I relax at his thoughtfulness.

"Yeah, I did notice we didn't use anything. But I've been on the pill for a while, so we're good."

"I'm sorry I didn't ask if it was okay to go bare, but I wasn't thinking. I just wanted to be with you," he says as he gets into bed with me after discarding the washcloth.

"G, it's not a big deal. I would have said something if I wasn't comfortable without a condom." I smile at him as I rest my head on his arm and cross my leg on top of his.

"Thank you for agreeing to be bound to me," he says, those deep brown eyes shining full of love.

"Yeah, G. We're bound to each other." He captures my lips with his, and we get lost in each other one more time.

Chapter 17

Gabo Godoy

B

I just woke up, and Bella's side of the bed is cold. I know she's still in the villa; otherwise, the security team would have alerted me. I wonder why she got up so early. Even though she said she wanted to be bound to me, I still feel she's holding back. I know after our conversation about her parents, it won't be easy for her to fully trust me. That's something that will only come with time. And now that she decided to take a chance with me, I have all the time in the world—I'm not going anywhere, and if we decide to have kids, we'll be the best parents who ever lived.

After stretching and splashing water on my face to wake up, I go looking for her. It doesn't take me long to find her. She's in her studio, her back to me, wearing one of my white dress shirts. She's painting a large canvas that I had set up for her when I offered her a space to create.

"Good morning, Bella mia," I say as I make my way to her. She turns to face me, a beautiful smile on her face, and the view takes my breath away. She's not wearing anything under my shirt, and it's unbuttoned, teasing me with glimpses of her delicious body.

"Morning, G." She stands on her tippy-toes to kiss me. "This morning, I woke up with an idea that wouldn't leave me alone, so I came to work on it," she tells me as she turns and continues to make soft strokes with her brush.

"I like it; it has character," I tell her honestly after looking at the blend of colors and shapes she's creating.

"Thank you. I won't tell you what it is until it's finished. You'll figure it out by yourself."

"Deal. Do you want breakfast?"

"I'm not hungry yet, but a cup of coffee would be lovely."

"Coming right up," I tell her as I make my way out of the studio.

"G?"

"Yes?" I turn around to face her.

"Thank you for creating this amazing space for me. I'm so in love with it. I'll create many, many pieces here. I can feel it," she tells me, those azure eyes shining bright like the ocean at noon.

"You're welcome, principessa. I'm glad I was able to make it happen for you."

After dropping off the coffee and a few pastries for her in the studio, I go for a swim in the pool. I need to get my own inspiration for the palace I need to design.

The water is crisp and refreshing, perfect to cool me down on this hot summer day. I do freestyle laps, not really counting how many, letting the repetitive motion clear my head.

After a while, lines start forming in my brain. A beautiful castle starts to take shape. Tall walls, smooth colors, and jewel shapes give me a visual of what I can create.

I stop swimming after my arms and legs start burning, the lactic acid building up in my muscles, so I get out and towel off the excess water. Bella's studio has a huge set of French doors that open to the garden. I see her lost in thought, still painting her canvas.

A rush of lust takes over me, and I feel I will die if I don't have her right now—in her element. I walk slowly, trying not to disturb her. I get behind her, and even though she hasn't looked back, she presses her back to my front.

"I was wondering when you were going to make your way back to me."

I grab the brush and the paint palette from her hands and place them gently on a small table she has nearby. Then I place myself in the same position we were in a moment ago and start playing with her nipples. Bella tries to grab my cock, but if she touches me, this will end before it can start. I'm that ready for her.

"Only I get to do the touching, principessa." She whines in protest, but she gives up on her exploration attempts when my hand goes south to her core. I take advantage and keep her hand on mine while I use my other hand to play with her clit.

"Fuck, G. This feels so good," she moans against my ear, and my dick jerks in response.

Her arms go up, and her hands clasp the back of my neck, giving me better access to her pussy. I continue my ministrations, and once my hand is coated in her arousal, I enter her with a finger, then another.

"G, I'm going to come. Don't stop," Bella says as she rides my fingers, finding her release. Her little cries make me spread precum all over her ass.

Once she has calmed her breathing, I help her get her hands against her canvas. Some of the paint is still fresh, so we're making a mess, but when she turns to give me a smirk, that's all the permission I need to get inside her. I don't want to go slowly—I'm way too excited for that. I enter her from behind and start thrusting as deep as I can. Bella meets me thrust for thrust. This woman is so effortlessly sexy; it's surreal. Her heart-shaped ass hits my hips after every thrust, and I grab her long hair, clenching it in my fist. When she looks back at me, she licks her lips. I can't help but encase her lips with mine and nip at her lower lip. Bella moans inside my mouth, and that just encourages me to thrust harder into her. After a couple more thrusts, Bella lifts her hands from the canvas and places them behind my neck. I can feel the paint on my skin, and the sensation brings a wake of goosebumps to my neck.

"Bella, I want to see you when you come on my cock," I tell her as my dick leaves her pussy, and she whimpers at the loss.

Oh, this beautiful girl. My dick misses his cunt, too.

She holds my hand and gently pushes me down on the couch in her studio. Bella positions herself on top of me, straddling me, and my cock enters her smoothly. Her hands paint my chest as she starts riding me, and I let her set the pace—this is my favorite view of her tits, by far—bouncing to the rhythm of our lovemaking. When Bella starts making her little sounds, the telltale sign that she's close to reaching her orgasm, her walls close on my cock, and that's all it takes for me to come with a roar, feeling her milking my release.

"Fuck, that was amazing," I say against her head once she rests on top of me.

"It truly was," she replies as she lifts her head, giving me a sweet and sated smile.

"Wanna go wash off in the pool?" she asks, mischief in her eyes. I get up from the couch, holding her bridal style, and run toward the pool with Bella squealing. I laugh unabashedly—I don't think I've ever been this happy in my life.

"Are you ready for our next stop?" I ask over lunch on the terrace.

"What do you mean? I thought we were staying here all week," Bella says as she takes a bite of her risotto.

"We could if you want, but I was hoping we could spend at least a few days on my yacht." Bella's eyebrows go all the way to the sky, and I chuckle at her response.

"Oh, fun! But wait a minute, does your yacht have Wi-Fi? Remember, I have work to do, and the last thing I want is for people to think I'm being favored because we're together." I look at her, my eyes full of mirth, and she shakes her head in amusement.

"I know I should know better—you're a billionaire; of course, you have Wi-Fi. Plus, you seem to be the kind of man who enjoys different transport vehicles." I smile at her assessment.

"You're not wrong. I do enjoy my toys. And the yacht is pretty cool, if I say so myself."

"So where would we go?" she asks, giving me her undivided attention.

"On the other side of the Adriatic Sea, there's a small island in Croatia called Ilovik. We could visit there and also spend a few days in the ocean, with no one nearby to bother us."

"Sounds like so much fun. But then we need to go back to the penthouse. Remember, I didn't bring any clothes?" She gives me a pointed look.

"I know, but that's not an issue. Remember, we won't need clothes, anyway," I say with a wink, and she chuckles.

"But we can go shopping before we leave."

She surprises me when she says, "Okay!" with a shrug. I thought she was going to show more resistance to the idea. I can't wait to spoil her.

I have clothes here at the villa, so I pack a small bag for myself. I wasn't lying when I told her we wouldn't be needing many clothes.

Bella decides to wear the jean shorts she wore yesterday and styles them with one of my shirts. It's huge on her, but she looks effortlessly sexy. I'm not sure when exactly she took over my heart, but then she also went for my mind and my soul. I'm completely at her mercy—all I see is her.

On our way out, I inform Rocco and Aldo that they can go back to Bologna. Mario will go with us on the yacht. I pass my G-Wagon key to Mario, and he smirks at me.

Yeah, I'm riding in the back with Bella. Sue me, I think to myself.

"Are you going shopping with me?" Bella asks, batting her lashes. I chuckle because there's no way I could say no to her.

"Sure, where do you want to start?"

"I don't know Rimini, remember? You're the expert."

"Right. Well, let's go to Corso d'Augusto. It's a pedestrian street filled with stores."

Mario nods and drops us off at the beginning of the street. I get out and then help Bella out. The first store that catches her attention is by a very famous Italian designer. There's a dress in the window that I immediately know will look stunning on her. We go in, and she starts browsing the store, grabbing clothes here and there. From dresses and skirts to shorts and T-shirts—a little bit of everything. I ask the attendant to put the dress I saw in the window in Bella's changing room.

I grab a champagne flute offered to me by an attendant as I get comfortable on a sofa outside the changing rooms. Who would have thought going shopping with a woman would be so relaxing? I usually despise shopping for clothes for myself, which is why I have a personal shopper who takes care of all of my clothing needs.

"Are you ready, G?" Bella asks, peeking out her door, and I smile at her. She comes out wearing the dress I chose. It's made of pure silk with a yellow flower print. The bodice is doubled with lace, and the bottom hem is trimmed with lace inserts. I can picture her wearing this dress for a candlelight dinner or visiting a museum with me.

"Do you like it?" I ask her. Her blinding smile is all I need as an answer. "You look stunning, principessa."

She winks at me and goes back to the changing room. She tries on more dresses and looks absolutely mesmerizing in every single one. Once she's satisfied with a pile of clothes that's taller than her, we go to the cashier to pay. She tries to get her wallet out of her purse, but I place my hand on her forearm. She looks up at me, confused.

"You're not paying, Bella. This is on me."

"But I can pay for it, you know?"

I smile at her as I pass my black Amex to the clerk. "I know you can, but I want to spoil you, principessa."

She closes her eyes as a timid smile forms on her lips. Resting her forehead to my chest, she murmurs, "Thank you for taking such good care of me, G."

I place a kiss on her head and grab the bags to go to the next store.

By the time we're done shopping, we're starving. We grab a table at a small cafe nearby, and Bella sits as she tells me, "Just feed me, G. My legs are killing me."

I chuckle at her antics but go inside and place an order for coffee and sliders.

"We'll just have an appetizer to tide us over. Dinner is ready and waiting for us on the yacht," I inform her, and she does her happy dance in her seat.

"I'm so excited, G. I've never been on a yacht." I love her honesty; no need to pretend to be someone she's not.

"Is there something crazy or over the top that you have always wanted to do?" I ask.

She thinks it over as the coffee and appetizers are delivered to our table. "Not really. I love the things I do. Namely, painting and dancing. But I've never considered doing something extreme, like jumping off a bridge or out of a plane. What about you?"

"I've always wanted to climb a mountain. I'm not sure if it's a snow mountain or just a regular one," I confess, feeling a blush creep up my face. She looks at me, analyzing me.

"I'm sorry, that sounded more adventurous in my mind. I guess maybe jumping off a cliff would be another cool thing to do," I say as I take a sip of my coffee.

"You don't need to apologize. If you think climbing a mountain is adventurous, then it is. I would totally do that with you. Jumping off a cliff, however? I'll wait for you on the yacht or something."

I throw my head back in laughter. "It's a deal. Maybe we should visit Gio sometime. From what I understand, he doesn't live far from the Blue Ridge Mountains."

"That would be lovely. Maybe he would even hike with us." I see the longing in her eyes; she misses her family. I make a mental note to suggest visiting her siblings as often as possible once I ask her to move in with me.

"Ready, boss?" Mario appears behind Bella, startling me. I look at her, and she's done eating her slider.

"Is everything alright?" I ask Mario as I get up from my seat, and Bella comes to stand next to me.

"Yes, of course. It's just the area is getting a little crowded, and we don't have backup. It's best to be safe."

"Understood," I say as I place my arm around Bella's back and start walking toward the car. I can't wait to be alone with her again and have her wear the lingerie we bought with a pair of *fuck me* stilettos.

Chapter 18

Isabella Bianchi

Waking up on Gabo's yacht was surreal. The main suite is on the top level and features 180-degree windows. We forgot to close the shades last night since we couldn't take each other's clothes off fast enough after dinner.

The crew was waiting for us on the main deck. At first, I felt self-conscious that all these people would hear me moaning all week long, but then they disappeared into their quarters, and I swear the only thing we could hear was the ocean.

my feelings at bay, every time I see him, my heart makes a somersault. Gabo is the man of my life. I'm still scared about being in a relationship and potentially hurting each other, especially if we have kids. But this incredible man, with his wit and charm, has taken up residence in my heart.

"Good morning, principessa. Are you ready for an ocean day?" Gabo asks, pulling me close to him. My back is to his front, and I can feel his hard length between my ass cheeks. We fell asleep naked. I shake my ass, making him groan, and I giggle.

"Do you want to take care of that before we go downstairs for breakfast?" I ask him, his hand on my breast already.

"I always want you," he whispers in my ear as he enters me from behind. I hope this feeling of belonging every time I'm with him never goes away. It makes sex that much more special.

After our breathing calms from that decadent quickie, we take a quick shower and then head downstairs for breakfast. The crew is already working on their different tasks for the day with bright smiles on their faces. I'd be a happy camper, too, if my view were an endless beautiful ocean.

"What's the plan for today?" I ask Gabo after a dreamy bite of roasted salmon and capers on rye toast.

"I thought we could enjoy the yacht today, go for a swim. Have lunch on the yacht's bow. Maybe you could get some inspiration and draw something? I know I'm always inspired so long as you're with me."

I melt on the spot. "That sounds like fun. You know what? I thought about something that I consider crazy and would love to do with you."

Gabo's eyes open wide, expectant about what I'm going to say next.

"Do you have jet skis?"

"Now I feel offended," he scoffs, and I laugh.

"You're right, silly me. So maybe we ride those for a while and then we swim?"

"Do you know how to use a jet ski?" Gabo asks.

"No, but I know you'll teach me."

"You're absolutely right. Let's go. We need to put our gear on," he says as he extends his hand to me.

"What gear are we talking about, exactly?"

"Wetsuits, of course. The water will hit you like needles at the speed we'll be going."

"Hold on to you for dear life. Got it," I tell him, and he laughs out loud.

"You're adorable. Did you know that?"

"Among other things, yes," I answer.

"Yes, adorable, confident, smart, determined, sexy, beautiful, kind. Should I keep going?" he asks as we get to our room. He then goes into his closet, looking for swimsuits, I assume.

"It's doing great things for my ego, so I wouldn't mind if you keep going," I tell him with a giggle.

"I'll never stop praising you, Bella mia." He gives me a soft kiss as he hands me a wetsuitthat looks like the perfect size for me.

"Did you have this here already?" I ask, curious how he had it on hand.

"Yes, there are a bunch of sizes for both men and women. Anytime I had friends over, they could wear these. But now I'm going to order a custom-made wetsuit for you."

I chuckle at his extravagance, but I know it's a moot point to tell him no, so I leave it at that.

Gabo rides incredibly fast on the jet skis, and all I do is hold on tight to him. Even though I'm terrified of having a freak accident, I know I'm safe with him. After a few laps around the yacht, I feel more comfortable and let go of the vice grip I had on his middle. He slows down the jet ski and brings it to a halt.

"Is everything okay?" he asks, concern in his tone.

"Yes, G. Everything is great. I'm just feeling more comfortable now, so no need to hold on so tight to you."

He releases a breath and moves around the jet ski until I'm in the driver's seat. "Let's go, principessa. Take us for a ride." He places his hands on mine and shows me how to push the throttle as I let go of the brake. After a few tries, I get the hang of it and start riding around the yacht, faster each time. The time flies by, and before I know it, we're having a candlelight dinner and watching the sunset. Another blissful day with my guy.

—⟨⊕⟩—

Tomorrow, we're heading back to Bologna. Gabo has to go back to work, and I need to go back to my summer class. I've been trying to work on the project for Gabo's firm, but the man refuses to let me work. I don't want to look like I'm just taking advantage of my title as his girlfriend, so I've been waking up early to log in for at least a couple of hours of work each day.

Gabo decided to give the crew the day off so they could enjoy the island, leaving the yacht for ourselves. I've been sketching all morning. Gabo wasn't lying when he said I could get lots of inspiration here. It's been beautiful to see how the color of the ocean changes according to how the sun's rays hit the water. I've been trying to work on something I want to give Gabo for his office, but having him around all the time makes it difficult to surprise him. He has been sketching portraits of me, and I'm in awe of his talent. It's been fun getting to know each other more. I always thought I enjoyed the silence while painting, but talking with Gabo has been a nice change.

"Hey, G. What was your favorite soccer team growing up?" I ask him. It's unbelievable, but we've discussed every single topic under the sun, and we agree on most important things, yet we haven't talked about soccer. I wonder if he's not as into it as my brother Luca and his friends are.

"I grew up following *La Católica*, but to be honest, besides the Soccer World Cup, I don't pay much attention to soccer anymore. What about you?"

"My brothers are huge fans of *Alumnos de la Plata,* so I grew up watching that team. But now that Cata plays for the Golden Warriors, that's my favorite team. Besides the Argentina National team, of course."

"Is Cata one of your friends?" Gabo asks as we continue working on our projects.

"Yeah, she's my best friend, actually. Her sister is married to one of Luca's friends, and we met at a concert years ago. We've been best friends ever since," I share, reminiscing about the amazing Eras concert we attended in Buenos Aires.

"Oh, so she's Colombian, right? I heard all of Luca's friends married Colombian women."

"She is, and she's the most badass soccer player I've ever seen. It wouldn't surprise me if she ends up playing in a bigger league soon."

"I hope she comes to play in Europe. You'll see her often, then."

My brain screeches like a broken record. "What do you mean?"

"Well, now that we're together, I'm thinking you'll spend more time in Europe. Am I wrong?" he asks.

I focus my gaze on what he's painting. Today, it isn't me; it's a palace. He told me all about it the other day, and I'm so proud of him. I mean, a sheikh hand picked him to design a palace. Not many people are talented enough to tell that tale.

"I don't know, G. I honestly haven't thought that far out. Yes, we're together and we're having fun, but my original plan was to be here only for the summer and then open a gallery in Santiago," I tell him honestly, forcing my brain to deal with the tough conversation I know we need to have.

He puts his pencil down, and I mimic his action, giving each other our undivided attention.

"I told you I'd be patient and show you with my actions that I meant it when I said you're not a fling to me, but you have to meet me halfway. If your dream is still to open the gallery in Santiago, I will support you in any way you let me. I could have my interior design team work on the gallery, and I can host a meet-and-greet of new artists in Bologna or anywhere in the world you want. But I'd hope you'd consider living in Bologna for at least part of the year.

"A long-distance relationship isn't ideal because I seem to have to be close to you all the time, but if that is what will bring you happiness, I'm willing to do it. I'd move to Chile for part of the year as well."

This man is so incredible. Here he is, a billionaire willing to compromise leaving his empire for me. I feel like a spoiled, selfish little child.

"Don't let this get to your head, but you're right, G. I promise we'll figure out a schedule that will work for both of us. The fact that you're considering even going to Chile for me means everything. Your life is here, yet you're willing to make sacrifices for me."

"Are you serious, Bella mia?" Gabo says as he lunges for me, and I giggle at his eagerness.

"Why would I lie? We'll figure this out."

"Thank you," he says as he kisses me, carrying me bridal style to the bow of the yacht.

"What are you doing?" I ask him, curious what he has in mind.

"Sealing the deal the only way we can," he says as he places me gently on the outdoor sofa. His swim trunks are off and on the floor, and my bikini follows. I sit up and grab his cock to taste him, but he swats my hand away.

"I need to taste you first." He goes down on me, and he always does a great job pleasuring me, but this time, he feels different, like an animal that has been starved for days. He flicks and sucks my clit, and I can't help but yelp in pleasure, then he spits on my pussy.

He spits! Oh, my God.

I never thought that would be sexy, but seeing him so feral almost made me come. He continues with his assault, and when I'm feeling close to release, Gabo grabs my ass and turns me around, putting me on all fours. Damn, this man.

"Fuck, G. That was so hot." I hear him chuckle, and the vibration against my clit gives me the push I need to jump off the cliff. He continues licking and sucking until I'm spent.

"My turn, G. And you can't say no." I get up and motion for him to lie down on the sofa.

"Wouldn't dream of it," he says as I take his cock into my mouth. I've never thought cocks could be described as beautiful, but Gabo's is. It's thick and long with a vein going around it, as if labeling him as a stallion. I get as much as I can inside my mouth and start sucking, Gabo moans in appreciation and holds my head, trying to set a pace, and I let him. I love the way he owns me, the way he commands me in bed.

When I release him with a pop, he says, "Bella, I need to be inside of you. Now." His tone is urgent and desperate. So I straddle him. We both moan in unison and it's the best sound in the world. It's incredible how in sync we are.

The sun is warm against my skin, and beads of sweat drip down my chest and fall onto Gabo's. We're a tangle of limbs, sweat, and arousal, and fuck if this primal sex isn't the best we've had so far. Gabo starts playing with my nipples as I ride his cock, setting the pace. The feeling of being naked in the middle of the sea, having sex with the most thoughtful and amazing man on early is just like Gabo said, the only way to seal our bond.

Gabo sits up and starts nibbling at my neck. "I never thought it could be like this, principessa. Everything's better with you," he confesses against my skin, and even though I feel the exact same way, I can't form words. I'm too entranced by the way he's making me feel, so I do the only thing

I can manage at the moment: I kiss him. Slow and steady, matching the way his cock enters my pussy. Gabo's hands go to my ass, pulling me flush against him, making him go deeper, which I didn't think was possible.

When Gabo hits that magical spot inside me, a shot of pleasure courses through me, and I see stars. The sensation is so powerful that I shout the only word that seems to be able to form on my lips.

"Forever."

Chapter 19

Isabella Bianchi

I thought it would be weird to be back at uni after how things went down in Fuoco, but Giacomo turned out to be a decent guy. The first thing he did when he saw me at school was apologize.

"Hey, Isa. I wanted to say that I'm not usually the way I behaved in Fuoco. It must have been the alcohol talking. I didn't realize you were with someone, but it shouldn't matter. You were clear you didn't want to dance with me, and I kept pressing like an idiot. I just thought we could have _____ _____ you know? I guess I should have seen it earlier _____ _____ to a second date, but I also thought _____ _____ You're funny, smart, gorgeous _____ _____ conscious _____ I really _____ off now.

Friends?" Giacomo extends his arm for a handshake, and I genuinely accept it.

"Thank you so much for clearing the air. I appreciate you as a friend and think you have great talent," I tell him honestly, and he smiles.

"Last week, I had time to talk with a few acquaintances and asked around for up-and-coming artists. There are quite a few interested in learning about your idea for a gallery in South America." I beam at his words.

This is so exciting.

"Thank you so much, Giacomo. Maybe we could do a meet-up tomorrow? I can find a place after school today," I tell him, already thinking about texting Gabo for help.

"Sure, do you need help with that?"

"No, I got it covered. Thank you, though."

Class goes by in a blur—we have a new instructor this week, and we're working on sculptures. This is definitely not my forte; I've been struggling all afternoon trying to create a flower pot. It looks like a cup of french fries. Checking out the time, I realize there are only five minutes left in class anyway, so I start packing my stuff and head toward the parking lot.

Aldo and Rocco are outside the building, and I nod as I pass them. They follow me with a good distance between us, and if they didn't have such burly faces, they could blend in as students.

"Miss Bianchi, hi," Professor López greets me from the other side of the pathway.

"Hello, Professor López. I thought you had gone back to Geneva already," I say as I walk toward him.

"I'm leaving tonight. I had a few things to take care of while here in Bologna."

I nod in understanding. I'm sure he has contacts here at the Museum of Modern Art.

"Any chance you could join me and my boyfriend for dinner? I spoke so much about you; he's curious to meet a fellow Chilean," I say with a chuckle.

"I'd love to, but I already got the train ticket; I leave in an hour. Maybe next time, we can plan in advance. I'd love to have dinner with you and your boyfriend. I'm sure he's as interesting as you are. Anyway, it was a good thing I saw you before leaving. I'm hosting a meet-and-greet at the museum where I work next month, and I think it'd be the perfect opportunity for you to mingle with other young artists."

"This is amazing. Thank you so much for inviting me."

"Absolutely, here's my card so we can keep in touch. Have a good evening, Miss Bianchi." He waves, and I wave back.

I look at the guys sitting on a bench. They look so funny trying to blend in with the students walking around campus. I think they would be more successful in their jobs if they were wearing linen pants or even shorts, not expensive black suits.

Once I get to the penthouse, I check the fridge, and even though there's enough food to feed a small army, I want to cook something special for Gabo.

"Hey, guys, I'm going to the small market at the end of the street," I tell Aldo and Rocco, and Rocco gets up to go with me.

"Anything in particular you're looking for, Miss Bianchi?" Rocco makes small talk as we get on the elevator.

"Well, dinner is already in the fridge, but I was thinking about a nice dessert. We ate so well at the yacht this past week. I want to keep it going," I answer him as I feel the blush rise on my cheeks, and he chuckles.

"I hope you don't think I'm too forward, Miss Bianchi, but you are good for Mr. Godoy." Rocco surprises me with his words, and I look at him, curious to know more. "Yes, ever since you moved in, he's been different. He seems like he has found something he was missing."

"Like what?" I ask him, wanting to know everything.

Rocco rubs his face in frustration. "I shouldn't have said anything; I'm terrible with words."

I chuckle. "No, no. You started this. Now you have to tell me." I press further, and he releases a frustrated breath but continues talking.

"I'm just trying to say that before you, he used to be around women who wanted to be with him for his money and influence. Since you arrived, he's been more relaxed. It's a Mr. Godoy we didn't know before. I think you have brought out the best in him."

"Awww, Rocco. You're happy for your boss? That's such a nice thing to say. I've never been happier in my life, and I feel

Gabo has been a great influence on me, as well. So I'm glad we bring out the best in each other." He nods, then goes back to his burly stance—the bodyguard is back.

We enter the small store, and I look up the recipe I want to create on my phone: flower vanilla berry cake. I get fresh vanilla beans, acai berries, wild violets, borage, and mint leaves. The lady who owns the store packs me a loaf of bread for free, saying Gabo and I need to eat healthier. I chuckle at her way of saying we're too skinny, but thank her and leave a few extra Euro bills on the counter as she gives a sweet treat to Rocco.

"This looks delicious. What's the occasion?" Gabo asks as he gives me a kiss after coming home.

"I just felt like making a yummy dessert to go along with the nice dinner the chef had prepared for us," I tell him as I plate our food, and he opens a bottle of wine. I finally learned Gabo's secret to always having the fridge stocked with cut fruit and ready-to-eat meals: he has a chef who comes twice a week.

"Do you remember the project I'm working on?" he asks as I take a bite of the delicious pasta we're having.

"The palace? How can I forget? I still can't believe you're designing one. It feels so royal," I tell him with dreamy eyes, and he chuckles.

"That's the one. I need to go to the Emirates tomorrow and see the area where the sheikh wants it built. One thing is seeing pictures; another is being there, feeling the wind on my fac, you know?"

"I definitely know. That's how I am sometimes when creating a new piece; I need to get inspiration from the source. Sometimes pictures and videos aren't enough," I tell him, and he smiles brightly. I love how we both take our art so seriously.

"Do you think you can come with me?" he asks, and my immediate response is to get giddy about it.

"Perfect, we'll take the jet after breakfast, and we'll come back after dinner," Gabo says, joy radiating from him.

"Oh, wait. I'm planning a meet-and-greet with young artists tomorrow. Long story, but Giacomo approached me today." The moment I say his name, Gabo goes rigid. "Relax, G. He just wanted to apologize for the way he behaved," I say, and Gabo releases a breath.

"And you told him you're with me?" I chuckle at his possessiveness and roll my eyes.

"No, G, he noticed that himself. But if I had felt there was a need to mention you, I would have." I wink at him, and now it's his turn to chuckle. "Anyways, he mentioned he had contacted a few artists who would be interested in being part of my gallery, so I need to meet with them. I actually called the PR department of Godoy *Construzione* today, and Francesca set up a space and refreshments already," I tell him as I start playing with my food. My appetite is ruined now that the excitement over traveling with him is gone.

"It's alright, principessa. I love that your plan is starting to take shape. There will be more opportunities for you to go with me and see the Emirates. Maybe we'll be invited to the palace inauguration." I swoon at his thoughtfulness. He truly is my biggest cheerleader.

"You're right, there will be more chances later on," I tell him, and we continue to enjoy our meal in comfortable silence. When it's time to have dessert, Gabo grabs the cake and offers me his hand.

"I have an idea. Come with me."

I follow him, curious to see what he has in mind. We go to the terrace, enjoying another beautiful summer night. The little garden Gabo has out here is in full bloom.

"Undress," he says in a low voice, and I raise my eyebrows.

"Excuse me?" I ask with a hand on my waist to add sass.

"You heard me, Bella. Undress."

"Why are you so bossy all of a sudden? At least ask nicely." He rolls his eyes, clearly frustrated I'm not following his game, and I chuckle internally.

"I want to eat this delicious cake off of you. Undress. I won't ask again."

His words are cold, and they should upset me, but the rush of desire that goes through my core is undeniable. I start undressing as he commanded. I remove my shoes, then unzip my dress and let it pool down by my feet. I'm not wearing a bra, which earns me a disapproving glare, and I giggle.

"Do you think that's funny, Bella? Those tits are mine. Just the thought of any asshole on the street ogling those perfect tits has my blood boiling." He grunts; he looks so funny when he's upset. But I refrain from laughing—I need to use my words instead.

"Good thing no one saw them, only you." He pulls me to him and leans down to suck and lick at my breast. Then, one of his hands finds my pussy, and he starts playing with my clit through the flimsy lace thong.

"Weren't you going to eat cake?" I ask in a breathy tone, and he releases my nipple with a pop, which only makes me hungrier for him.

"Those peaks were calling me. Who knew that being a possessive ass would turn you on." He gets some of the cake frosting on his finger and paints my breasts with it, going back to his delicious torture of licking and sucking.

When my knees start bending because his attention to my breasts and clit has me weak, he lays me down on the couch where he was sitting.

"I got you, Bella." I know he does; he's been an amazing influence in my life, not only supporting my dreams but also showing me how a loving relationship can be.

"Open your legs for me," he commands as he stands to remove his clothes. I watch him take off his vest and then unbutton his shirt. My mouth starts watering as I see his hands work effortlessly, popping the buttons off. When his chest is on full display, my hand goes to my clit; the sight of his abs and taught arm muscles sends shots of electricity through me.

"What do you think you're doing? I thought I told you to open your legs, not to start playing with yourself," he tells me in a stern tone that only makes him look hotter. I bite my lip to stop the smile that wants to form on my lips, but this only makes him more determined. He removes his belt in one swift move, and the next thing I know, he's tying my hands above my head with it.

"G, that's not fair," I whine and pout. But I love how possessive he is tonight.

"That's what happens when you're not the *good girl* I thought you were." He kisses the pout of my lips as he removes the rest of his clothes. He's buck naked on our terrace, and the sight is a balm for sore eyes. Gabo's cock is a work of art. I make a mental note to ask him to let me create a replica with silicone, so I can at least have his big cock with me when I'm in Chile.

Gabo goes back to painting my body with the cake frosting. The motion tickles, but I try to focus on what he's writing on my belly. I'm too aroused to think straight, so I take a couple of deep breaths to relax.

Once he starts licking whatever he just painted, I pay extra attention to what his tongue is tracing, and when he finishes, I whisper, "*Sempre mia.*" (Always mine.) The moment Gabo hears my words, his eyes lock with mine, and I see every single feeling I have for him reflected there for me.

Before I can continue speaking, Gabo disappears between my legs and starts nibbling and sucking my clit. I want to pull his hair, grab him, and put his cock into my mouth... something. But he tied my hands, and I can't move them. The restraint just makes me more aroused.

What the hell? I have never experienced this kind of ecstasy—I guess I'm truly Gabo's good girl.

The moment he enters me, a jolt of pain mixed with pleasure hits me. He's pounding into me mercilessly, and I welcome the invasion.

Gabo reaches for some of the cake and puts it inside my mouth, along with two fingers. It's too much and not enough at the same time, so I work on eating every bit of the cake and frosting off his fingers as he continues pounding me.

Out of nowhere, one of Gabo's fingers—from his other hand—enters my ass, and I come immediately on the spot. His fingers muffle my cries as I continue to ride the wave of pleasure. Once my breathing has calmed, Gabo removes his cock from my pussy and strokes it at a fast pace, while moving up toward my face. When the first shot of cum hits me, I move my tongue around to try to lick as much of it as I can. Gabo grunts his release as I lift my head to reach for his cock, and lick it clean.

Gabo unties me, and after rubbing and kissing my wrists, he cleans my core with a wet napkin and his hands, as well.

He then lies down with me on the couch, and we fall asleep while watching the stars. No words are needed when the night we just had was everything and more.

How on earth am I going to survive without him in Chile? I need to think of a better plan than dividing my time between the two countries.

Chapter 20

Gabo Godoy

back out. I just spotted an entourage of camels—I can't wait to be able to ride one and get to the top of the dunes.

After sipping a delicious tea, I ask what the name is. One of the butlers informs me that it's called Sulaimani and is made of mint, lemon, and cardamom. Taking a picture of my view, I shoot a quick text to Bella.

Gabo: Wishing you were here enjoying this view with me.

Bella: Ugh, don't do this to me *crying emoji* I should have gone with you. It looks incredible.

Gabo: Don't worry, principessa. We'll come back together.

Bella: You're too good to me, G. Miss you. *kiss emoji*

Gabo: Miss you, too. See you tonight.

I pocket my phone, and after finishing my Sulaimani, I go where the camels rest. The person in charge helps me up on one of the camels and gives me a quick rundown on how to handle the camel properly and not fall like a fool.

It reminds me of that time I was back at my parents' villa in Chile, and I decided to be a tour guide for the day. It was the summer before I moved to Bologna for school, and I thought I was the next big thing. My idea was to tour the actual vines, not the ones we have close to the gift shop, and everyone would use a horse. I could tell Fernando, the villa manager, wasn't too pleased with the idea, but he bit his tongue and let me do as I wanted. Next thing I knew, everyone was out of control, going as far as the eye could see. I was running around like a fool, trying to wrangle as many tourists as I could. Needless to say, I was the laughing joke for days at the villa.

When I get the hang of it, we start crossing the dunes. I stop from time to time to take pictures, check the strength of the wind, and enjoy the spectacular view.

Even though I'm a billionaire, and my life has been everything but normal, I can't help but take a moment to be thankful for everything I have. I'm grateful for all the professional achievements I've obtained while still being young, for all the lives I've been able to touch—helping my employees make their dreams come true, and providing them with more than fair salaries and a healthy work environment. I'm proud of helping the town of Monterosso maintain its charm and lifestyle, ensuring investors don't take their houses and land for a couple of Euros, and making my parents proud by being a good son. And best of all, finding love with the most amazing woman I've ever met. Bella is what my life was missing; she has given me a renewed purpose, a new reason to work harder. Life is no longer about me; it's about *us*.

I would love to visit a local jewelry store once we're back in Abu Dhabi. When I ask the team, they nod, affirming my request. I've heard the jewelry here is exquisite, and I need to find something for Bella.

After we return from the dunes, the team takes me to an enormous mall with countless jewelry stores, but the security lead shows me one in particular. The moment I enter, I'm blinded by the amount of gold and precious stones.

"Welcome, Mister..." the woman behind the counter says, and I reply, "Godoy."

She smiles at me and says, "Welcome, Mister Godoy. Is there anything in particular you are looking for?"

I smile at her as I start looking around for blue stones. "I want something for my girlfriend. She has the most beautiful azure eyes, and I want something that matches."

The woman nods as she motions for me to follow her. "Right this way, sir."

We get to a display of sapphires: rings, bracelets, necklaces, earrings, hairpins. Everything is beautiful, but I need to find something that screams Bella the moment I see it. I start looking more closely at each piece until I spot a set that makes my heart skip a beat.

"Can I see this one?" I point to it, and the woman immediately places it in a velvet tray for me. The moment I grab it in my hands, I know this is what I want to gift Bella. It's unique, exquisite, one of a kind. Just like her. "I'll take it. Please wrap it up."

"Right away, sir. How would you like to pay?" I take out my black card, and her smile widens.

I can't wait to get back to Bologna and see Bella wearing this. It's perfect.

⚊⊸⊛✦⊛⊶⚊

Last night, by the time I arrived, Bella was already in bed. I decided to pull an all-nighter and finish the initial draft of my design. I had the basic idea already on my design app, and after seeing the location in person, I made a few changes to the design and the materials I want to use. As Bella had once described my style, I decided on a very intricate yet modern flare for the sheikh's palace.

Finally, around five in the morning, after showering, I get into bed with Bella. Her soft breathing immediately changes when I pull her closer to me.

"What time is it?" she murmurs, still asleep.

"Not time to wake up, yet. Keep sleeping, principessa," I whisper in her ear. She wiggles her ass against my dick, and it jerks like it's finally home.

In the morning, Bella surprises me by waking at the same time I always do. After we shower together, I prepare acai bowls for breakfast.

"I'm done with the first draft for the palace. I'm turning it in today," I tell her as I pour two glasses of orange juice.

"Can I see it? Or is it top secret?" she asks with a smirk.

"Here, tell me your professional opinion."

I fire up the tablet for her and show her the blueprint. Bella grabs the tablet and starts going through the design. She pauses at certain spots, making me curious about what she's focusing on, but then she continues scanning. I love how much attention she's paying to every detail.

After almost half an hour, she passes the tablet back.

"I love it, but it doesn't scream sheikh to me. Maybe you need to add a few more touches," she says this timidly, almost afraid of my reaction. I was expecting her to praise my design, but I can't deny I'm intrigued to learn her feedback.

"What would you add?" I ask her honestly, and she seems surprised by my response.

"Do you really want my opinion? I'm not an architect."

"No, but you're an artist. Maybe you could help me improve my design." She smiles brightly as she goes to her bag and grabs a pencil and her sketchbook.

"I'd make all the windows look like mirrors so that the palace would be a mirage in the middle of the desert. The heat that the windows collect, because you know they're going to get hot, could be used to power at least part of the palace. It would be amazing if it could be a self-sufficient building. I would also add some other colors besides those mimicking the sand. Maybe the light that passes through the windows could be heat-activated, so the hotter it is outside, the darker it becomes inside, saving on cooling costs.

"Also, you could create an indoor Eden Garden. Imagine being able to visit a tropical forest in the middle of the desert or take a book and sit by the luscious plants while having tea. Finally, I don't think there's anything cooler than an indoor pool with a slow river connecting it to the outdoors. Fit for a sheikh." She finishes with a flourish, and I give her a standing ovation.

"Are you sure you don't want to join my team permanently? These are great ideas, Bella," I tell her as I place a kiss on her hair.

"Thanks, G. But no, I'd rather continue my work. I'd love to be your personal consultant, though. You can pay me with orgasms." A grunt escapes me as she lunges to run away, giggling all the way to our room. I'd chase her to the ends of the universe if necessary.

After arriving at the office way too late, I get an inquisitive look from Dom.

"What?" I ask him as I fire up my computer in my office and see him closing the door behind him.

"I've known you since college, *Fra*. And this is the first time you didn't get to work on time. What the fuck is going on?"

"Good thing it's my name on the building. Did someone die?" I ask him without looking at him; I'm not sure what he's trying to get at.

"Holy fuck, you've really got it bad for Luca's little sister, huh?" Dom says with a cackle.

"Bella. Her name is Isabella. And yes, I'm in love with her. But this has nothing to do with her. I didn't realize I had to ask you permission to work from home after flying in and out of Abu Dhabi in a twenty-four-hour period."

"Woah, sorry, man. I didn't mean anything bad by it. I just didn't realize you were serious about her. You've never been serious about a woman before."

"None of them were *her*." I give him a pointed look, hoping he'll drop this topic. I don't feel like explaining myself when I haven't told her I love her. "Now, if you'll excuse me, I have matters to attend to." Dom raises his hands in surrender and makes his way to the door, but before he leaves my office, I say out loud, "Go scratch that itch you've had for years with Mario. Maybe then you can stop minding other people's business."

"Fuck you." He gives me the finger as he leaves my office, and I laugh out loud.

I get back to approving designs and checking emails. One from the design team in particular catches my attention.

> Dear Mr. Godoy,
>
> I simply wanted to say we are impressed by the quality and the turnaround time in which Ms. Bianchi has been working on the project she was assigned.
>
> To be honest, I didn't know what to expect from her since I wasn't involved in her hiring, but she has been

critical in having the designs ready for your approval. Not only does she provide quality work but also valuable feedback.

If for some reason she would like a permanent position on the team, we would be happy to have her.

Regards,
Angelo Cabrissi
Design Team Leader
Godoy *Construzione*

My chest fills with pride to see others recognize what I've seen in Bella all along: a hardworking, driven, and bright woman. I can't wait to tell her. I'm about to reply to Angelo when my office phone lights up.

"Excuse me, Mr. Godoy. The sheikh is on line two and would like to speak with you," my assistant informs me.

I raise my eyebrows, wondering what the sheikh would like to speak about; I thought my trip went smoothly yesterday.

"Mr. Godoy, I just wanted to personally thank you for coming to my country yesterday and sending the first draft of my palace today," Sheikh Khalid says, and I'm deeply honored he called me instead of having his team contact me.

"It's my pleasure, Sheikh Kahlid. Do you approve of the design?"

"I'm pleasantly surprised with the additions you recommended after our initial conversation. Admittedly, they're my favorite part of the palace now. I'm looking forward to seeing them once completed." He's praising Bella's ideas. I can't wait to tell her.

"Thank you very much. I must admit, those ideas are my significant other's. I cannot claim them as my own."

"Oh, you have a bright woman by your side. I didn't expect less from you. Please extend my praise to her. Talk soon." The sheikh hangs up, and I decide to send a text to Bella.

> **Gabo**: We're going out for dinner tonight. Wear white, Bella mia.

> **Bella**: Oh, fun, where are we going? Should I wear something fancy?

> **Gabo**: Yes, the fanciest dress you have.

> **Bella**: Okay. *happy emoji*

I type and delete those three words I want to tell her over and over again, but I have to wait to tell her in person. I need to see how her azure eyes sparkle when I tell her I love her.

I get to the penthouse before Bella returns from uni, which is a good thing because if she were here, we wouldn't be going out. I take a quick shower and put on one of my Brioni tuxedos.

As I'm putting on the cufflinks, she enters our room. She hasn't seen me in my closet yet, but I have a perfect view of her. Her hair and makeup are done, and I love that she went the extra mile to get all fancy tonight. She's always gorgeous, but tonight, I wanted to roll out the red carpet for her.

"Hey there, principessa," I tell her as I leave my closet. She yelps as she practically jumps out of her skin, and I feel like shit because I didn't mean to scare her.

"Gabo, *pelotudo*. You scared me." She swats my chest as I try to hug her.

"Please forgive me. I didn't think I was going to scare you," I tell her, and she huffs a breath before lifting her face for a kiss.

"Give me five minutes to put on my dress and shoes, and we can head out," she says after one more kiss, and I lustfully watch her walk back to her closet. I don't know when we became so comfortable with each other, but all this feels so normal. Sharing a bed, having her own space in my penthouse, and having her studio in my villa—all of it feels right.

I feel my hands getting clammy and my heart racing. I'm only planning to tell her I love her, so I can't imagine what a mess I'll be when I ask her to marry me.

"Ready." Bella comes out of her closet, and my brain short-circuits. She's wearing a floor-length beaded dress that hugs her perfect hourglass figure, with a deep V neckline in the front and a bare back. Her hair is up in a chignon. She's a fucking angel who has come to Earth to bless my life for eternity. What did I do to deserve her? Only God knows, but I'll be thankful for the rest of my life.

"You like?" she asks, a blush creeping up her neck.

"Like? You look stunning, principessa." I go closer to her, and once I have her hand in mine, I help her spin to see her better. She's glowing.

"Here, I brought you something from Abu Dhabi." We walk to a table near the sofa I have in my room. I pick up a velvet box, and when I open it, Bella gasps, and her hands cover her mouth.

"You got that for me?" she asks, incredulous.

"Of course. Let me help you." I take out the necklace, and Bella gives her back to me, so I can clasp the necklace at the back of her neck.

"There's only one of these in the world. Fifty sapphires and one hundred and fifty diamonds arranged in a raindrop pattern." I place a kiss on the back of her neck once I'm done, and goosebumps appear on her skin. She's wearing a different perfume tonight. It's flowery and citrusy. I like it.

"Gabo, this is too much. I don't have anything to give you," she says as she touches the necklace, admiring it on her neck.

"You don't need to give me anything, I simply love spoiling you," I tell her as she turns around and crosses her arms behind my neck.

"Thank you, G. You make me infinitely happy."

I see her eyes sparkling, and I take her lips with mine. I cradle her face with my hands and deepen the kiss. It's tender and slow but intense and binding at the same time. I reluctantly let her lips go, and after one more peck, I place my hand on the small of her back, showing her the way to the garage.

"Which car are we taking tonight? Or is Mario driving us?" she asks as the elevator doors open.

"We're taking the Rolls Royce," I inform her as I get the key from the panel where I keep all of the car keys.

"Oohhh, we're really fancy tonight. Are you sure there's no way you'll tell me where we're going?" she asks as I help her get into the car. Her dress is a little tight, and as good as she looks, I can't imagine it's easy to sit.

"No, principessa. You'll have to be patient until we get there," I say as I start the car and make my way out of the garage.

"I wouldn't be so sure about that, Mr. Godoy. I have my ways," Bella says while wiggling a bit in her seat.

I have both hands on the steering wheel, looking straight at the road. It's the kind of focus I clearly need to stop worrying about how she will react when I tell her I love her. I'm a successful billionaire who has made businesses with powerful men around the world, but telling my girlfriend how I feel about her has me on edge. The power this woman has over me is something I've never experienced before, and maybe that's what has me nervous. I'm playing over and over in my head how I'm going to tell Bella I love her when I feel her hand on my pants.

"What are you doing?" I ask, intrigued.

"I told you I wasn't so sure about being patient." The next thing I know, Bella is leaning down, her head getting closer to my lap, and ever so slowly, she unzips my trousers.

"Holy fuck," I say, stunned.

"I told you. I have my ways to get what I want."

Bella takes my cock out and starts moving her hand up and down my length as she puts it in her mouth. It doesn't take me long to get rock-hard. I start breathing through my teeth and grabbing the steering wheel for dear life.

"You taste so good, G. I can't wait to swallow every last drop of your cum," Bella says, and I press the gas pedal. She chuckles, and it only makes me want to get deeper in her mouth, so I thrust hard, and she chokes.

"Bella, you don't have to do this," I tell her, worried she's not enjoying it anymore, but she surprises me.

"I'm not a quitter, and I want you all the way inside my throat. So thrust away, G. I'm a big girl, I can take it." Her words awake a madman inside me. I keep driving as fast as I can as I start thrusting my cock into the back of her throat. She starts moaning, and the vibration of her vocal cords is the extra push I need to jump off the proverbial cliff and empty myself in her.

"Fuck, Bella. That was the best orgasm of my life," I say, completely satiated.

"Good, because now you're going to tell me where you are taking me," she says as she fixes her lipstick and rearranges herself in her seat.

"I'll do you one better. I'll show you. We're here," I say as I park in front of the National Art Gallery.

"What's this?" Bella asks as she looks outside the window.

"We get to have dinner in the museum. Just the two of us and hundreds of historical pieces."

Bella does her little happy dance, and I chuckle at her excitement. After helping her out of the car, we make our way up the stairs to the building, and I can't help but look back. The fountain behind us, the soft glow of the street lamps, Bella next to me, shining like the star she is, and I'm smiling like the luckiest bastard in the universe—it's a spectacular view. The best part? Mario snapped a picture of this moment. I can't wait to ask him for it so I can use it as a screensaver.

When we get inside, a table for two is waiting for us in one of the rooms dedicated to the paintings of the fifteenth century, Bella's favorites. I remember she talked about this particular room all night long after she visited with her summer class.

"G, this is incredible. I can't believe we'll be having dinner here," she says as I help her take a seat. The dinner is amazing—all the dishes come from a pop-up restaurant run by a Michelin-starred Danish chef currently in town. Everything is farm-to-table, earthy, and organic.

"So, G. You know I love being with you, whether eating a sandwich at a tourist cafe or having an eight-course meal prepped by a Michelin chef, but is there a special reason why we're having dinner here tonight?"

Holding her hand, I release a deep breath. "Since the moment you arrived in Bologna, my life has turned for the better. I know you have trust issues, but I'm here to tell you that I love you, Bella, and whatever path life takes us, I'll always be by your side."

Her azure eyes are filled with emotion like the deep blue seafaring a storm.

"G," she begins, but her voice breaks. I squeeze her hand twice, letting her know it's okay. She rewards me with a crooked smile.

"I'm not ready to say the words yet, but you know what you mean to me, right?"

And I know—I feel it, too. The way she cares about me, the way she gives herself to me fully and unconditionally. It might take her some time to realize it's okay to verbalize what her heart feels, but I know she'll get there. We'll get there.

I take my phone out of my pocket. After opening my music app, "Lose Control" by Teddy Swims starts playing. I place the phone on the table and extend my hand to Bella.

"Would you allow me the honor of this dance, principessa?" She chuckles but takes my hand. I direct her to a slow dance, my hard body flushed to her soft one. With her hands crossed against the back of my neck, her head resting on my chest, my hands on her ass—I'm a shameless motherfucker, but without a doubt, this is the best night of my life. I can't wait for what the future holds for us.

Chapter 21

Isabella Bianchi

Last night, I truly felt like a principessa. Everything was so luxurious; the food was divine, and the location was unbeatable. I'm thankful I paid attention to Karina before coming here and got this gorgeous beaded dress at her friend Dani Garcia's store.

I have way too many emotions to process; I need to talk to someone, and obviously it can't be Gabo. How on earth am I going to tell him how far gone I am for him when I'm not ready to say I love you? There's only one option: I need my

"You know you'll never interrupt me. How's everything going?" My soccer star bestie beams at my question.

"It's going great. The team is doing amazing, and we're in the playoffs! I still can't believe I might play the final match for the Argentine Women's Soccer Tournament."

I chuckle at her excitement. "Of course I can believe it. You're the best soccer player I've ever seen."

She rolls her eyes at me. "Nah, it's either because you're my best friend or because you don't watch enough soccer. Regardless, I appreciate the support."

We fall into a comfortable silence. I'm trying to think about how to bring up the subject, but Cata beats me to it.

"So, are you going to tell me? Or do you want me to ask you until you come out with it?"

Yup, that's my best friend. A straight shooter, on and off the pitch.

"So, I'm dating Gabo," I tell her, ripping off the proverbial band-aid.

"You what? Karina's brother?" Cata shouts, and I cackle at her reaction.

"Yeah, I don't think we know any other Gabo."

"You're right. I just didn't think it was true."

What does she mean?

I make a confused face, and she immediately continues talking. "Oh, well. You know how the boys are always checking on each other. And the last thing Mati shared was they were doing an 'interfriendtion' so Luca would stop getting in your business."

I throw my head back in laughter at the image that forms in my head: Luca being scolded by his friends because of me.

"Oh, I guess it worked because since he left, he hasn't contacted either of us," I share with Cata as I wipe the tears from my face. It was a good laugh.

"Damn, you know from what Sofi has said, Luca has always been a little overbearing with Karina, but she knows how to put him in his place. I didn't realize that would extend to you, as well. But it makes sense; I mean, you're his sister. Even Franco tried to scare Mati off from dating me, arguing that I was his little sister, and he didn't want Mati to hurt me."

I open my eyes wide. I had no idea all this had gone down.

"What the hell? I mean, he's known Mati since they were kids. Why on earth wouldn't he trust one of his best friends?"

"That's exactly what the boys told Luca. They said Gabo was a man, not a boy trying to have fun with a *mina* for the summer."

I feel my cheeks warming at Cata's comment. In a way, I feel bad Luca gave Gabo so much shit knowing it was me who didn't want anything serious.

"What's that face for? Isabella Bianchi, what aren't you sharing?" Cata puts her face closer to the camera, and I burst out laughing.

"You know me too well," I tell her, and then I take a couple of deep, cleansing breaths.

"The thing is, *I* was the one who told Gabo to just have fun and see where things go. I don't want any attachments, Cata. Look at my parents. They had three kids, then dumped them and never contacted them again." I hate how this topic always makes me so sensitive; I feel water pooling in my eyes, and I wipe them before they fall.

"Isa, that's beyond your control. And it isn't fair to Gabo to compare what you guys have to your parents. I am one hundred percent confident that if at some point you decide to have kids, you'll be the best mom in the world, not because you had a good example, but because you'll do everything in your power to be the complete opposite of your parents."

I can't help it—I break down in tears. All the anger and frustration I've buried in my chest over my parents finally leaves my body. Cata doesn't say anything; she simply lets me cry. When I look at her on the screen, there's not a drop of judgment or pettiness on her face, just understanding.

Once I feel I have no more tears to waste on my parents, I wipe my face off and get a bottle of water from the fridge.

"Feel better?" Cata asks, and I smile at her.

"Good. Now tell me what is going on with Gabo. Aren't you happy with him?"

"Are you joking? That man is amazing. I've been having the time of my life. So much so that I'm reconsidering going back to Chile once the summer is over," I say as I bite my nail.

Cata shouts so loudly that Rocco comes into the kitchen to check if everything is okay. I show him my phone and Cata, who is losing her mind while fist-pumping the air in her car. He chuckles at the scene. Once she calms down, she waves at him.

"Oh, hello, Mister. I didn't realize my friend wasn't alone. But you don't look like Gabo."

I crack up at her comment, and Rocco's lips form a tiny smile.

"No, Miss. My name is Rocco. I'm Miss Bianchi's bodyguard."

"*Ay, jueputa*" (Oh, fuck). "That's right. Gabo is a billionaire. I sometimes forget what the life of a billionaire is like."

Rocco makes a confused face, and I'm surprised at how much he's interacting with Cata since he's usually so stoic.

"I'm Cata, good to meet you. My family and I have had our share of bodyguards. My dad is one of the most powerful people in Colombia, and for many years, we had to have bodyguards, but now, they are less frequent."

Rocco nods at her, then at me, and leaves me alone again—back to his burly bodyguard facade.

"Okay, so little detour there. If you're clearly so into him, what is the issue?" Cata asks the million-dollar question.

I sigh, frustrated at myself for not being able to tell Gabo what I feel.

"Cata, the man told me he loved me, and I couldn't say it back."

I think she's going to yell at me, but she surprises me when a kind smile forms on her face.

"*Ay,* Isa, you're just scared shitless to get your heart broken. It was one of the issues Mati had, but he's been going to therapy, and let me tell you, he's improved so much. We might not have a perfect relationship, but I wouldn't change it for the world."

And there it is. Something doesn't have to be perfect to be amazing. I need to simply jump with Gabo—I know he'll catch me.

—◦✦◦—

I'm relaxing, taking a bubble bath in the penthouse after a full day of painting and experimenting with colors for my class when I decide to check my emails. There's one that has me giddy with anticipation—I hope it's the news I've been waiting for.

Dear Miss Bianchi,

It's my absolute pleasure to extend to you an invitation as a distinguished guest to our annual Latino Artists Association gala, which will take place on the twenty-sixth of the month at six in the evening at the Modern Art Museum of Geneva. Please be advised we'll have a spot reserved for one piece of your choosing to showcase your work. Please RSVP at your earliest convenience.

Regards,

Dr. Martín López

Curator.

Modern Art Museum.

Geneva, Switzerland.

Reading Professor López's email has me so excited. I can't wait to share my news with Gabo and ask him to be my plus one. I'll have to go to the villa tomorrow to finish the painting I've been working on for Gabo. That's the one I want to use for the gala.

While waiting for Gabo, I go to my closet to see what I have to wear for the event. I definitely don't want to wear the dress I wore for our special night. Maybe I'll wear it again when I tell him I love him— a full-circle moment.

"Hey, G. How was work?" I greet him as he leaves his bag in the living room.

"It was fine, nothing exciting. I've been thinking about you all day," he says as he kisses me.

"Oh, yeah? Anything in particular about me?" I ask him, a shot of electricity running through me.

"Why don't I show you instead," he says as he lays me down on the kitchen counter. Even though I can't wait to have him inside me, I've been waiting all afternoon to share my news.

"Before you show me, do you think we can talk?"

Gabo's face of horror makes me giggle, which earns me a glare.

"Bella, you just used the famous last words. How can you be laughing? Are you really this cruel?"

I roll my eyes at his dramatics.

"G, relax. All I meant to say is that I have something exciting to share with you."

He pretends to wipe sweat off his forehead and takes a seat at the breakfast bar.

"So remember Professor López?"

"Yes, the one you invited to have dinner with us and bailed?" I make a disapproving face but continue talking.

"That's the one. He emailed me inviting me to a Latino Artists Gala on the twenty-sixth of this month. It's in Geneva, and I thought you could be my plus one. I'll even get a chance to present one of my pieces."

Gabo opens his eyes wide, pride evident in his gaze.

"That's amazing, principessa. Congratulations! I would love to go with you."

"You're the best, G. Thank you." I throw my arms around him, kissing him with an overwhelming feeling of appreciation and that deeply rooted feeling of love I refuse to admit out loud. But before I could get lost in my haze of uncertainty, he lays me on the counter and distracts me with multiple orgasms.

Chapter 22

Gabo Godoy

T͟ **͟** **obal** **erc**
͟ **͟** **wa** **ou**
the m **͟** **I** **ad**
morni **͟** **͟** **hen**
ence **͟** **nt**
and **͟**
je **͟**

͟op
͟ **de t**
generous **͟**

Bella drove to Geneva yesterday despite me telling her I'd happily rent a jet so she could sit comfortably on a quick flight instead of a seven-hour drive in her old Bug.

"G, you know I've never driven in northern Italy. Why would I take a plane when I can drive and sightsee?" she asked when I brought up the jet.

"Principessa, we'll have time to do all the roadtrips you want. Why don't you take me up on my offer, please? I want you to be safe," I pleaded with her, not really knowing why it was so important for me to have her fly rather than drive.

"I'll be safe. Aldo and Rocco will be following me the entire time, remember? Besides, when you and I go on a roadtrip you know the last thing I'll be paying attention to is what's outside our car," she said as she kissed me. My resolve vanished once I had her in my arms. She'll always win.

Bella's gala is in one hour, and I'm still stuck in Sweden. And to make matters worse, I haven't been able to reach her since I told her my jet was grounded.

Is she mad? Why do I have a sinking feeling in my gut?

"Any luck contacting Rocco and Aldo?" I ask Mario, who came with me on this trip. The fact that he's not meeting my gaze is all the confirmation I need to know that something bad happened; I can feel it.

I heave a deep sigh while I pace the hotel room. I'm not sure where else to look or who to call.

Suddenly, a light bulb goes off in my head. "Dom," I whisper as I take my phone out to call one of my best friends and business partners.

"Dom, where are you?"

"Hello to you too, man. I'm in the office. Why?"

"I need you to take a couple of the security guys and go to Geneva. Take the same route Bella took with Aldo and Rocco. None of them are picking up the phone, and I'm stuck in Gothenburg."

"Fuck. What does Mario say?" Dom asks, and I can sense from his stern voice that he's taking this seriously, too. This shit has never happened in the time we've worked with Mario's security company.

"He's been on the phone for a while, but he hasn't said a word. I'm beside myself," I say in an exasperated tone.

"Okay, let me see who's available here besides Luigi to come with me. I'll call you as soon as we have something."

"Thanks, man. I owe you big." I disconnect the call and take a big swig of my whiskey. I've been drinking since I learned there's no way I can make it to Geneva on time. It's not how I usually handle stress, but I need to calm down if I want to think about an effective solution to this mess.

Starting to get more and more impatient with Mario's inability to get answers, I stand up and walk to the large window. This is the perfect storm: shitty weather and zero communication with my Bella.

Where is she?

Scratching the back of my head, I pace back and forth, straining to hear what Mario is saying and who he's talking to.

When he finally hangs up, he looks at me and says, "Something's wrong."

"No shit, Sherlock. What the fuck is going on?" I ask him.

"Aldo and Rocco can't be reached. Their last location is the hotel where Miss Bianchi is staying. We contacted the hotel, and they said their security feed has been deleted. They're working on figuring out what happened."

"What? This sounds like a plot out of a movie," I say, scratching my jaw in disbelief.

"I sent a crew in another jet to do recon and find any leads on their whereabouts. They'll gather information while we're en route, boss."

"Where's Bella? Is she safe?" I ask, my heart rate skyrocketing.

"We don't know, boss. The hotel management said they haven't seen her."

"Fuck," I shout, grabbing my whiskey glass and smashing it against the window.

"We'll find her, boss. We're already on it."

"Find us a way to Geneva. I can't sit here a minute longer."

Mario nods, and I head to my room to get my suitcase.

This shit can't be happening.

"Boss, I just got a text from the pilot. We've been approved for takeoff," Mario says, a big look of relief spreading across his face.

"Let's go," I say. I snatch up my suitcase and leave the hotel as fast as possible. I get into the back of the car while Mario sits in the front with the driver. I take out my phone and start typing a text. I delete it, type again, and delete it several times, not sure if it's wise, but I'm losing my mind.

Gabo: Hey, is anyone available?

A few minutes go by before my brother Vicente replies.

Vicente: Hey, bro. What's up?

Gabo: I'm still in Sweden. Just got the word we can lift off after a terrible storm. But Bella is in Geneva. I was supposed to be there to attend a gala with her.

Vicente: Aww, she's mad at you because you chose work over her?

Gabo: Fuck, I don't know. But neither she nor her security team can be reached.

Gio: What? What do you mean they can't be reached?

Gabo: Yeah, we can't find them.

Texting this to my brother and my closest friends seems surreal.

Vicente: I'm on my way.

Gio: Me too.

Luca: Fuck you, Gabo. I told you to take care of her. I can't leave Karina alone; she's due any day now.

Luca: You all better keep me posted.

Chapter 23

Isabella Bianchi

My head is spinning, and I'm nauseous. For a moment after I wake up, I can't feel my legs. Panic sets in but no sound escapes me.

Where am I?

This doesn't feel like my comfy bed at the hotel; the mattress is cold and stiff against my back. The last thing I remember was heading back to my room from the hotel lobby after picking up something Gabo had sent me. For some reason, the hotel staff wasn't allowed to let the delivery person

[text obscured] think anything of it; I just thought I'd grab
[text obscured] back to my suite to finish getting ready,
[text obscured] let the [text obscured] give me, I
[text obscured] to call [text obscured] I remem-

Slowly, I try to open my eyes, but my eyelids feel heavy, as if weighed shut. When I try to move, the cut of metal digs into my wrists.

What the heck?

I move my arms, but they seem to be tied to something. My wrists ache, chafed and raw from rubbing against something for a while. My skin feels irritated, burning painfully.

Am I chained?

A cold sense of dread takes over.

"Easy, Isabella," a familiar voice says.

I stop moving, trying to figure out where the voice is coming from. When the person doesn't speak anymore, I try to ask, "Who are you? Where am I?" My voice is a whisper; it even hurts to swallow.

"There will be time for that later. Rest for now." The voice draws closer, and I feel a pinch. Then, my brain goes blank.

—◦❖◦—

I have no clue how long I've been out, but at least now, I can open my eyes. When they adjust to the light, I notice I'm in a cabin; everything is made out of wood. And I am indeed chained to a bed.

What the actual fuck?

There are trees outside, too many to see beyond them.

Who would have wanted to hurt me this way? Why did someone target me? Maybe they got the wrong person? Or am I here

*because I'm involved with Gabo? He has never told me why he is
so adamant about me having a security detail, but maybe there
was a threat I wasn't aware of?*

*Ugh, this is so frustrating. I wonder if Gabo has noticed I nev-
er made it to the gala. And what happened to Aldo and Rocco?
Maybe they got captured, too?*

"Aldo, Rocco. Are you guys there?" I shout as loud as I can,
but all I hear is silence. I won't let my mind spin to the worst
possible scenario; they need to be okay. I've grown fond of
them. I love how they are so careful and respectful with me,
like a set of older brothers.

"Hey, I need to use the restroom. Let me out."

More silence. I start rattling the chains, but they don't
budge. My wrists are bruised—*how long have I been here?*
Suddenly, the door opens, and a man enters the room. I assume it's a man because the figure is tall with defined muscles. He wears a mask that covers his entire face except for
the eyes. Slowly, he removes the locks on each of the chains,
pinning me to the bed— first my feet, then my hands.

"Do not try to escape. There's nowhere to run," he warns
me.

The thought crosses my mind, but I'm too weak and disoriented to try to run. I need to find out what's going on
before I do anything.

Once I'm free of the chains, the man helps me to my feet.
My legs are wobbly, and it takes me a couple of minutes to
start walking. Once I do, I start to scan my surroundings. The

room is simple; it only has a bed, and the chains are attached to the floor. *Has this man held someone captive here before?* The mere thought gives me goosebumps.

Once outside the room, I notice the rest of the cabin is a large open space with a small kitchen and a living area. On the opposite side of the room, there's another door. The man points toward it, and I walk, assuming it's the bathroom. When I open the door, it's pitch black. I touch the wall, looking for a light switch. When I finally find it, I turn on the light. The bathroom is very small: a sink, a toilet, and a one-person shower. There are no windows, which explains the complete darkness. I do my business, and while washing my hands, I try to think of ways to escape. Then, there's a knock on the door.

"Time's up, Isabella. Come out now," the man says, and I sigh deeply. I need to find a way to let Gabo know that I'm okay.

Once I'm out of the bathroom, I scan the living space, looking for anything to use as a weapon, but so far, there's nothing. Everything is made of wood; there are no pillows, no blankets, no decor. Nothing. The man grabs me by my arm and guides me to the breakfast bar by the kitchen. I try to pull my arm away, but he only tightens his grip until I wince.

"Why are you doing this? Do you want money? I have plenty. Let me make you a wire transfer, and you can let me go."

The evil cackle that comes out of his mouth is frightening.

"You're more naive than I thought. You are here to pay for the sins of your family. I couldn't care less about your money."

I open my mouth, but nothing comes out; I think my brain is still foggy from whatever drug he used to sedate me.

What on earth is he talking about? Is this about my parents? Maybe they owe this guy money? But their social circle is in Argentina.

Nothing makes sense.

"There are many things you don't know about your brother."

I bring my eyebrows together in confusion.

"The one you think the world of."

I'm still confused; I love both of my brothers. When I don't say anything, he continues talking.

"Luca ruined my life. I've waited patiently to get my revenge. Never in a million years did I think his little sister would cross paths with me, but here we are."

My head starts spinning. *What is this guy talking about?* The moment he takes off his mask, my eyes grow as big as saucers, and my hands fly to cover my mouth. I can't believe this.

"Hi, Isabella. Do you know who I am?"

When I don't answer, he says, "I'm the last person you'll see before you die."

Chapter 24

Gabo Godoy

W___ en I h__d i_
__ __e t___a___
about ___ __ and w___
heart ___ __ to ju___
  "H___ ___ w___
evi___

___ng
___ed all
__l with B___
  "Don't ___
selves, al___

"Let me stop you right there, Vicente. First of all, you're not their savior, and second, they must have done something wrong because Bella isn't where she was supposed to be."

Vicente sighs in frustration, but I can't be bothered. My brain is laser-focused on finding Bella.

Mario leads us to a waiting car, and I get in with Vicente.

"Mario, any news?" I feel like a broken record, but I'm blind, and I cannot take it.

"No, boss, but I already contacted Interpol. They are working on restoring the video feed from the hotel."

I nod as I bite my thumbnail. The stress is killing me.

"What about the gala? Has anyone checked there?"

Silence.

"Mario, what the actual fuck? How long have you been in the security business?"

"Twenty years, boss."

"Twenty fucking years and so far you haven't done anything to find Bella?" I shout, and Vicente flinches next to me.

"Bro, you're mad. I get it, but remember, everyone here is trying to help. Being angry and behaving like an ass won't bring Isa back any faster."

"Since when are you the voice of reason?" I ask Vicente, hating that he's right.

"Ever since my brother started losing his mind, I've had to be whatever he needs me to be," he says, giving me a pat on my shoulder.

"I'm sorry, Mario. I have no excuse for yelling at you. You have been a remarkable employee. I'm just worried sick about her."

"Don't worry, boss. We'll find her." I nod at him—I hope he's right because she has become everything to me. I'm not sure I know how to do life without her anymore.

"Has anyone contacted Dominic and Luigi?" I completely forgot I had asked Dom to come, driving the same route Bella used.

"Yes, boss. I instructed Luigi to be on standby. There's no need for them to retrace the steps from Bologna," Mario informs me, which seems logical. I'll have to give Dom a vintage bottle of wine as a thanks for always having my back.

We get to the hotel and head to Bella's room. The moment we enter, a pang of panic invades me. Her gala clothes are displayed on her bed. She was getting ready to go, but she never made it there. When I enter the bathroom, all her makeup is on the counter. I can smell her perfume—citrus and flowers. When I see the necklace I gave her on the counter, tears start running down my face.

God, I might not be a devoted believer, but please keep her safe and help me find her. Bring her back to me.

"Hey, Aldo and Rocco are here," Vicente informs me.

I wipe the moisture off my face before making my way to the suite's living room.

"Boss," they say in unison as they get up to greet me. My hands form fists inside my pockets as I nod at them, and they nod back.

"There is nothing that can justify what happened to Miss Bianchi. We were in contact with her the entire time. The only time we didn't have eyes on her was when she was in her room. Other than that, we were always with her," Rocco begins.

"And the bathroom, we didn't go in there with her," Aldo adds.

Rocco hits him in the ribs with his elbow. "That goes without saying, *idiota*."

Mario and Vicente laugh, I would have, too, if Bella were here with me.

"I'm sorry, boss," Aldo says without lifting his gaze.

"Anyway, as I was saying. We always had eyes on her. We spoke with Miss Bianchi two hours before the gala. She said she would let us know when she was ready to go.

"Five minutes later, we got room service. Even though we didn't order it, it came with a note from Miss Bianchi. We didn't think anything of it since she's always so nice to us, so we decided to eat before going to the gala. Next thing we know, we were being woken up by the hotel management under Mario's order." Rocco finishes his retelling, and even though I want to be mad at them, I can't. I would have eaten the damn food, as well.

"So one thing we know is that whoever has her knows her well. They knew about her security and how her relationship is with you guys," I say. There's a knock on the door, and Mario goes to open it.

"My contact from Interpol is here," he announces as a tall man in uniform enters the room.

"Mr. Godoy, I'm Francois Dubois."

I extend my hand to greet him, and I see Vicente is ready to shake hands with the officer, as well. I guess it isn't often that there's more than one Godoy in the same room.

"We were able to recover the hotel security feed. The person who deleted it made a mistake, and that's the only reason we could recover it. From the footage, we can tell it's a team."

"Can we see it?" I ask, already making my way to the door.

"Yes, of course. Here." Officer Dubois clicks a tablet screen a few times. I'm not sure how I missed that he was holding it.

He passes the tablet to me, with Vicente on one side and Mario on the other. The screen shows a feed from the elevator. Bella seems asleep, and a man is holding her up on each side. She's wearing one of the comfy fleece tracksuits she loves, but her hair is in a pretty bun. They get off on the third floor, and the feed switches to another camera. They head to the utility stairs, carrying Bella as if they aren't doing anything wrong.

The next feed is from the garage. They cover her with a white sheet, and panic rises within me. *What did they give her?* When they are about to exit the garage in a tiny car, I pause the video. Finally, we have a clear view of the men who took Bella. I can't believe my eyes. I look at Vicente, wondering if I'm imagining things, but his face is as aghast as I'm sure mine is.

"I cannot fucking believe this," I manage to say.

Rocco and Aldo come to watch the video, and when they look at the screen, they seem surprised.

"That's Bella's instructor, Professor López," Rocco says.

"Fuck." Vicente lets out the curse with a deep rumble. "No, Rocco. That's Max von Willer. He was a family friend back in Chile and was blackmailing our sister when she and Luca met. Luca ended up unmasking him and bought his family's vineyard since they had to flee Chile—he was in deep shit with the mafia."

When I look around the hotel room, everyone's flabbergasted. Yeah, I would be, too, if I didn't know Bella is in real danger now.

"Okay, now that we have a name, what do we do? Bella is in danger," I say urgently. There's no time to waste. This man came for revenge.

"How the fuck did he find her? Did he pretend to be her teacher to get close to her?" Vicente asks no one in particular.

The fuck if I know. This seems to be too coincidental for my liking.

"The best thing you can do, Mr. Godoy, is to stay here and wait for any news. Maybe they'll call asking for ransom. I'm going to start my search with my team. I'll keep in touch," Officer Dubois says as he leaves the hotel room.

I'm about to protest when Vicente places his hand on my shoulder, silently telling me to remain quiet. I reluctantly follow his advice. I can't just sit here doing nothing while my Bella is out there with a crazy motherfucker.

"Mario, tell me you know people who can go on a hunt with us right now," I say as soon as Dubois leaves the room.

"Yes, boss. I contacted them the moment we landed."

"Good man, let's go. There's no time to waste."

Chapter 25

GABO GODOY

W___ drove to ___
___ired ___ I ___
just go___ pan___
down___ nev___
a bui___ ___o___
"___

> **Gio**: Just landed. Tell me where you are, and I'll meet you there.

Fuck, with all this ordeal, I forgot Gio was coming.

> **Gabo:** We're on our way to get you. Hang tight.

I pocket my phone as I scan the room. There are a bunch of computer screens and a team of about twelve people, all checking traffic feeds and satellite images. This is next level, and I'm glad Mario has this sort of contact. We needed it.

"Bella's brother just landed. We need to pick him up at the airport. But do you guys have any leads yet?" I ask, a mix of nerves and anticipation invading me. I keep my hands in my pockets to avoid the more noticeable shaking. I'm a live wire ready to burst.

"Actually, we do. Once we were able to identify who took her from the hotel, we followed them on the street. They got her in an old yellow Fiat. Here." Elio points to a screen, so Vicente and I lean in, trying to see the grainy feed.

"We were able to track the car. It appears it was abandoned at a gas station, forty-five minutes from the city, in a mountainous area in France."

"Fuck, if we're not careful, this could end up being an international debacle," Vicente says out loud, and I can't believe the shit he's worried about.

"I couldn't give two shits, Vicente. Bella, my principessa, is in a precarious situation for something she had no part in.

If something happens to her..." my voice breaks before I can finish the sentence, and I bite my knuckles to keep myself in check.

"Sorry, bro. My CEO mode just came out," he says as he pats my back.

"We're ready to go, Mr. Godoy. If we go now, we can use the darkness as the coverage. We need to scan the forest without being seen. Otherwise, we can wait until dawn. It's your call," Elio says, and I take a deep breath.

"It's showtime."

We pile into two black vans, and I can tell they're bulletproof. The windows are tinted, and the interior is packed with every single gun and ammo under the sun. I can't help but swallow hard at the sight. It feels surreal to be in this situation all because a deranged asshole decided to blackmail my sister years ago. And now my Bella is the one who has to pay. When I thought life had given me everything I could ever want and more, a blast from the past comes to bite me in the ass and threatens to take the love of my life away from me.

When we get to the airport, Gio is pacing the tarmac, ruffling his hair as he talks on the phone. I can't shake the feeling that Bella's siblings will resent me for this for the rest of our lives. She was under my care, after all. I promised them

I would protect her at all times. But when they learn who has her, Luca is going to lose his shit.

"Hey, man. Do we have proof of life yet?" Gio asks as he hangs up the phone and gets into the van with Vicente, Rocco, Aldo, Mario, and me.

"Ha, and you thought I was being inconsiderate," Vicente chirps. I would smack him in the head if he were next to me.

"Sorry, did I say something wrong?" Gio asks, looking a little flustered.

"No, no. I know you have Bella's best interests at heart, you're her brother, after all. It's just that I'm on the edge. That's all."

Vicente chuckles as he shakes his head at me. I glare in return.

"Okay, yeah. I can see why you would be losing your ever-loving mind," Gio says with empathy.

"So, where are we going? Where is she being held captive?" Gio asks.

Mario takes out a tablet. "According to what we know, the car she was taken in was abandoned at a gas station. When we look at the satellite imagery of the area, it's an untouched forest, but there are a few paths that are visible from the data taken during winter. I want to take those trails and see where they take us. Elio and his team have more advanced equipment and will be tracking footprints."

Gio nods, mulling the information he just got from Mario. "Do we know who has her?"

When I don't immediately reply, Vicente fills him in. "Max von Willer. He's a former family friend."

Gio interrupts Vicente as he takes out his phone. "Fuck, Luca's nemesis. Isa has to be okay." He calls Luca and starts talking rapidly, filling him in.

Bella has to be safe. There's no other option.

Chapter 26

ISABELLA BIANCHI

I in an alternate universe? How does Professor López know Luca? And why does he want to kill me?

I've been replaying the last few weeks in my head, over and over, trying to see if he ever gave me reason to think he was an evil person. But nothing comes to mind. He was always kind when I approached him with questions, never made me feel unsafe, and didn't treat me differently than he would the other students.

Damn, he's good.

"So what's your plan? Kill me and send me back to Chile?"

He laughs, waves his index finger, signaling no.

"That's too easy. I want them all to see." Vicente turns, beginning to pace. "After your brother—"

them. I left a few morsels of information so they could find us. I want them to watch you die, helpless to save you."

What did Luca do to this man?

The thought of Gabo seeing me die is like a knife to my heart. He'd never recover from this. I know he loves me as much as I love him. I need to keep this man talking; maybe if he gets ruffled, he'll slip up and say something I can use against him. I mean, if Luca was able to take him down once, I could do it, too.

"What did Luca do that was so bad? I'm sure my brother never had bad intentions."

He turns on his heel and gets in my face.

"What did he do?" he snarls, making me flinch. "Your brother ruined my life. I was supposed to marry Karina. We were supposed to join our families' vineyards and create a wine monopoly in Chile. But your brother decided to charm Karina with his Argentine swag, and she fell for it," he says as he slams the plate of food I had in front of me against the floor. I try not to flinch, but it's impossible. My nervous system is a wreck.

"Then, he decided to tell my family about my little secret—my drug addiction. When my parents learned about my not-so-holy addiction and the debt I had with the mafia, they quickly sold the vineyard, not really caring to who. We left our country like pariahs," he says slowly, each word dripping with venom. His voice shakes with barely contained rage, his eyes wild and unhinged.

I try not to react to this news, but fuck, Luca basically took his life away from him. Not that I blame him, though. Luca and Karina were made for each other. I have never seen him as alive and happy as when he met Karina and bought the vineyard for her. I just didn't realize all this drama was behind my brother's ultimate romantic gesture to get his girl.

No, I need to stop thinking about my brother and ask this guy more personal stuff. Maybe this will make him open up to me.

"But you're such an amazing professor, you had me fooled. I honestly thought art was your passion."

It's the first time I've seen him smile—a genuine smile.

"It is. Art brought me back to life. It's something I truly enjoy doing. Curating art for the Museum of Modern Art has been the medicine I needed to mend my broken life. When I realized you were related to the bane of my existence, all those repressed feelings resurfaced," he says as he passes his hand across my cheek, and I flinch. A touch has never disgusted me so much in my life.

"Please don't touch me," I plead as bile rises in my throat.

"I wasn't thinking about it, but maybe I should try for myself to see why Gabo is head over heels for you." He licks my face, and I scream at the top of my lungs. I try to get away from him, but he holds me by my arms; he's incredibly strong.

I manage to lift my leg and hit him in the balls. He folds in pain, but when I try to flee, he knocks me down.

I fall face-first to the floor. There's a metal taste in my mouth—I'm sure I ripped my lip open. Blood stains the floor.

"Where do you think you're going, Isabella? The fun is about to start," he says in a low tone against my ear, pressing himself against me. I arch my back with all the strength I can muster and hit his chin with my head. "You bitch, if I didn't want to kill you in front of them, you would be dead already," he says as alarms go off. The deafening sound engulfs the room as I try to find the source, but I can't see anything. No screens, no phones. Nothing.

"They're here. Let's go, it's time to party," he says as he lifts me from the floor. Instead of turning off all the lights, he turns everything on, including the outside lights. The little cabin is like a beacon in a sea of trees and darkness.

We head outside to the front yard. He ties my legs together and then my hands behind my back. Finally, he places a piece of tape on my mouth.

"You stay here. I want them to see you when they approach the cabin. Don't try anything stupid; the house is protected by a minefield. One wrong step, and you can go *kaboom*," he says with a cackle.

I can't help the tears that roll down my face. I'm terrified not only of dying but of potentially seeing Gabo die if he's the one who's near.

Fuck, why did I have to end up in the middle of this shit show?

I'm not sure how long I stand there in the cold night. I don't move, afraid if I do, I might trigger a landmine or, worse, make enough noise to put Gabo in danger. Everything is eerily still. There's no breeze, no moon shining down. The sky is covered in clouds—like time is frozen. The calm before the storm.

Suddenly, I think I hear the crunching of leaves. Maybe I'm imagining it? My body is exhausted, and I'm not sure how much longer I will last standing. The only thing keeping me upright is the fear of messing up. I hear it again: *crunch, crunch*. I don't look behind me to see if Professor Lóp—Max—noticed. I don't want to alert him in case he didn't hear.

"I know you're out there, Gabo. Come get your girl," he shouts.

I try to press my lips together, but I can't—the damn tape is too tight around my mouth.

Out of nowhere, a figure appears in the distance. I can't tell who it is, but I'm sure it's a man. He approaches the cabin slowly, with measured steps and hands in the air. When I see him, I can't help but cry harder. He came for me. And now he's going to die because of me.

"Bella mia," Gabo says as he walks faster toward me. His voice is rough like he's been yelling a lot. I can't imagine the nightmare this has been for him, too.

"Stop. There are landmines," someone shouts, and Gabo freezes.

"You brought professionals. I didn't think you were here alone," Max says from behind me, safe from the landmines on the cabin's front porch. He pulls out a gun and points it at me. I want to charge and knock him down, but I can't move. And I don't know where the landmines are. My legs start wavering; I'm so tired, but I need to be strong for *him*. For us.

I try to take calming breaths, but it's in vain. Seeing Gabo so close yet so far away is killing me. When he extends his hand to me, as if to say, "I'm here. I got you," I lose it. My body doubles over in pain. I'm desperate to be in Gabo's arms.

"Aww, such a beautiful moment, Gabriel and Isabella finally reunited," Max says in a mocking tone.

My thoughts shift from sadness and stress to murderous rage. I've never been a violent person, but knowing that Gabo is here and is in danger makes me rabid.

"What do you want, Max? A formal apology? I can have Luca on the phone in two seconds," Gabo asks.

"Oh, so he's not here? I guess he doesn't care about his family as much as he made it seem all those years ago."

I grit my teeth. Can *someone shut this idiot up?* My brother is the most caring person ever, so if he's not here, it is precisely because he's taking care of his family.

"No, he couldn't make it. His wife is ready to give birth to their first child any day now," Gabo says.

I hear a loud noise behind me. When I look back, Max is angrily kicking a rocking chair, over and over, until it becomes a pile of wood. I'd rather he take his anger out on the chairs than on me or Gabo.

"I saw their wedding pictures and how happy they are together. It should have been me marrying her. I didn't realize Karina was so close to giving birth. I guess I've been distracted planning this little reunion," Max yells, so much anger in his voice.

I stay rooted on the floor, terrified of what's coming next.

"No, that should have never been you. Karina and Luca are meant to be." I would recognize that voice even in my sleep. I can't believe Gio is here, too.

I fall to my knees as I see him walk toward me and stand next to Gabo. This has to stop now before I lose two of the most important people in my life. I hope they have a plan because we're really going to need one to get out of this mess.

"Ah, the smart brother. Gio, right? Yeah, I've read about you. Smart and lonely. Ever since Ruin vanished. Poor soul, may she rest in peace."

Gio transforms from cool and collected to a wolf ready to draw blood.

"Keep Ruin's name out of your filthy mouth," Gio shouts with such a stern voice that even I get the chills. I'm not sure I've ever seen him so mad.

"I'm here, Max. Talk to me and leave my family the fuck out of this." Luca emerges from the shadows, and I see everyone's faces transform in pure shock. I'm shocked, too.

How did he make it from Chile? Oh, my God. This is madness.

"I was just making sure my wife was safe before I came to end this charade once and for all."

I cannot believe this. Everyone I love is here. Gio remains next to Gabo, and there's no one else on the periphery. At least, no one I can see.

"So glad you could join us, asshole. It wouldn't have been the same without you," Max says as he rearranges his hair and cocks the gun. I whimper. I hope Gabo has a plan because right now, I feel helpless and useless.

"Who's going to be brave enough to come and get Isabella? Remember, the perimeter is a minefield, so make sure you know where to step," Max says in a chirpy tone; he's enjoying this too much, and I hate him more for it.

I plead with Gabo not to come. I hope he can see it in my eyes because it's the only way I have to communicate with him.

When no one moves, I feel Max getting impatient behind me. "Come on. No one? Okay, I'll go first," he says as he descends the porch stairs and starts skipping around the cabin's front yard. "See, it's easy. You just have to know where to step."

I roll my eyes because, honestly, this man is an idiot. Such childish behavior.

"You're skipping around so carefree because there are no mines. You're bluffing," Gabo says in a strong voice.

I really want to believe his words, but how is he so sure?

"It's your word against mine, Gabriel. Why don't you come and try for yourself?" Max challenges him. I scream with all my might for Gabo not to accept, but all that comes out is a muffled sound. The moment I see Gabo start walking toward me, my heart skips a beat. I have acute chest pain—this must be what it feels like to have a heart attack. When nothing happens, and Gabo continues walking, I start breathing a little easier. Maybe this idiot was bluffing after all.

Gabo keeps closing the distance between us. When he's ten feet away, Max steps closer to me, his gun pointed at my head with intent, and Gabo rushes toward me. I try to get up to meet him halfway, but there's a deafening gunshot before I can reach him, and I fall back to the ground. A strong body lifts me, and I inhale his scent—a mix of whisky, tobacco, and sandalwood.

Gabo got me.

When I'm sitting upright, I touch him from head to toe, making sure he's unharmed. When he catches on to what I'm doing, he hugs me hard.

"I'm fine, I'm okay. You're the one I'm worried about." He slowly lets me go and very gently starts checking my body, making sure I'm fine.

I look around, trying to see what happened to Max, but chaos has broken out all over. Luca, Gio, and Vicente rush toward Gabo and me. Luca has a gun in his hand—this is ludicrous.

Since when does my brother know how to use a weapon? Did he kill Max? Oh no, I hope we're not in trouble.

"It's over, principessa. I got you. My team disarmed the minefield. As soon as they gave us the all-clear, nothing was stopping me from getting to you," Gabo says as he peppers kisses all around my head, my face, and my neck. He removes the tape from my mouth as gently as he can, grimacing as he sees the blood from the cut in my lip. I notice how badly he's trembling when he removes his radio earpiece. He cups my face in his hands, his expression a mixture of relief and sorrow. Seeing this strong man almost at his breaking point makes me cry harder. I can't believe this nightmare is over. Everything is still a jumble of thoughts and memories in my head.

"Isa, thank fuck you're okay," Luca says as he falls to the ground next to us. When I see him and Gio, I try to hug them, but I'm still handcuffed. Gabo shouts for someone to help me, and a man wearing all black military gear materializes immediately next to me and removes the chains in no time. Once free, I hug my brothers, and the three of us start crying uncontrollably.

"I'm so sorry you had to go through this, Isa. Please forgive me. You know I love you and care about you deeply," Luca says, sobbing as Gio tries to comfort him, but it's in vain; he's in shock.

"There's nothing you have to apologize for, brother dearest," I murmur. The nickname earns me a small chuckle from him, so I continue. "You just fought hard for what you wanted, and you got her. It's not your fault this idiot is a mess and tried to ruin everyone's lives." Luca nods, absorbing my words as he continues to let his tears run free.

I feel a strong hand on the small of my back. After my initial shock, I look back. When I realize it's Gabo, I relax and turn around to hug him. He cradles my face with his hands, and I feel at home again. "I love you, G. I love you so much."

My tears mix with Gabo's, and all the stress from this harrowing situation starts to melt away.

"I love you, too. Always," he says against my lips. We kiss slowly and gently, careful around the swollen cut. We kiss like we have all the time in the world. Because we do.

I hear someone clearing his throat near us, and I remember my brother and Vicente are here, too. Reluctantly, I end the kiss, and after giving Gabo a cheeky grin, I hug my brothers again.

"What are you guys doing here? I thought Karina could give birth any day now?" I ask them, even though I know full well he'll go to the end of the world for me.

"Well, your Gabo here texted all panicked that something was wrong. I knew I needed to come and support any way I could. Besides, I needed to keep Luca in check. The man was losing his mind," Gio says, and Luca winces as he wipes the tears from his face.

"Yeah, the moment this *boludo* texted us, I knew I had to come. I brought Karina with me just in case. We even brought her doctor in case of an emergency."

I know the situation isn't funny, but this is my brother in all his glory—extra until the end of time.

I see Vicente approaching us with Rocco and Aldo, and I sigh in relief to see them alive and well. I hug them, but they remain immobile, likely looking to Gabo for approval. I don't care if we're breaking protocol. I thought they were dead.

"I'm so glad to see you guys. I promise I'll never ever complain about having you as my security team again." They both chuckle, but I can tell they're still shaken by the situation.

"We're so sorry, Miss Bianchi. We failed you, but we're really thankful you're safe and sound," Rocco says, and Aldo nods.

"Okay, that's enough. Bella, come with me," Gabo says, and I warily chuckle at his possessiveness but go to him anyway. I'm still shaking from all the adrenaline.

We walk toward the spot where a military team has detained Max. He's been shot in the shoulder, and several people are helping him out. This team seems to be the real deal.

"You worthless piece of shit," Gabo says as he lunges to punch Max in the face.

"Noooo, G," I shout and try to go after him. I don't want him to get arrested because of that psycho.

"It's okay, Isa. He needs to let all that pent-up energy out," Gio says as he holds me back.

I sigh but hug my brother.

Gabo gives Max a few good punches, and Max starts laughing uncontrollably. It's almost maniacal. How can one laugh when there are bones crunching and blood flying left and right?

"Do you think a few good punches are going to do anything to me, Gabriel? What your family and the Bianchi's did to me and my family is far worse than a few punches. And maybe this time my plan didn't go as I thought it would, but time will tell who has the last laugh." Max spits on Gabo's shoes. Gabo lunges to hit Max again, but Rocco and Mario hold him back this time.

Vicente approaches him with his aloof demeanor. He is the typical powerful billionaire: cool, calm, and collected.

"You caught us by surprise this time, Max. But make no mistake, the Godoy's and the Bianchi's are not to be messed with. We wouldn't want to take away anything your parents have been able to acquire since you all moved to Switzerland," Vicente says with a low growl, making everyone's hair stand on edge.

Max sneers but doesn't reply. He knows he's lost.

"And I was the one who shot you, in case you were wondering who took you down, *asshole*," Luca says as he approaches Max and presses his thumb into Max's wound. Max's shriek of pain is deafening. I cover my ears as Gio hugs me tighter. The next thing I know, Max is on the floor, unconscious.

"Hmm, who would have thought that actually worked? I saw it in a couple of movies and always wanted to try it," Luca shares as he approaches us while cleaning his hands.

"Officer Dubois, what a pleasure to see you here," I hear Gabo greet a man in uniform. I wonder when they met. There's a lot for us to still talk about.

"I wish I could say the same, Mr. Godoy. I thought I had been clear enough when I said to wait at the hotel while my team worked on the case."

I laugh but try to cover it with a cough. This man should know Gabo has no chill, especially when I'm involved.

"I'm sorry, officer. I just couldn't sit there doing nothing."

The officer nods at Gabo and then motions for two officers behind him to get Max.

"I'm a Swiss citizen! You don't have jurisdiction over me," Max shouts as he is woken up by the officers' rough hold. He tries to break free but immediately winces in pain.

"Good thing we're Interpol. There's a warrant under your new name for stealing art from an English collector." Max's face goes pale, and he suddenly has no words.

"Karma is a bitch, huh, Max? Or should I say, Professor López?" I'm too excited to learn this man will spend a long time in jail. He glares at me as Interpol officers push him away.

"So am I to assume you came here with just your security team?" Dubois asks Gabo.

He presses his lips together, trying to hide a smile, but I can see it.

"Yes, officer. Mario, my security lead, is familiar with the area."

Mario nods.

"You all are lucky this didn't go sideways. Mario, please come with me. I'm assuming you're the one who shot von Willer?"

A silent understanding passes between Mario and Gabo as he puts a hand across Luca's chest to stop him from stepping forward.

"Yes, sir. Here's my gun." Mario disappears with the officer, and Gabo comes back to where I'm standing with Gio, Luca, and Vicente.

"I guess I'm glad Officer Dubois wasn't in earshot when I told Max I was the one who shot him," Luca whispers, and we all cackle. "Wait, is that why Mario lent me his gun?"

"Mario is a professional and won't be prosecuted like you would be. However, you shouldn't worry about that, brother-in-law. With our fortunes combined, we could easily get you out of jail this lifetime and all the rest," Gabo tells Luca, who glares at him and then dissolves into a fit of laughter.

"That brother-in-law title has a whole new meaning now, huh?" Luca asks, and it's Gabo's turn to chuckle.

"Let's go home," Gabo says as he kisses my hair.

Everyone falls into step with us. I breathe him in, and I don't think I've ever been more thankful to my guardian angels in heaven. I'm finally safe in my happy place.

Chapter 27

GABO GODOY

W........ing ...ne.....
.....oup..of......
heaven.....ense we.....
but Gi........and......
"G...............n....
my............

.....rea...
...g and ......
...o attend.....
with *her*.

"I don't know, G. I'm still a little tired, but I guess we should check on Gio and Luca at some point. Then maybe go to the villa? I could use some relaxing time," she says as she stretches her arms above her, still lying down. Her breasts rise out of the covers, and I take one of her pebbled nipples in my mouth. I can't help it. Her moans are all the fuel I need to know she wants this, too. Ever so slowly, I make my way to her core, leaving a trail of kisses in my wake.

"Yes, G. I need you," she tells me, a beautiful smile on her face.

"Are you sure, principessa? You've been through a lot in a short period of time." I double-check—I need to make sure this is what she wants and that I'm not forcing her to do something she's not ready for after the ordeal she just went through.

"Yes, G. I need you," she repeats as she pulls my hair, placing me where she wants me—my mouth on her pussy. The moment my tongue touches her clit, and the flavor of her arousal hits my tastebuds, I feel like everything is right in my world. I make her come on my tongue and fingers, and then I enter her slowly, enjoying how she stretches inch after inch to adjust to my size. Bella is looking at me with such adoration and so much love in her eyes that I know no matter what life has in store for us, we'll always face it together.

"Stay with me, Bella," I plead with her.

"I'm right here, G," she replies in a breathy tone.

"I mean, stay here, in Bologna, with me. I can build you a bigger house, a bigger penthouse. Anything you want is yours. Just stay," I tell her against her neck as I kiss and nibble my way to her ear. Bella is panting with need, letting me know she wants more, so I pick up the pace. Her hands go to my ass, and I love the sting that her nails leave on my skin.

"I'm yours, G," is all she says before we both find our release.

Once our breathing has calmed, I go to the bathroom for a washcloth to help her clean up. She seems quiet; maybe she still needs time to process everything that went down.

Maybe I shouldn't have asked her to stay with me just yet.

There's a knock on the door, and I groan as I discard the washcloth in the bathroom and put on sweatpants to answer.

"I'm sorry to bother you, boss. But we have a problem downstairs," Mario says as he presses on his earcom. "We need to get you, Miss Bianchi, Mister and Mrs. Bianchi, and Dr. Bianchi out of here." I'm startled by the urgency of his tone—he's usually a relaxed guy, so whatever is happening must be serious.

"Okay, let me get changed, and we can leave," I tell him as I close the door. When I turn around to tell Bella we have to go, she's sitting on the bed, her phone in one hand while the other hand is covering her mouth.

"What is it?" I ask her. When she lifts her gaze to me, her eyes are full of emotion. She passes me her phone, and I look at the screen.

"Chilean and Argentine Billionaire Families Involved in International Scandal." That's the headline of the article she's reading. I scroll down and see a picture of the outside of my penthouse building. At least one hundred people are outside, waiting for a statement.

"Fuck, I'm sorry, principessa. It's best if we get ready and get out of here," I tell her gently. I know she's still very shaken, and this will only make things worse. She nods and gets up, disappearing into her walk-in closet. I throw on a white tee and a black cap, socks, and shoes before going to find Luca and Gio.

"Hey, man. What do you want to do?" Gio asks me as he gets out of his room. I go knock on Luca's door. Gio is looking at his phone; I think he was on FaceTime with someone.

"Mario says we need to get out of here. Maybe go to the villa, or somewhere the media doesn't have access," I tell him, and he nods slowly. Thinking.

"No, we need to give a statement. Put me in front of the cameras," I hear Luca say as he comes out of his room, my sister behind him. I sigh in frustration.

"Haven't you done enough, Luca? Bella almost died because you didn't do a good enough job getting rid of that piece of shit," I tell him, and I see my sister flinching at my words, but I'm tired of his meddling.

"I deserve it, Gabo. I know I do. We haven't have the chance to let it all out since we were all still on edge, but I'm so fucking sorry Isa had to go through all that because of Max. And as bad as I feel, how was I supposed to know he was looking for revenge after all this time? They vanished, and like a normal person, I didn't keep tabs on them," Luca volleys back, and I know, deep down, this is not his fault.

"I know, you're right. But you have to understand that I'm also tired of you butting in at every single turn. I love your sister. That's a fact. It would be nice if the guy who calls himself my best friend would actually trust me and let me take care of what's mine," I say, suddenly tired after all we've been through.

"Yeah, bro. All you have to worry about is Karina and the baby. Let Isa and Gabo handle this the best they can. I'm just here to support in any way I can," Gio tells Luca in that older brother tone similar to the one Vicente uses when he means business.

"Fine. I know you're right, Gabo. I'm sorry, man. I know I've been a pain in your ass, and I should have trusted you from the get go like you've trusted me with Karina," he says as he goes to kiss my sister on her forehead.

"I'll apologize to Isa later when the dust has settled," Luca says honestly, not a smidge of sourness in his tone. He gives me a bro hug, and I return it in kind. I'm glad he has finally come to his senses. I'm just sad it took almost losing Bella for him to realize I'm all in with her.

"You've finally seen the light, *guachito*. My brother and Isa can finally be at peace," Karina says as she hugs Luca, and Gio and I burst with laughter.

"Careful there, Karina Bianchi. I have ways to make you pay later on," Luca says as he kisses my sister.

I gag. "Okay, we have to draw a line, man. I don't want to see you getting it on with my sister, and you don't want to see me with Bella. Let's leave those comments and behavior for when you are in private."

Gio rolls his eyes as Luca flips me the bird and continues kissing my sister.

Okay, two can play that game. Let's see what he says when I'm kissing my woman.

"Time to face the music." Bella appears in the living room, dragging two huge pieces of luggage behind her. I can't help but chuckle at her attempt to pack light because we have to get out of here.

"What?" she asks in mock defiance, raising a brow.

"Nothing, principessa. I see you're ready." She nods as if to say, "Good answer."

Gio murmurs, "Yeah, Gabo has it bad for my sister."

"I detect no lies," Luca says with a chuckle, and I shrug. I don't care who knows; Bella Bianchi is the beginning and the end of my love life.

We get in my G-Wagon—Mario will drive Gio and us while Aldo and Rocco go in a car ahead of us with Luca,

Karina, and her doctor. Luigi and the other security team are in a car behind us.

When we make it out of the garage, the police are trying to keep all the journalists and camera crews away from our cars, but it's impossible—they've turned into a mob. Bella gently pats Mario's shoulder as she tells him to stop the car. She opens the moonroof and stands, her upper body emerging from the car.

"I simply want to thank each and all of you for caring so much about my story. I went through a very traumatic event, so I would appreciate privacy and space after this statement. Neither the Bianchi nor the Godoy families have ever been involved in any illicit or dubious businesses. The man who took me against my will has had psychotic issues for a while, and now that he's with the proper authorities, I hope he'll get the treatment he deserves. I'm going to move on and leave behind all the pain and suffering this experience has caused me and our families, and I urge you all to do the same. Please respect our privacy. Thank you." Bella gets back inside the car, and I kiss her hard, not caring that Gio is in the backseat.

"You were amazing. Is there anything you can't do? Artist, designer, public speaker." I praise her, and she beams, her azure eyes shining bright.

"Don't know yet. I'll let you know when I find out."

I bark out a laugh as Mario starts driving again, leaving the media circus behind us.

"I don't want to burst your bubble, guys, but I need to head back to the States. Any chance you can drop me off at the airport?" Gio asks, and I wonder what he has going on that he's so pressed to head back. Mario looks at me for instructions in the rearview mirror, and I mouth *airport* to him.

"Oh, Gio, I'm so sorry I didn't have much time to chat with you this time around," Bella tells her brother, and I marvel at how caring and loving she is when she's the one who was kidnapped.

"I'm just glad I was able to be here for you," Gio tells her honestly.

"Aren't you supposed to be teaching by now? I thought the semester had already started at the uni where you work," Bella asks, and I shake my head in disbelief, a full-on billionaire still teaching lectures.

"Actually, I resigned from my job in Raleigh."

I raise my eyebrows as Bella shouts, "What?"

Gio seems a little nervous, and he scratches the back of his neck before continuing to talk.

"I met a kid in the lab where I work, used to work, and he was telling me all about his hometown in the North Carolina mountains. They're about to lose their home because there's a big corporation trying to buy out the entire town to build a ski resort or something."

Bella and I look at him, incredulous. I mean, Gio has always talked about being a scientist and how much pride he has in his research. It's astounding news.

"So what's the plan? Save the town?" Bella asks, and Gio chuckles.

"Something like that. I just think it's time for me to find a simpler life. There's a community college nearby where I could teach, and maybe I could use my resources to help this town flourish," he says with a shrug.

I think there's more to it than he's letting on, but I'm sure he'll share more when he's ready.

"Well, I can't wait to go visit you at... What's the town's name again?" Bella asks.

"Azalea Creek, North Carolina."

"We'll definitely go visit," I reassure him as we make it to the airport.

After goodbye hugs and promises to keep in touch and visit him soon, Gio gets on his jet. Luca comes closer to Bella while Karina stays a couple of feet behind, trying to chat with me. All I want to do is become a fly and listen to the conversation that's about to go down between Luca and Bella.

Chapter 28

Isabella Bianchi

"Hey, Isa. Is this a good time?" Luca asks.

I look at him with curious eyes. "A good time for what?"

"Well, I think there's no time like the present. I owe you a big apology, Isa. Time after time, I told you I was going to respect and support your decisions, only to do the complete opposite. I behaved like an ass, and it took you being in danger to finally realize how wrong I was," Luca says as he plays with the hair on the back of his neck, the only telltale that

"Thank you for acknowledging how dense and ridiculous you've been since I came here." Luca chuckles, and I join him. "Imagine if someone had given you so much shit for dating someone you honestly liked. Even worse, giving me shit for dating one of your best friends. Did you honestly think Gabo would hurt me?" I ask him, curious to know why he was so crossed about me being with G.

After a long sigh, Luca says, "To be honest, Isa, I have no excuse. Deep down, I know you're not my daughter, you're my sister. But I guess I've taken the role to heart, and I just panicked about you getting involved with someone the moment you started to fly solo, so to speak."

I bark out a laugh. Honestly, only my brother, with his sense of humor, would make me laugh after what I went through.

"Oh, brother dearest, you're the best. I needed that. Flying solo..." I dissolve in a fit of laughter all over again.

"You're welcome, Isa. But I truly am sorry for everything. Not just for being a pain in the ass about your personal life."

And here it is—the elephant in the room. I guess we needed to address it at some point.

"Luca, you're not responsible for Max's actions. It was not like he targeted me for years and waited until I came to Italy. It was just the right time and the right place for him to do something stupid," I tell my brother.

He sighs, his shoulders sagging. He's going to blame himself for this for a while, and all I can do is support him in his healing process any way I can.

"Thank you, Isa. Honestly, thank you for being the best sister I could ever ask for." He comes to hug me, and I notice he's shaking a little.

Is my brother crying? God bless him.

After more hugs from Luca and Karina, they board their jet, and G and I get back into the G-Wagon.

"Where to now?" he asks me.

"Take me home, G," I say as I snuggle with him in the backseat.

"Mario, to the villa."

He nods as he gets on his comms to tell the team where we're heading.

Home.

Chapter 29

Isabella Bianchi

It's been two weeks since Max kidnapped me. Not a day goes by that I don't think about those excruciating hours where I didn't know if I was going to make it out alive. I was lucky enough that Gabo put a team in motion to find me when he couldn't reach me. And even luckier that no one was harmed while saving me. The only scars I have now are the ones that can't be seen.

After years of trying to contact my parents and never hearing back from them, I got an email from my mom the day after the interview that went viral:

us, we would love to see you. I heard you're dating a Godoy. We would love to meet him, and maybe talk business with him."

The nerve of this woman, asking for a flight and an appointment with Gabo. I guess I needed this to happen for me to believe what my brothers have been trying to tell me all along: our parents only care about money. Now that they know their sons are billionaires and I'm dating a billionaire, they want to be part of our lives. The math is mathing.

I don't want to add more invisible scars to my heart, especially to give a space in my life to people who don't deserve it. After a lot of thinking, I decided to block her email and never think about my parents again.

I'm lost in thought while letting Margareta spoil me with a delicious fresh pastry and a coffee when I get an incoming video call from Luca.

"Hi, brother dearest. How's everything going?" I ask once the video connects.

A warm smile spreads on my face as I see my brother is positively shining.

"Oh, everything is peachy. Is Gabo around?"

I twist my eyebrows in confusion. Why does he need Gabo? He could have just called him.

"No, he went into the office today," I say. The moment my brother moves the phone and Karina comes into view, holding a precious bundle of joy in her arms, everything makes sense.

"Well, it's his loss. We wanted you guys to be the first to see Enzo Bianchi," Luca says, his voice full of emotion.

"Oh, my goodness. Hi, baby. Hi. I'm Auntie Bella." I coo immediately at the phone, and Luca moves closer to Enzo. He's happily asleep in his mommy's embrace. His face is scrunched up, but he's the cutest baby I've ever seen. My heart expands with love for this tiny boy who I'll be able to spoil for the rest of my life.

"Isn't he the most gorgeous baby you've ever seen?" Karina asks, a beautiful smile on her face.

"He sure is. How are you doing, Kari?"

"I'm okay. The pain meds are working, so I'm feeling great."

I chuckle, and she gives me a small wave as she readjusts her position; maybe she's going to nap while Enzo is asleep. I've heard that's what moms are supposed to do.

"Thank you for calling us first. I can't wait to tell Gabo when he comes home tonight."

My brother smiles at the screen; I don't think I've ever seen him this happy. He's shining brighter than when he married Karina, and that says a lot.

"Just promise you and Gabo will come to meet your nephew soon," he says as his voice breaks. I hate that he has no family in Chile with him. I mean, Karina's parents are amazing, but I'm sure he wishes he had some support, as well.

"Of course, I can't wait to meet him. Gabo has some things at work that he needs to take care of, but I promise as soon as his calendar clears, we'll make our way to Alamo Peaks."

We chat a little bit more before saying goodbye, and once we do, my heart is full. I love my family.

⸺⸻❖⸻⸺

We've been staying at the villa since the kidnapping, and I don't want to ever leave. Gabo has been going to the office in Bologna twice a week, and he's been handling everything else from home.

I've been trying to paint and dance, trying to get my groove back, but so far, nothing sticks. I didn't want to finish the summer class at school. I want to focus on getting better before I go back to uni, and I'm sure the gossip is running wild about the fraud of a professor who kidnapped the billionaire's girlfriend. Giacomo even reached out to check in, and I told him I wanted to postpone our project, which he completely understood. So maybe next summer, I can pick it up again when everything has died down.

I finished the assignment for Gabo's company since that was something I could work on remotely. I honestly loved it, so it was no hardship to finish my task. Both Gabo and the design team leader praised me, and although it felt good to be recognized for my work, I wanted to focus on my mental health first.

Every trace I make on the canvas reminds me of the cabin, the chains, and the weakness I felt when I woke up on that bed. I want all this pain to go away, lock all these memories away in a box, and throw the key as far away as I can. But that's not how life works, and I know I need to face my demons, but I'm not ready yet. I don't know if I'll ever be.

"Principessa," Gabo calls my name as he enters my studio. I turn around to face him, and he's looking so good in a pair of dress pants and a white shirt. This is his relaxed fit when working from home.

"Hey, G," I say as I extend my neck to kiss him.

"What are you doing?" he asks as he stares at my canvas.

"Nothing." My shoulders sag.

"This is not nothing, this is art."

"This is the mess I have in my head, G. I don't like it. It's heavy and sad and depressing. I don't like it," I say, pouting like a little kid who doesn't get her way.

"Bella, don't you see, my love? This is amazing. You're creating something beautiful out of all that pain and sorrow. You're creating light out of darkness. This needs to be celebrated too. It tells a story—a story of resilience and strength, of love and healing."

I love how he sees things in a different way. And he's right. I can see it now. The forest, dark and heavy, with clouds full of water covering the sun, a small log cabin that seems to blend in and disappear into the forest. I can see it all. The strokes are thick but determined, reflecting the anger I felt while painting this piece. The colors are dark, but there's a small ray of light. Gabo. He has been that little morsel of warmth and light that has transformed my life for the better.

"Maybe I need to see someone." I finally say out loud what's been on my mind ever since we got out of that forest.

"What do you mean?"

"Maybe I need to see a therapist. Cata said Matias has been seeing a therapist for a while, and it has helped him a lot. I know it's for different reasons, but maybe I need to speak with a professional as well."

"Hey, hey, come here," he coos as he opens his arms, and I go to him without protest.

"If that's what you feel you need to do, I fully support you. You know that." I smile against his chest, a reassuring feeling in my chest that this man is it for me.

"I know there are still many emotions to process. Many memories, many things... it's better to start now, Bella. Don't suppress those feelings. If you think speaking with a therapist will help, do it. Yell if you need to, trash this place, we'll rebuild. Do whatever you have to do to get those feelings off your chest," Gabo says as he places a kiss on my head.

That does it. My tears start flowing freely, and I yell against his chest as hard as I can while gripping his shirt.

"That's it, Bella. Let it out," he tells me softly as he caresses my hair.

I continue yelling and crying, not sure how long we stay like this, but I'm so thankful Gabo is my rock. He's been trying every single day to assure me it's okay to do this, that it's actually beneficial for me. It took me two weeks to believe him, but he never wavered. He was always kind and sweet, showing me his unconditional support. And if that isn't love, then I don't know what it is.

"I want to stay here with you, G," I tell him with a watery smile. I lift my head from his chest and look up at those deep brown eyes of his.

"We're here, love," he tells me, a little confused by my words.

"No, I mean, I want to live here with you."

Gabo lifts me from the ground and twirls us around the room. "Are you serious, principessa?" he asks, full of hope.

"Yes, I want to open a gallery in Bologna. I want to live here at the villa, at least during the warm months. I want to see you every single day, not just when I can travel here or when you can make time to see me in Chile. I want you, Gabriel Godoy. All of you," I say, a crooked smile on my face.

"Fuck, yes. I want it all with you, too."

We seal this promise with a kiss, our lives officially bound. Forever.

Epilogue

Isabella Bianchi

One Year Later

After another great day at the village market, I come home with all the ingredients for dinner and a beautiful bouquet of flowers. I even got dessert—a gelato that Giussepe and Maria named in our honor: *miscela perfetta*, or perfect blend. That's what they say Gabo and I are, the perfect blend, and I couldn't agree more. He's my anchor, and I'm his muse.

After everything that went down last year, I decided to focus my energy on the gallery instead of going back to finish my class. I will officially open my gallery next me, but he also designed it to flow effortlessly. The transition from one area to the next creates opportunities to see more art. It starts with new artists, giving them the chance to wow potential clients first. Deeper into the gallery, the work of more seasoned artists is on display.

On the second floor, I decided to have a studio for when I work in the city or if a piece is too big for my home studio at the villa. This is also a multipurpose space where I plan to offer summer classes for kids and provide a venue for meetings or art clubs to meet and share ideas.

The first exhibit will feature all the art I've created since moving to Italy. It will include the paintings I made for Gabo, all the pieces inspired by my time in captivity, and the happier, more colorful art that came after. This exhibit is called *Origins*. It's a story of new beginnings and self-discovery.

The entire family is expected to attend the inauguration, and I couldn't be happier to have everyone in the same city—something that doesn't happen often.

Gio is coming in from the States with his partner, Vicente from London with his family, and Cata and Matías are even coming from Spain. They've been living there for about six months since Cata became a player for the Bears, and I've loved having her only an hour and a half away—by jet, of course.

Luca, Karina, and Enzo are coming from Chile. It'll be my nephew's first trip across the ocean. We went to meet him last Christmas, and I think Gabo and I got baby fever, though we haven't discussed it.

Even Gabo's parents are scheduled to come; they've welcomed me into their family with open arms.

"Principessa," Gabo greets me as I enter the kitchen, my hands full of bags and flowers. I kiss him when he gets closer to take the bags out of my hands.

"Hey, G. Are you done with work for the day?" He smiles as he takes all the ingredients from the bags and places them on the counter.

"Yes, I'm all yours."

I smirk at him. "You're always mine." I put one of my hands on my waist and cock an eyebrow.

"Touché."

"Do you feel like cooking with me?" I ask him as he wraps his arms around my back and starts slow-dancing with me.

"I feel like doing many things with you," he whispers in my ear.

"Oh, yeah? Like what?" I ask him as I nibble and kiss his jaw—it's my favorite thing to do while we're this close and playful.

"Like making a baby."

I stop dancing. My eyes grow big.

"Sorry, I brought it up so abruptly. It's just something I've been thinking about nonstop lately."

"Maybe since we met Enzo?" I ask him, wanting to know if we've been in tune all this time.

"Yeah," he says with a sigh. "Just the thought of you growing our baby, seeing your belly swell with the seed of our love, and creating a new life with you makes me feral," he says as he lifts me and takes me to the patio.

I giggle all the way there.

"Yeah, I've been thinking about it, too. And honestly I don't see why we should wait. I have plenty of things lined up for the gallery, and I can always hire people if I feel it's becoming too overwhelming." I share my thoughts with him.

His face lights up. "Should we get engaged first? Fuck, I should have brought the ring with me."

I raise my eyebrows.

"Do you really think I don't have a ring for you already? I've just been patiently waiting for you to tell me you're ready," he says, his voice shaking.

"Gabo Godoy, are you nervous?"

He chuckles as he exhales a deep breath. "Well, yeah. Marrying you is another thing I'd love to do with you."

And now is when I truly feel bad.

"Gabo, why do we need to get married? That's just a paper to confirm what we already know. You are my partner, my lover, my best friend, the only man I've ever felt this way for." I try to make him understand that I really don't need anything else other than what we already have.

"You're right. We're bound in all the ways that count," he says.

I breathe a little easier.

"Now let's go make a baby," he says as he takes me to the couch. There, under the stars, we add one more member to our family.

Do you want a sneak peek into Bella and Gabo's life down the road?

Subscribe to my newsletter and download the exclusive Extended Epilogue.

https://BookHip.com/JJCRCTM

Acknowledgments

Writing this book has been an experience all in itself. This book is what it is because of my amazing team, the women who give me countless suggestions and don't bat an eye when I come up with crazy ideas. Marissa and Lox, you are the butter to my bread. I'm forever in your debt.

My family, who always give me space when I need to write. Who doesn't complain about having an easy dinner because I have to work. I love you endlessly.

Amarilys, Emilia, Carol, Ivelisse, Marylou, Maritza, McKinley and Joscelyn: Thank you, ladies, for being the best **Beta team** I could ever ask for. Your comments and suggestions helped shape this book into the amazing story I was able to share with the world. You ladies have created a safe space for not only me but all of us, and I can't thank you enough. Love you all.

Liss Montoya's tribe & Liss' Party girls: Thank you for supporting me and my books. You ladies rock! I love you all!

To all my book friends who always have my back: I love you big!

My illustrator Jess, thank you for bringing my ideas to life. You're so incredibly talented!

To Jessica, for hitting the ground running since the moment I contacted you for PR help. Thank you so much!

To the amazing ARC readers who signed up to review and help promote my book: **THANK YOU** from the bottom of my heart. It means the world to me that you took a chance on my book.

To my author friends who never hesitated to lend a hand or an ear when I needed it: Thank you, ladies! Jocelyne Soto, Lily Baines, LJ Evans, J. Hutchison, Alexandra Hale, Rebecca Jenshak, Daphne Elliot, and many, many more. Thank you, thank you, thank you! You all are amazing!

And lastly, the biggest **THANK YOU** goes to you, the reader. Thank you for taking a chance on my book. It means the world to me. I hope you enjoyed it!

Do you want a sneak peek into Bella and Gabo's life down the road?

Subscribe to my newsletter and download the exclusive Extended Epilogue.

https://BookHip.com/JJCRCTM

Much love,

—*Liss*

What Comes Next?

Ready for more Kinsmen Billionaires?

Preorder Lodged, Gio's book coming this fall, now.

https://www.amazon.com/Lodged-billionaire-romance
-Kinsmen-Billionaires-ebook/dp/B0D3WX1JT8

More By Liss Montoya

With You Series

  A Lifetime With You Marco & Daniela

Going The Distance With You Luca & Karina

Moving On With You Franco & Sofía

Entangled With You Matías & Cattleya

Read free in **KindleUnlimited**

Kingsmen Billionaires

(UN)Bounded Coming August, 2024

Stay Connected

Email: authorlissmontoya@gmail.com

Amazon Author Page: https://www.ama-zon.com/stores/author/B0C7HBXMVM

Instagram: https://www.instagram.com/lissmon-toyawrites

Newsletter: https://subscribepage.io/lissmontoy-anewsletter

Bookbub: https://www.bookbub.com/profile/liss-montoya

Goodreads: https://www.goodreads.com/author/show/32361230.Liss_Montoya

TikTok: https://www.tiktok.com/@lissthebooklover

Facebook: https://www.facebook.com/lissmontoyawrites

Facebook Reader Group: Liss Montoya Saucy Readers

About The Author

L iss Montoya is an author of Contemporary Romance with new adult characters that is full of emotion, spice and all the latin flavor.

Liss was born and raised in Colombia, South America and moved to the United States in her early twenties to pursue a PhD degree. She later became a biology teacher. But after meeting her husband and having their first child, she decided to stay home with her kids and her rescue dog, Luna.

When she's not writing, you can find her playing personal assistant to her kids and her dog, catching up on tv shows with her husband, or reading saucy books.

Printed in the USA
CPSIA information can be obtained
at www.ICGtesting.com
CBHW071942310724
12396CB00013B/38

9 798330 306503